VENICE BEACH

Emily Gallo

Cover photograph by Jim Stripe

The author may be reached at ecegallo@gmail.com

ISBN-13: 978-1505456219
ISBN-10: 1505456215

For AK, PK, LK, BC, BS, CS, ES and DG

Prologue

THE FURNITURE AND HOUSEHOLD ITEMS WERE SOLD, *the books and records shipped, and the clothes donated. Super Shuttle would pick him up at 3 a.m. It wasn't worth trying to sleep for just a few hours. He had spent most of the day running around the city, emptying out what was left of his bank account, changing his address with the post office, and arguing with Judith for an advance. His financial situation was so grim that he had even scrubbed the apartment so he could be sure to get his deposit back. By the time all that was done, it was after eight and he was starving. But more than that he was thirsty, so he decided to spend his last evening in New York at the White Horse Tavern. The food and service were lousy, but Finn wasn't looking for a superb culinary experience. A well-done burger and some cheap Irish whiskey would be just fine.*

The White Horse was crowded because it was still the dinner hour. Everything was always later in New York. People went to work later in the morning and stayed later in the evening. Thus dinner hour usually started at 8 p.m. and went on until midnight. He found space at the bar and plopped himself on a stool for what would be a long night. Service was especially slow so by the time he had a drink in front of him, it was after nine. He wasn't sorry that the bartenders were busy. He was in no mood for conversation.

He had visited Kate in Los Angeles a few times and although her house was comfortable, he was not happy about living on the west coast. It wasn't that he was so enamored with New York. In fact there was a lot he didn't like: the noise, the grime, the weather. But it was familiar. He doubted he'd ever get used to a life that revolved around cars. He hated driving. Luckily Kate lived in Venice Beach, one of the few communities in Los Angeles where walking was an option. And he did love the ocean.

After a few drinks, he thought it would be wise to eat something. Maybe the food would keep his mind off the anxiety and dread he felt about moving to Kate's. The whiskey had already kept his mind off the sadness and melancholy he felt grieving for Maggie.

He walked back to the apartment at two when the tavern closed. He sat on the kitchen counter waiting for the Super Shuttle. It was the only place to sit other than the floor or the toilet and neither of those places seemed particularly enticing. At three he took one last look around the apartment, picked up his suitcase and went downstairs. The van was already there when he walked outside. He didn't want to wallow in his anguish over what lay ahead so he would sightsee on the way to the airport. At that hour it was especially bleak driving through the industrial areas of Queens, but at least it would keep his mind busy. The writer in him was always searching for new stories and new ideas so he would use this time for creative collection.

He was soon on the plane where he could finally close his eyes and get some much-needed sleep. And that is exactly how he *spent the next 6 hours before disembarking at LAX into the worried and apprehensive arms of his daughter.*

1

THE SUNLIGHT HAD JUST STARTED TO STREAM through the stained glass window that was the centerpiece of the dining room. Finn sat at a large antique oak table in his now faded and well-worn bathrobe. He stared at the blank computer screen. The table was covered with mounds of paper and there were piles of books and newspapers stacked haphazardly on the floor. He sipped periodically from a cup of coffee and glanced around the room that was now his office. It had the original oak built-in shelves and beveled glass cabinets that adorned all the Craftsman style houses built in Venice in the early 1900s.

Kate had bought hers just before the market soared and he guessed she could sell it for at least a million dollars. He doubted that would ever happen, though. She had always been good about saving money and she had managed to furnish it with antiques on a teacher's salary. It was her pride and joy, an immaculate showpiece. He wasn't sure how she had become such a neat freak; certainly he had had nothing to do with it.

There was a thud as something hit the house. Finn got up and went to the front door. He bent down to pick up the *Los Angeles Times* and glanced at the stately grandfather clock in the front hall. It said 5:30. He threw the newspaper on a side table and returned to his dining room/office. He sat motionless, staring at his computer and sipping from his cup. When the clock struck six times, he went back to the front door and walked out onto the porch. He searched up and down the street, cursing under his breath. Finally a car drove up and slowed just enough for the driver to hurl a newspaper onto the lawn and then sped off. "It's nine o'clock in New York and you can't get the paper here before now?" Finn yelled after him. "And you're supposed to put it on the porch, you idiot!" He picked up the paper and stormed back inside the house. He decided he needed a new cup of coffee to go with his *New York Times* diversion.

The kitchen was newly remodeled and spotless. Finn leaned against the counter, glancing at the front page, while he waited for the coffee to finish brewing. Kate entered, dressed in running clothes and holding the *Los Angeles Times*. She was an attractive, athletic, forty-two year old with a short pixie haircut, slightly built and spry like her father.

9

"Why won't you at least look at the LA paper, Dad?" Kate asked. "You should learn more about the city now that you're living here."

"I'm not interested."

Kate playfully mussed his hair, a typical Irish full mane of white. "Oh, don't be so inflexible. Would you like me to make you some breakfast?"

"No thanks. I'll just have more coffee." He poured himself coffee and handed the pot to Kate.

She filled her own cup and placed the pot back on the burner. "What are you going to do today?" she asked as she opened the *LA Times*.

"Read, write, eat, drink and be merry," he muttered.

"Are you really going to write?"

"What's that supposed to mean?"

"I wonder how much longer the publishers are going to wait."

"They can wait 'til I'm good and ready."

"You don't have the luxury of waiting 'til you're good and ready. You're broke."

"Thanks for reminding me."

She smiled. "Happy to oblige. See you in an hour." She kissed him on the top of his head and jogged out the back door and turned toward the beach. The Venice bike path that ran along the boardwalk north toward Santa Monica teemed with bike riders, skateboarders, rollerbladers, joggers and walkers in the early morning hours so she went the opposite way, south toward Marina del Rey. It was usually deserted in that direction.

Finn went back to the dining room, took a bottle of whiskey out of the cabinet, poured some into his coffee and returned to stare at the computer screen. Since Kate was on her morning run he didn't have to hide it so he drank with more gusto. More than a week had gone by but he hadn't left the house except when Kate forced him out to a supermarket or restaurant. He pretended that he had to stay home to unpack and write, but he had done little of either. He didn't expect to be here that long so why bother. But then, where else would he go? New York no longer held any appeal for him. He had become such a recluse since Maggie's illness that he hardly had any friends left and the city, itself, was just a reminder of all his losses. He didn't want to admit that he might be sliding back into the abyss of drugs and alcohol that had consumed him after Kate left home and before he had met Maggie. But it was a similar period; unable to write, aimless and adrift, wanting to be alone but knowing it was the worst thing he could do. The isolation that ate at his soul only served to compound his grief and it certainly didn't help him overcome his writer's block. At least he had the wherewithal to know what he shouldn't do, so he went upstairs to get dressed. He wouldn't stay in his bathrobe all day. That was a positive step.

A Month Ago

ONLY THE RUSTLING OF THE NEWSPAPER PAGES *interrupted the rhythmic pulsing of the oxygen machine. The hospital bed hadn't moved from its upright position in more than a week, ever since Maggie slipped into a coma. At first Finn tried to force ice chips into her mouth, but he soon realized there was no point. She couldn't swallow on her own. The only relief for her chapped lips was the jar of Vaseline that sat on the night table along with the syringe and the box of tissues he used to wipe the drool off her chin. Antoinette, the hospice nurse, had removed the pill bottles a few days before and exchanged the bedpan for a box of Depends.*

He had bought the recliner for Maggie after her surgery, but now it was where he spent most days and nights, biding time as he waited for the inevitable. His coffee was cold by now and although he had read every word of the New York Times*, he doubted he could recall any of it.*

She was only sixty-four when she was diagnosed a year ago. The doctors thought she had more time. But cancer is a crapshoot. They opened her up, only to close without removing any of the tumors. It had spread too much. At first he didn't accept it. He wanted to take her for second and third opinions. Maggie was a pragmatist, though, and refused. She chose to live her last months with Finn as fully as she could. They had managed to travel some in the beginning, but the decline was rapid and debilitating.

He was dressed in his uniform of late. The bathrobe had been a gift from Maggie when they first married twenty-five years ago. He hadn't worn it much then. He had always been an early riser, usually out of the house by eight. But now the robe had started to show signs of wear.

The bedroom was dim; just a faint glow came from the floor lamp behind the recliner. There was no need for much light anymore. Maggie had always loved it when the sun streamed through the windows in the morning. She kept all the lights on in every room of the apartment. She said the brightness made her feel like she was at the beach. They had always spent a couple a weekends every summer on Fire Island. They couldn't afford a house there, but luckily they had friends who could.

They had met after both of them had gone through a dark period. Maggie had weathered an ugly divorce and Finn was in some sort of midlife crisis. His daughter had graduated from college and moved across the country. He had retired from the school district and had been trying to write but without much success. He had spent the last couple of years tucked away in his apartment with only his beloved bottle of Jameson for company.

He had mustered up the strength to go to a gallery opening one evening and saw her across the room. It was the first time he had been out and about in the New York art scene for a long time. Their eyes met and he smiled at her. It was a shock to him that he remembered how. Their courtship was short. He asked her to marry him just a couple of months after they met. They explored the city as if they had not lived there for the last thirty years. He could control his drinking to social occasions only and he devoted himself to writing and to her.

2

HE STARED AT THE BLANK COMPUTER SCREEN for another half hour, but this time in street clothes, hoping he would get motivated to write. He quickly switched to the Google page when he heard the back door open and close. He could always claim he was doing research. Kate entered, panting and breathless. "Why do you do that to yourself?" Finn asked.

"Do what? Exercise and take care of myself? It wouldn't hurt you to take a walk. We live by the beach, for heaven's sake, and the weather is beautiful today. And by the way, corduroy pants and flannel shirts are not really appropriate."

"That's the problem with this place. The weather's too perfect. And leave my clothes out of it."

"Oh, Dad," she sighed. "Do you ever stop complaining? Try being positive for a change." She left him muttering to himself like a clichéd caricature of a cantankerous old man.

"Nothing worse than a Pollyanna who always has to find the goddamn silver lining." He stood and stretched, and glanced out the window. "Oh, what the hell." He put a pen in one pocket and his wallet in another. He folded the newspaper, stuck it under his arm, and went into the kitchen for the spare key hanging on a hook. He was going to call up the stairs to Kate and then decided to leave without telling her. He didn't want her to know that he was following her advice.

The city of Venice Beach is a jumble of diverse housing. On the beach there are multi-million dollar homes as well as once shabby apartment buildings, most of which have been refurbished into condos and hotels. The further you get from the beach, the neighborhood becomes a mixture of slums and ordinary ranch houses. Along the canals, however, you can find architecturally stunning, interior-designed mansions. The contrast continues in the shopping choices from trendy restaurants and boutiques on Abbott Kinney Boulevard to the storefronts selling cheap T-shirts and shoddy trinkets on the boardwalk. The vendor tables that sell art and jewelry on the boardwalk range from high-end, gallery-ready to a childlike masterpiece only a mother could love.

Then there are the "middle class" homes on the walk streets extending out from the boardwalk where cars are not allowed. They used to be affordable, but are now out of reach for most.

Abbott Kinney Boulevard is named after a tobacco millionaire, a casino owner who founded Venice in the early 1900s after winning the land in a coin toss. His dream was to have a resort town modeled after its namesake in Italy with canals and gondoliers, oceanfront walkways, and Venetian style buildings. He envisioned an amusement park on a pier that included a heated, salt-water plunge as well as the typical carnival rides. It was a huge success but in 1920 Kinney died, the pier burned down, Prohibition was established, and tax revenue took a plunge.

By 1925, Venice's politics were out of control. Its roads, water and sewage systems were in disrepair and couldn't handle the huge increase in population. The city of Los Angeles annexed it in 1926 and started paving over the canals. After an outcry, a few of them south of Venice Boulevard were left intact. In 1930 oil was discovered generating a financial boom for Venice, although short-lived. The oil wells also brought in air and water pollution and by the fifties, its heyday was over. It became the "Slum by the Sea," ripe for the "Beat Generation" and the subsequent hippies of the sixties to move in. Soon after that, the popular musicians of the time and some of Hollywood's A-list discovered it and Venice was reborn as an eclectic artistic community.

16

The two-and-a-half-mile cement promenade called the Venice Beach boardwalk is unique and mind-blowing. It is not your usual family-friendly, seaside walkway. It certainly has its share of cheap clothing and souvenir shops, and pizza and ice cream parlors, but it is also home to a distinctive, motley cast of characters. It serves as a soapbox for political activists and New Age philosophers, as well as a marketplace for artists and entertainers. You can have your name written on a grain of rice or have your fortune told. You can get a prescription for marijuana from Dr. Kush, and get it filled at the attached dispensary.

Directly on the boardwalk is an outdoor fenced-in area packed tightly with exercise equipment. It is called Muscle Beach and it is rumored that Arnold Schwarzenegger got his start there. Next to Muscle Beach are paddle tennis courts that are similar to regular tennis courts but smaller. The racquets are made of wood instead of aluminum or titanium and the game is a lot faster.

Further up the boardwalk where it meets the sand are the Venice Public Art walls where artists with a valid permit are allowed to express themselves. Next to them is a huge skate park that is usually filled with daredevil athletes ranging in age from six to sixty. They fly through the air, twisting and turning and contorting their bodies, and still somehow land back on their skateboards. There are several sand volleyball courts and a basketball court where several NBA players were supposedly discovered.

Running alongside and between the promenade and the sand is a twenty-two-mile-long bike path called The Strand that stretches from Will Rogers State Beach in Malibu, north of Venice, south to Torrance County Beach, past the LA Airport. The beach itself is flat and expansive and it can be a long, hot-on-the-toes trek to the ocean from the boardwalk when the weather is steamy. And of course, being southern California, there are the surfers who tend to crowd around the breakwater that consists of a sand bar, pipes and rocks and juts out into the ocean.

Finn walked slowly along the boardwalk, stopping to watch different performers. He stopped at some of the tables to admire the wares.

A myriad of musicians played guitars, banjos, ukuleles, keyboards and drums and their skill level also ran the gamut. There was even one man on a regular-sized spinet piano, playing only classical music. He dragged the piano onto the boardwalk every morning to a spot in front of a sidewalk cafe. He must have had permission from the cafe to keep it inside, as he was the only person who had a "regular" place on the boardwalk. The others all vied for the 205 precious spaces that were on a first-come, first-served basis. There were singers and dancers doing everything from reggae to hip-hop to eye-popping break dancing. A muscular man wearing a bright royal blue speedo whizzed past on rollerblades followed by a man adorned with twigs and leaves walking on stilts. There were acrobats walking across tightropes and jumping over a line of six or seven people touching their toes. A man did a twenty-minute interactive show walking barefoot on broken glass as professional as any you'd see in Las Vegas. Clowns, dressed in wild and crazy homemade costumes, made balloon animals. There was a man who had painted his entire body gold.

Finn had to admit that the Venice Beach boardwalk was entertaining. He decided to be adventurous and detour onto the sand. He walked toward the ocean and stuck his toe in the water. The air was still cool and the water cold so he moseyed on back to the boardwalk to do his favorite activity: people-watch.

3

EARLY IN THE MORNING THE BOARDWALK TEEMS with joggers, rollerbladers and bike riders while the homeless sleep on benches and between buildings. After the exercise fanatics go to work and the sleeping bags are rolled up and put away, the tourists come out to watch the performers. Mixed in between the fancy houses and the boardwalk schlock are streets with cheap restaurants and small grocery stores and in between these streets are the alleys and walk-streets.

Jed walked past an overflowing dumpster in one of these alleys. He was a thin yet muscular middle-aged black man and his clean-shaven, angular face radiated a subtle sensuality. He was neatly dressed in mismatched but clean clothes and had on a large, bright yellow backpack with a sleeping bag tied to the bottom. A black and white spotted cat rode on top of the backpack. She slept soundly. She was obviously accustomed to this precarious perch. Jed's stride was easy yet purposeful. He was obviously not a man who dawdled or stumbled blindly through life, even if he didn't have any particular place to go.

He walked by the back door of a Mexican restaurant where Luis, a slightly overweight man in his fifties wearing a cook's apron, stood outside smoking a cigarette. "Buenos dias, Jed."

"Hey, Luis."

"Can you work tonight? Another dishwasher got deported."

"Six?"

"Si senor. Seis."

"See you then."

"Hasta luego."

Luis went inside and Jed continued walking down the alley to the street and onto the boardwalk. He stopped at a trashcan, took out a Styrofoam container and looked inside. A half-eaten hamburger and a few French fries swam in a pool of ketchup. He took a paper napkin out of his backpack and wiped the ketchup off the fries before closing the container. He carried it with him as he walked to Muscle Beach. When he got to the row of benches in front of the exercise machines, he put the container on the ground and removed his backpack and lay it down gently. The cat didn't flinch, but then jumped off and stretched before moseying over to the container. Jed broke up the hamburger into small pieces and did the same with the fries. "There's your breakfast, Mother." Jed watched the cat eat voraciously.

Finn approached the bench and sat down. He and Jed sat in silence until the cat rubbed against Finn's leg and climbed onto his lap.

"Friendly cat," Finn said, petting the loudly purring cat.

"Do you mind?" Jed asked.

"Not at all." They continued to sit in silence for a few more minutes. "What's its name?"

"Mother."

"Interesting. What do you call her for short?"

"Mother."

"Some nickname."

"I don't need to call her much. She's always with me."

"I'll bet she's good company."

"Yep."

Finn looked at the backpack and sleeping bag. "Just moved here?"

"Nope."

"Are you going on a trip?"

"Nope."

Finn looked at him curiously, and then continued petting Mother. "I'm Finn, short for Finnegan."

"Jed, short for Jedidiah."

Jed stood abruptly and put on his backpack. Finn took the cat off his lap and handed her to Jed.

The cat crawled up Jed's arm and onto the top of the backpack. "Nice meeting you, Jed."

Jed nodded but didn't answer. Finn stared at him as he walked away. "Strange fellow," he thought.

Finn got up and walked on, pretending he had somewhere important to go. He remembered seeing some stores and restaurants on Pacific Street. He found a cafe a few blocks away and stepped inside. It was filled with Hollywood wannabes all dressed alike in designer jeans and T-shirts. Some were alone typing on laptops while others talked animatedly to their clone tablemates.

He ordered a cup of coffee at the counter and scanned the tables while he waited. None of them were empty so when they called his name, he grabbed the cup and sauntered outside to the patio. He sat down next to a young woman who didn't fit the mold. She was more a throwback to the sixties with long blonde hair and a flowing paisley skirt. She was alone, busily typing on her laptop. He opened his newspaper and pretended to read but really he was eavesdropping on the conversations surrounding him. He soon realized that there was nothing of consequence to listen to so he folded the paper in half and started working on the crossword puzzle. The young woman at the next table stopped typing and took out a newspaper already folded. "What'd you get for seven across?"

"Excuse me?"

"I said what'd you get for seven across?"

"This is the New York paper."

"I know."

"How did you know?"

Harper scanned the tables, turning her head dramatically. "You just don't look like the type to be reading the *Hollywood Reporter*. So what did you get?"

"I haven't gotten there yet. I just started."

"I'm sure you'll have it done in no time."

"Why do you say that?"

"Because you're doing it in pen, for one thing. That's always a sign of a proficient puzzler." Harper closed the lid of her laptop, picked up her stuff and moved to Finn's table. "Do you mind? I need some help. I can usually only finish Mondays and Tuesdays and sometimes Wednesdays without resorting to a dictionary."

Finn shrugged his shoulders. They sat in silence, each doing their own puzzles. "Resurrect."

"That's it! Now I can get seven down. I got 780 on my SATs, graduated Barnard with a double major English and Creative Writing, but I have the worst vocabulary ever."

"I always told my students that crossword puzzles would improve their vocabulary."

"Yeah, my professors told me that, too. What did you teach?"

"High school English."

"No shit. Oops, sorry."

Finn smiled. "Not a problem."

"I've entered a story of mine in a contest and they're supposed to pick the winners today or tomorrow. I'm almost too nervous to work."

"What work is that?"

"Waitressing."

"That was one expensive degree so you could be a waitress."

"You sound like my parents."

"I guess all parents sound the same." He returned to his puzzle and she resumed typing on her laptop.

After a few minutes she sat back in her chair and closed the computer. "I need a break. I think I'll go to the boardwalk. Want to come?"

"I don't know. I just came from there and the sun doesn't treat Irish skin well."

"Aw c'mon."

He pretended to look at a watch. "Oh all right. I guess I can fit it in between my coffee break and lunch."

Harper laughed. "You're a funny man Mr. . . ."

"Finnegan. Finn for short."

"First or last?"

"First."

"I'm Harper."

"First?"

"Yeah, after Harper Lee. My parents are proud southerners." Harper packed up her laptop and the various items she had spread over the table and then paused with an incredulous look as Finn zipped through the crossword puzzle. "Wait a minute. Are you Finn McGee? The author?"

"One and the same."

"Oh my God! You're kidding! I love your books! I read them like three times. I can't believe it. You were like a God to my Creative Writing Seminar class. What are you working on now?"

"I'm having a bit of writer's block, you might say." He was flattered and secretly hoped her words would inspire him but he doubted it.

"Really? Even great authors like you can get writer's block?"

"I've never met a writer who hasn't had it. It goes with the territory," Finn added.

"Hey, would you read my story and critique it?" Harper asked.

He shook his head. "No, I'm sorry, but I don't do that anymore. My teaching days are long over."

"That's okay," she said, trying to hide her disappointment. "I guess it is asking a lot. It's not like it matters now anyway, since I've already entered it in the contest."

Finn finished the puzzle with a flourish of the pen. "There. Done." He stood, put the pen in his pocket, walked to a trashcan and dumped his coffee cup and newspaper.

"I knew you'd finish it quickly," Harper said. They walked out to the front of the cafe and started down the street. "Oh wait, I'll be right back. I forgot something." She went back and took Finn's crossword puzzle out of the trashcan. She put it in her backpack and rejoined him.

They strolled down the sidewalk to the boardwalk. "So, Harper, how did you wind up here after graduating from college in New York?"

"The usual reason kids wind up three thousand miles from their family."

"Ah yes. Just to be three thousand miles from their parents."

"You guessed it."

"So it's not because you wanted to break into Hollywood, I gather."

Harper laughed. "No way. Hey, you did it too. I remember from your book about how you left Ireland at eighteen and moved to New York."

"That's true. Good memory."

They continued to walk down the street. Harper talked animatedly as Finn sported a bemused smile. He realized that it might have been the first time he smiled since arriving in California. Maybe even since Maggie had gotten sick.

"I loved living in New York but my parents loved visiting too much."

"I gather they're not thrilled that you're here."

"No, they're not. Six hours on a plane is not as easy as six hours in the car. What about you? I didn't know you had moved here."

"It was a recent move."

"Do you miss New York?"

"Some things."

"Pizza? That's what everyone out here says."

"No. Not pizza." Lucky for Finn, they reached the boardwalk. The conversation was getting a little too personal.

"This is quite a circus," Finn said as he watched a sword-swallower and a fire-eater vying for people's attention.

"Is this your first time to the boardwalk?"

"No, but I used to just walk across it to go to the beach."

"You don't live in Venice?"

"I'm staying with my daughter."

"How long are you staying?"

He hesitated, unsure how to answer. "I'll be here a while."

He paused to read some of the political signs and pamphlets piled on a table, while Harper stopped at a vendor displaying jewelry. They are not technically allowed to sell jewelry or clothing on the boardwalk because of the shopkeepers who pay exorbitant rents to sell their wares, but they manage to get around that ordinance most of the time. "You're not exactly dressed for the beach," she chided playfully. "Next time you really should wear shorts."

Finn grunted. "I don't think I've put on a pair of shorts in thirty years."

"Well, now's as good a time as any to start."

"Yeah, first day of the rest of my life. Hah!"

"See you at the cafe tomorrow?"

"You never know."

Harper waved goodbye as she ran off. Finn decided he would take advantage of the smorgasbord of entertainment before him. He headed for the musical street performers but was sidetracked by a man at a table with a sign that said Venice Beach Homeless Shelter. Charlie, thirtyish, earnest and upbeat, stood behind the table and smiled at Finn. "Come check us out. We can help you."

"Who, me? Oh no. I don't need your services."

"We won't ask you any questions. And we're nondenominational. We're just here as a resource center."

"I'm sure you do great things but really, I don't need it."

"Why don't you take one of our brochures? You never know when you might need us. We serve breakfast on the boardwalk and supper at the shelter. We also have computers and phones available."

"Fine, I'll take one of your brochures."

Finn looked through the brochure as he walked off, amused but also curious. He glanced up when a large commotion erupted. A crowd had gathered around a scuffle, some of them yelling to call 911 and others egging the fighters on. A young teenager, dressed from head to toe in expensive Italian leather, escaped from the midst of the hubbub with Jed's cat.

Jed ran out of the crowd after him, throwing his backpack and sleeping bag on the ground. A second teenager, a clone of the first, picked up the backpack and ran into Finn, knocking him down. He continued running until he caught up to his partner. Mother hissed, squirmed and scratched at them as they tried to escape but Jed was close on their heels.

Davion and Ty, a pair of Jamaican street dancers in their twenties, stopped their performance and sprinted after them, catching the cat thief and wrestling him to the ground. Jed jumped on the thief and punched him repeatedly. Davion pulled Jed off and Mother scampered off in one direction while the teenager scurried off after his friend. "Cool it, mon," Davion panted, "You're gonna kill him."

Jed squirmed out of Davion's grip. "Let go of me!" Jed ran down the boardwalk, yelling and shoving people out of his way.

Meanwhile, Charlie had rushed over to help Finn up. "Are you okay? Your head is bleeding."

Finn brushed himself off and felt a cut on the side of his head. He looked at his hand, shocked at how bloody it was. "I'm fine, just a little shaken up."

"You have to be careful around here."

"I can see that."

"Especially with those Beverly Hills bullies."

"Those two are from Beverly Hills?" Finn asked.

"Oh yeah. Matt and Luke are well known around here. They love causing trouble, especially with the homeless."

A breathless Jed walked up to Finn and Charlie. He took a handkerchief out of his pocket and handed it to Finn. "Don't worry. It's clean."

"I wasn't worried. Thanks." Finn held the handkerchief on his bleeding cut. "I'll wash your handkerchief and get it back to you."

Jed started to walk off and waved his hand dismissively. "Don't bother."

"No bother. Where can I find you?" Finn called after him.

"I'll find you," Jed said without turning around.

Mother emerged from behind a building and scampered up to Jed. He scooped her up and put her on his shoulders, and then proceeded west toward the ocean to clear his head. When he got to the water he put Mother down carefully, stripped off his shirt and shoes, and dove in. He swam for twenty minutes or so and returned to the sand where Mother sat patiently guarding what was left of his few possessions. He sat awhile, drying off, then dressed and put Mother back on his shoulders. He headed north up the sand toward Malibu and the Santa Monica Mountains. It was a six hour round trip walk, but he knew that there was enough time before he had to be at Luis' restaurant, and he also knew that it was necessary.

Meanwhile, Finn walked home holding Jed's handkerchief to his head. When he got to Kate's, he went straight to the bathroom to search for bandaging material. Of course she had every possible size of gauze, tape, and Band-Aids as well as an array of ointments. He picked out what he needed, wrapped his head, and headed straight for his office to eradicate the pain with the contents of his beloved Jameson.

He brought the bottle into the living room along with a copy of his book and made himself comfortable. It didn't take long for the whiskey to do its work and he drifted off.

A Month Ago

FINN WALKED OVER TO THE DRESSER and picked up a framed picture of him and Maggie. It had been taken on Fire Island about eight years ago, when all was still right in the world. He looked in the mirror and saw a very different countenance staring back. He was still slender and spry, but the lines and dark circles of age and stress now crisscrossed that once boyish and serene face.

He put the picture down next to the old stereo. He had dragged it from the living room to the bedroom so Maggie could listen to music. They were still vinyl aficionados, not yet having made the jump to digital music. He found the album he was looking for and put it on the turntable. Van Morrison's "Moondance," the song that had been their song, came on.

He heard the key in the lock and the sound of the front door open and close. The familiar padding of nurses' shoes came closer until Antoinette stood in the doorway of the bedroom.

"Good morning, Mr. Finn. Shall we give Mrs. Maggie some light?" She was only a few years younger than Maggie, but her smooth black skin looked more like a woman in her forties.

"No, Antoinette. No light."

She fluffed the pillows and tightened the blanket. "Shall I give her the insulin shot?"

"No need. I gave it to her an hour ago."

33

Antoinette took the empty bottle of insulin and some dirty tissues off the night table and threw them in the wastebasket. "I can sit with her if you wish, give you a little break."

"No, I want to stay."

"Would you like some more coffee?"

"That would be nice." Antoinette took the empty cup and went to the kitchen.

Finn's eyes followed her out of the room. He checked the clock and then took a syringe off the night table and another bottle of insulin out of his pocket. He stared at Maggie's sallow, bony face and tried to replace it with the beautiful, vibrant one he remembered. He filled the syringe and placed the bottle back on the table. "I love you, Maggie." He kissed her gently on the lips and injected her. He put the syringe in his pocket and stood next to the bed, gazing down at her. He lifted her hand and felt for a pulse. Then he kissed the hand and laid it down gently. When he turned around, he saw Antoinette standing in the doorway, her eyes wide with shock. Their eyes met and they stared at each other for a moment. He looked away and neither one said a word for several moments.

Finally he stiffened and cleared his throat. "Maybe you could sit with her for a minute." Antoinette handed him the coffee silently. He felt her eyes follow him as he left the room.

He entered the kitchen and took a bottle of whiskey off a shelf, poured some in his coffee, and peered out the window at the New York skyline as he gulped it down.

Antoinette came rushing in shouting, "Mr. Finn! Mr. Finn!" He put his cup down and hurried out.

Finn stood to the side while two EMTs lifted Maggie, her body and face covered with a blanket, onto an ambulance gurney

34

and wheeled her out of the bedroom. Antoinette followed them out. He listened to the front door close and the padding of her shoes down the hall, probably for the last time.

"Shall I clean the room while you go to the hospital?"

"Yes, that would help a lot."

"I'm very sorry, Mr. Finn. Mrs. Maggie was a lovely woman."

"Thank you." He watched her leave. He would never hear that lilting Jamaican accent again either.

That evening Finn entered the apartment and turned on the lights. He placed his keys on the table and his coat on the sofa. It had been a long, harrowing day, dealing with the hospital and the funeral home. He watched his account balance creep dangerously downward as he wrote check after check.

The kitchen was spotless and smelled of Lysol. He never understood why Antoinette had to use it full strength when the directions called for diluting it. He took the whiskey and a glass off the shelf and filled it to the top. Leaning against the counter, he downed the whole thing and poured out the rest of the bottle. His eyes turned to gaze out the window at the lights of the New York skyline, a sight that never ceased to amaze him.

He had arrived in New York at age eighteen after a dirt-poor, miserable childhood in Ireland and never went back. It was the usual cause: an absent, alcoholic father who beat both *him and his mother. She had endured it silently, which made it even worse. Most of his childhood was spent afraid of his father and angry with his mother. When he got older and he got tall enough to outrun him, he transferred the anger from his mother to his father. After he graduated from secondary school, his mother encouraged him to leave their dysfunctional household and it was then that he started the process of forgiving her.*

He had always wanted to be a writer and one of his teachers had given him books by Norman Mailer, James Baldwin, Truman Capote and T.S. Eliot. He devoured them and imagined himself in heated drunken discussions with these esteemed authors at the White Horse Tavern in Greenwich Village, the bar made famous by Dylan Thomas.

His arrival in New York mirrored one of Horatio Alger's stories. He had little money but hoped to meet the wealthy mentor who would "discover" him and bring him fame and fortune. After several months of typical menial jobs, he didn't meet a wealthy mentor, but he did meet a woman who supported him while he went to college. He had intended to major in English in order to hone his writing skills, but when she became pregnant, he started taking the required courses for his teaching credential. The baby arrived, he started a job teaching high school English, and his wife died, all in the same year. There would be no time for writing or alcohol-fueled conversations in the White Horse Tavern. He had a child to raise . . . alone.

The phone rang and he walked into the bedroom to answer it. The bed had been stripped and the night table emptied. He would call the medical equipment company in the morning to remove the hospital bed. "Hello? Oh, Kate. Yes. This morning. I haven't called anyone else yet. Can I call you tomorrow? It's been a long day and I'm exhausted. Thanks. Bye."

He hung up and went to the stereo. He placed the needle on the record and turned up the volume. He had always played music softly in the bedroom for Maggie's sake, but now he could play it as loud as he wanted. He turned out the light and sat on the recliner. He gulped down the second full glass, put the glass on the table and leaned back. His eyes closed as Van Morrison's "Into the Mystic" filled the room.

When the song was over he went back to the kitchen, opened the cabinet, and rifled through the cans and jars. But he found nothing that would quench his thirst. He went to the phone and dialed a number he had obviously called often. "Hello. This is Finn McGee. Send up three bottles, please. Yes. I have it. I'll pay when you get here." He hung up and took his wallet out of his back pocket. There was no cash but he found a credit card that he hoped still had room on it.

He wandered around the apartment, going from room to room, picking up various items off the tables and bookshelves. Each one brought back a memory from the forty-five years he had spent in New York. There were none from his Irish roots. His only nod to that part of his life was his brand of whiskey and a reference to it when he wanted to be likened to the great authors from the Emerald Isle.

The doorbell rang and he rushed to answer it, his need for alcohol far outweighing his need to continue his trip down

37

memory lane. After paying the deliveryman, he took the glass and the bottle into the living room and flopped onto the couch, preparing to drink himself into oblivion and hopefully to fall asleep.

Apparently it had worked. He woke up on the couch still in his clothes from the night before and with a nasty headache. The phone rang and he waited for the answering machine to come on to see who it was. "Dad? Are you there? Pick up if you are, please. I have to leave for work so I won't be able to talk to you again 'til school's out at three."

He jumped up to get to the phone before she hung up. "Kate, I'm here."

"Dad, how are you doing? Are you okay?"

"I'm okay."

"I don't see how I can take off work to come—"

He interrupted her. "No need. She didn't want any kind of service. But I'll need to take you up on that offer. I'll give my thirty days notice on the apartment right now."

"Okay. And Dad . . . don't worry . . . things will work out."

Finn smiled. Although Kate could be stubborn and opinionated, she was also compassionate and dependable. "Thanks. I'll keep you posted." He hung up and went to the kitchen for his hangover remedy: Irish coffee. He knew that she hadn't expected him to move to Los Angeles. Never in a million years did she think he would leave New York. It surprised them both. He had no choice, though. He was broke.

Kate had gone away to college and never returned to New York except for the occasional visit and even those had become sporadic after he had married Maggie. He knew it was nothing against Maggie. She just had this perception that it was her responsibility to take care of him, even as a child. When he married Maggie, though, she relinquished that role.

Kate had spent her twenties in different countries experimenting with a variety of men of assorted ethnicities and cultures. She had a couple of disastrous long-term relationships and one short-term marriage, and Finn finally realized what Kate had already understood about herself. His daughter was probably happiest being a single person. Upon turning thirty, having saved quite a bit of money by teaching abroad and living in the houses of the rich people's kids she taught, she decided to return to the states and make a stab at a more conventional lifestyle. She bought a house, finished her teaching credential, and decided that her father had given her a calling. She followed in his footsteps and taught high school English.

Her relationship with Finn had never wavered from being warm and loving, but they had drifted apart due to distance and stubbornness. They were so alike in their quests to be independent and totally self-sufficient that they sometimes went months without any communication. She had many friends, though, and led a full, busy, satisfied life. But like anyone who lives alone for a long period of time, she had become set in her ways and less and less willing to compromise. This new living arrangement would be hard on both of them.

After shaving and showering, he opened his closet and peered inside. It had been a long time since he'd worn anything resembling business attire, but he thought it would be appropriate for his next activity.

He climbed the stairs of the Times Square Subway Station, along with a steady stream of office workers and tourists. He entered a large office building and got on the elevator. His eyes were focused on the doors in front of him, but his mind was far away. He was oblivious to the people jostling him on both sides as they entered and exited on various floors. When the doors opened on twenty-two, he walked purposefully toward an office door with JUDITH GOLDBERG, LITERARY AGENT written in large gold letters. The receptionist looked up from her computer as he entered.

"Hello Mr. McGee. I am so sorry about your wife."

"Thanks."

"Was Ms. Goldberg expecting you?"

"No. I guess I should have called first."

"She's here but she's in a meeting. Can you wait?"

"Sure."

The receptionist buzzed Judith on the phone. "Finn McGee is here to see you. He didn't have an appointment but - okay I'll tell him." She hung up. "She says she'll be done in a few minutes."

"Thanks." Finn sat down and folded the NY Times to the crossword puzzle. He wrote answers at a dizzying pace as the receptionist watched him in awe. When he finished, he looked around the room for a wastebasket.

"I can't believe you finished the puzzle so fast! That's amazing. You should be in a contest or something."

He shrugged. "Is there somewhere I can toss this?" She took the paper and threw it away.

The door behind the receptionist desk opened and a sixtyish woman appeared, heavily made up and garishly dressed with gold hanging from her ears, neck and wrists. A young man, dressed like he just stepped out of the J Crew catalog, followed her into the reception area. "Finn, darling, how are you holding up?" she gushed as she hugged him.

"I'm all right, Judith."

The young man's eyes widened. "Finn McGee? Wow! What an honor!"

Judith put her arm around the young man. "This is Trevor Smythe. He just signed with Random House."

"Congratulations," Finn said with blatant sarcasm.

"We're hoping he'll send me on my next trip to Europe. After all, you haven't paid for a trip for me in several years, Finn." She laughed but Finn didn't crack a smile.

"May I speak with you alone, Judith?"

She turned to Trevor. "I'll talk to you tomorrow and let you know when the book tour will start. Come on in, Finn."

He followed Judith into her office and sat across the desk. "Maggie's illness took a toll, Judith. I'm out of money and energy."

"I understand, Finn, but the publishers don't. You have two best sellers under your belt, but you haven't written anything in seven years. That's a long time in the publishing business."

"I know, Judith, but certainly they can give me a break under the circumstances."

"If you remember, Finn, they gave you a lot of breaks in the past when you were overdue getting your books finished."

41

"So I was late a couple of times."

"More than a couple. Your drinking binges cost them money. They had to cover up for you a lot. And, by the way, there are plenty of Trevor Smythes coming up the ranks."

"Yes, yes. I'm aware of that. And thanks for being so supportive!"

"Now Finn, you know I have your back."

"Listen. I have an idea for a new book. Would you set up a meeting so I can pitch it to the publishers?"

"I'll set up the meeting after you've started writing the book, Finn. I have to have something in my hands."

"I was hoping for an advance."

"It's not going to happen without something to show them. You need to win their trust again."

"For Christ's sake, Judith! I brought in a lot of money for them and for you!"

"Yes, you did, but that was a long time ago. Times have changed in the publishing business. The market is a lot younger now and everyone is self-publishing. You're going to have to get your act together and do things on time.   Publishers have to have guarantees and past best sellers aren't enough."

"Judith, I have nothing left. Nothing. I have to move in with my daughter, Kate, in California. Please talk to them."

"I'm sorry, Finn. Write a few chapters and send them to me. Then I can approach them about an advance." She busied herself rearranging a pile of papers.

"Dammit Judith!" Finn smacked the table with his fist, scattering them. "What kind of a half-assed agent are you!" He stormed out of the office.

4

FINN SLEPT IN AN EASY CHAIR in Kate's living room with the open book across his chest. The bandage on the side of his head was starting to unravel. The room was dimly lit, and an empty glass rested precariously on the table. The front door opened and closed and Kate entered the room. When she saw Finn's bandaged head, she rushed to his chair and shook him awake. "Dad! What happened?"

Finn stirred and opened his eyes. "What time is it?"

"About ten. What happened to your head?"

Finn reached up to the bandage and sat upright. "It's a long story. I'm fine."

"Why won't you tell me what happened?"

"Really, I'm okay."

"Did you fall or hit your head? Did you see a doctor?"

"It's nothing!"

"It's not nothing. You're hurt. It could be a concussion."

"For God's sake, Kate, I said I was fine."

"Did you go to the emergency room and have it looked at?"

"Stop badgering me!"

Kate flopped into the sofa and sighed. "You know, Dad, I'm sorry Maggie died and I understand that you're grieving, but I didn't ask to have my life turned upside down either."

"Dammit, Kate! It's not like I wanted to move in with you. I had no choice!" He stood and the book bounced off his knee to the floor. He teetered and fell into Kate on the sofa.

"Are you dizzy?" She tried to stay calm.

"No."

She picked up the glass from the table and held it up. "How much have you had?"

"It's none of your business."

Kate picked up the book and looked at the title: *Ode to Forgiveness: A Memoir* by Finn McGee. Her face softened and she smiled. "I haven't read this in years," she said.

"Neither had I."

"What made you pick it up now? Are you planning to write a sequel?"

"A sequel?" Finn asked. "You mean like there's been some resolution?"

Kate looked hard at her father and tears welled up in her eyes. She took his hand. "You've had a difficult life, Dad. A lot of pain and loss. I'm sorry. I don't think I ever said that to you."

Finn hugged her. "We've both had a lot of loss. I think you've done a better job of weathering it than I have."

"Why do you say that?"

"You don't resort to temporary relief."

"I just don't give in to it. I don't let it conquer me."

"How did I get such a smart, well-adjusted daughter?"

"It must have been my mother's genes."

He smiled wistfully. "Yes. She gave you many good genes. All I gave you was a stubborn streak."

"I like to call it a thirst for independence," she added.

He got up slowly and winced. She started to say something but decided against it. "See you in the morning, Kate."

"Okay." She watched him walk gingerly out of the room, not sure if he was in pain or just drunk. She opened the book and started reading.

She stayed over an hour, engrossed, with tears rolling down her cheeks. Sometimes they were tears of laughter, but mostly they were tears of sadness and regret. She wasn't sure who she was crying for more, her father or herself.

He had tried to create a normal childhood for her, despite the death of her mother when she was too young to remember her. She hated those feelings of being different and having to endure people's pity, but he had vowed to be a good parent and he had succeeded. She knew, even back then, that he had sacrificed a lot to give her a safe, loving environment. Some of it was financial but he also relinquished his own dreams in order to give her all his time and attention.

Finn's childhood, however, was another story. He had been raised in unimaginable filth and deprivation in an impoverished Irish ghetto. His father was a violent drunk who used what little money he earned for his own benefit while his family starved. He would stay away for days, only to return when he had nowhere else to go. He took out his resentment on his wife and son. Finn had learned at an early age that begging on the streets didn't provide much and that stealing was the only alternative. He also learned early on that he couldn't save his mother from his father's beatings. He could only save himself by running away. Soon he realized that he would have a better chance at a decent life by staying away. His mother died soon after he left and he never knew what happened to his father. He honestly didn't care. He wrote about all this in his memoir.

That's as far as Kate got that night. She didn't get to the part where he wound up in New York, went to college, met her mother, became a teacher and turned his life around. But she knew that part and she didn't need to read it to remind herself that he was a survivor, endowed with an enormous amount of courage and fortitude. He might be a cantankerous pain in the ass, but she couldn't be prouder of him.

Jed opened the back door of Luis' restaurant for a breath of fresh air. His brow was soaked with sweat and the rubber apron he wore was dripping soapy water. Mother slept on the ground next to the door. "Hey there, Mother. Getting tired of waiting?" He picked her up and went back inside the kitchen. He set the cat down on the counter and put the last of a large pile of plates into the dishwasher. There was an even larger mound of pots in the sink and he started to scrub them while Mother slept.

Luis, dressed up in a Mexican Guayabera shirt, rushed in with another tub of dishes. "Sorry, Jed, one more tub but that should do it. Whew. It was a busy night. Hey, what's your cat doing in here?"

"She's sleeping."

"You can't have the cat in the kitchen."

"She's not bothering anything."

"The Public Health Department would close me down on the spot. You need to put her out."

Jed's body stiffened. "I'm almost finished. We'll be out of here in a few minutes."

Luis picked up Mother and walked toward the door. "No, she has to go out now."

Jed pushed a pile of dishes onto the floor and rushed up to Luis, with eyes blazing. "Put her down!"

47

Luis backed up, alarmed, and dropped Mother. Jed took Luis by the collar. "Don't throw my cat!" Jed took off his apron, threw it on the ground, picked up Mother and stomped off. Luis stood frozen in shock.

Jed put Mother on his shoulders and stalked down the street toward the black ocean, muttering to himself. He knew he had to get back into the mountains to calm his temper. When he got to the sand, he turned right and started his trek. Sometimes he walked all night instead of looking for a place to lie down. His body seemed to be able to function on very little sleep.

He had endured many nights, both as a child and as an adult, lying awake, afraid to close his eyes. There had always been somebody or something to be terrified of and no one around who could do much about it. He was also used to handling extreme weather and extreme hunger. Even when he had not been homeless, food and comfort had not been easy to come by. He had learned how to accept all of that. He had a lot more trouble overcoming his angry outbursts.

5

FINN WAS TYPING AT HIS COMPUTER as the sun started to peek over the horizon. He had been awake for a couple of hours, drinking coffee and Googling about homelessness. The piles of papers and books had spread further and further out and were taking over his office, much to Kate's dismay. When the phone rang, he was relieved to relinquish his half-hearted researching, and he went to the kitchen to answer it. "Hello? No, Judith, I'm not home. That's why I didn't answer the phone," he retorted sarcastically. "Fine. Tell them I'll have something for them soon." He hung up and poured himself another cup of coffee. "Damn publishers," he grumbled.

He returned to his office and took the whiskey out of the cabinet. He had just finished pouring it into his coffee when Kate, in running clothes, entered with a laundry basket.

"Drinking already?"

"I'm rearranging things in the cabinet."

"Yeah, right. You're straightening up the cabinet." She glanced around the room. "Just like you neatened up your office."

Finn decided to ignore her cynicism for the sake of harmony. "Thanks for doing my laundry."

Kate's face softened. "You're welcome." She managed a small smile. "It's been a lot of years since I did your laundry."

Finn smiled back at her. "You were always a great folder, even when you were a little girl. You always had to have everything perfectly aligned. Even the sheets were perfectly creased."

"I started reading your book again last night."

"Oh yeah?"

"It's interesting to read it again years later. Now that I'm older, I have a different perspective on you and your views on life."

"In what way?"

"I guess I have more of an understanding of it and of you."

He smiled. "You mean you don't need to find fault with me as much?"

Kate got defensive. "What's that supposed to mean?"

"Are you going to tell me that you don't criticize me?"

"No more than you criticize me."

"When have I criticized you?" he asked.

"I think you disapproved of my choice not to get married again."

"Not at all. I just didn't understand it for a long time. Now I do."

"Well, you have a funny way of showing it."

"Why? Because I'm not as outspoken as you are about what you disapprove of?"

"That's right, Dad, if you're talking about your drinking."

"That would be what I'm talking about."

Kate pinched her lips closed. "I'll try to keep my disappointments to myself."

Finn took Jed's handkerchief out of the laundry basket and put it in his pocket. "I'd appreciate that."

"Since when do you carry a handkerchief?" Kate asked.

"It's not mine. Jed loaned it to me when I hurt my head."

"Who's Jed?"

"A homeless person on the boardwalk."

Kate looked at him warily. "You used a homeless person's handkerchief?"

"It was perfectly clean."

"It might have looked clean, but you don't know what or where—"

Finn interrupted her. "What happened to your keeping your disapproval to yourself?"

Kate pouted as she neatened the piles on the table. "So that's where you hurt your head? On the boardwalk?"

"Yes."

"Did you fall?"

"In a way. Someone—" He stopped himself. "I tripped."

She continued to try to make some order out of the surface of his desk and Finn scowled at her for doing so. "How will you find a homeless person to give him back his handkerchief?" she asked.

"I don't know. I'll look for him. He said he'd find me."

"Be careful, Dad. There are some really crazy people on the boardwalk."

"I'm a New Yorker. I'm pretty used to being surrounded by crazy people."

Kate picked up the laundry basket and muttered, "It takes one to know one," as she walked out.

The sun was bright when a showered and dressed Finn came out the front door onto the porch and picked up the two newspapers. He put the *NY Times* under his arm and tossed the *LA Times* on the floor inside the door. He descended the stairs onto the sidewalk and walked briskly down the street.

The inside of the cafe was crowded, so after buying a cup of coffee and a pastry he went out to the patio to look for an empty table. He found one and settled in to read his newspaper. It didn't take long for him to tire of the political shenanigans and the jewelry ads, so he folded it to do the crossword puzzle. He had just started to work on it when Harper appeared and put a piece of paper on the table in front of him. He looked down and then smiled up at her. "Well, look at that. You won the writing contest."

A beaming Harper plopped into the chair facing him. "Can you believe it? There probably weren't very many entries."

"Don't put yourself down. You don't know that. It's a great accomplishment and you should be proud."

"Thanks. At least it'll look good on my resume. Hey, what happened to your head?"

Finn felt the scab. "Oh, I, uh, hit it on the kitchen cabinet."

"Wow. It looks pretty nasty. Does it hurt?"

"Not really. It looks worse than it is."

"How's the puzzle coming?"

"I just started." He took a sip of coffee and made a face as he set it down. "This coffee stinks."

"Really? I like it here. This place is supposed to have the best coffee on the Westside."

"I like the one I make at home better."

"What kind is that?"

"The Irish kind."

She raised her eyebrows and grinned at him as he broke his pastry in half and offered her a piece. "No thanks. I try to eat healthy."

"Suit yourself. You're smart to eat well, but you know what they say: old people shouldn't eat healthy, they need all the preservatives they can get."

She laughed as he took a bite. "Your books never showed this funny side of you."

Finn shrugged his shoulders. "Probably because they were memoirs. There wasn't a whole lot to laugh about in my childhood."

"It did sound grim. You were so poor. I can't believe you didn't even have an indoor toilet."

"Where I lived in Ireland makes American ghettoes look palatial."

"I remember that you had to steal bread and milk so you and your family could eat."

"I'm not proud of what I had to do to survive."

"Well you sure did more than survive. You became a successful author."

"I was determined to get out of there as soon as I could."

"Have you gotten past your writer's block?"

"I'm starting to get inspired."

"Cool. What are you writing?"

"Let's just say I'm still in brainstorming mode." Finn finished his pastry and coffee and stood. "I'm going to stroll down to the boardwalk. Care to accompany me?"

"I can't. I've got to go to work. I just wanted to find you to tell you about the contest."

"I'm glad you won, Harper."

"Thanks. Reading your book really inspired me to write, you know."

"I'd like to read your story," Finn said.

"Would you really? That would mean a lot to me." She took it out of her bag and handed it to him. "Your opinion means more to me than the judges of the contest."

"Thank you, Harper, but I think your trust is somewhat misguided." He folded Harper's story and put it in his pocket. "I'll read it tonight." He put the newspaper under his arm and threw the coffee cup in the trash as he exited the cafe.

Finn walked aimlessly down the boardwalk, watching the vendors and performers set up their tables and props. Before 10 a.m. the only stores open on the boardwalk were the liquor stores, the food marts, and a couple of the restaurants. It was closer to eleven when the shopkeepers unlocked their stores and rolled out their racks of bikinis, T-shirts, and sunglasses. By then the people wearing T-shirts with stupid sayings had started to mill around, taking pictures and shooting videos. The musicians started playing and soon the boardwalk bustled as performers, political activists and hawkers vied for the tourists' attention.

Finn stopped to watch a violinist play a medley of rock, jazz, classical and bluegrass and wondered why someone with so much talent hadn't been discovered. He threw a dollar bill into the violin case on the ground and joined the crowd that had gathered to watch Davion and Ty. Their acrobatic dancing had the crowd and Finn in awe. He stood there quite awhile hoping Jed would show up. When the Jamaican pair took a much-deserved break, he went to the bench where he had first met Jed. He took out his pen and zipped through the crossword puzzle, looking up now and then to scan the crowd. When he finished the puzzle, he threw the newspaper in the trashcan and started to walk away but was startled by a voice that seemed to come out of nowhere.

"That's recyclable, man." Finn looked for the person talking and spotted a longhaired hippie about thirty, sitting on a bicycle with a guitar strapped to his back. "You need to recycle the newspaper. It goes in the green can over there."

"I see." Finn took the newspaper out of the trash and put it in the green can.

The young man approached Finn. "We don't have much time left, you know. This planet is on its way out, man. We've killed it. We have to do everything we can to save it. And us."

"Got it," Finn said as he started to walk away.

The young man reached into his pocket, took out a flyer and chased after Finn. "I'm Derek. Come to our meeting tonight."

Finn nodded and glanced at the flyer as he continued down the boardwalk. The meeting was for a group calling themselves "Save Our Earth." He threw the flyer away, being careful to put it in a green can. He continued down the boardwalk toward the skateboard park.

He noticed a short, plump, elderly woman, leaning on a shopping cart and sorting through a trashcan. She took out each item one by one, carefully turning it over in her hands, even holding it up to the sunlight. It was as if they were antiques or diamonds the way she evaluated them before deciding which items to put in her cart. She was neat and clean in a brightly flowered muumuu, but her hair was a tangled mass of frizzy gray. Her shopping cart was filled with old newspapers, tin cans, paper plates and cups, old paperback books - nothing of value or that could be called worldly possessions. She walked slowly to the next trashcan, pushing her cart, and sorted through that one. Finn was mesmerized. He continued watching her as she started walking toward the street, struggling to push her cart. He decided to follow her, always staying a few steps behind. It was a slow process.

They left the hustle and bustle of the boardwalk and walked a couple of blocks away from the ocean. She stopped at a trashcan and took out a yellow backpack that looked exactly like Jed's. He watched her open a couple of zippers, take things out and methodically sort through them. She took out a framed picture, some socks, a couple of shirts, a book, and a water bottle and carefully returned them to the backpack. She zipped the compartments back up and placed the backpack carefully in her cart. She turned right and walked over a bridge. Finn followed and found himself in the quiet, peaceful surroundings known as the Venice Beach canals.

All that was left of Abbott Kinney's glorious vision were four east-west canals and two north-south canals. There were no streets directly next to the water, just walkways with several quaint bridges to cross over. The canals were lined with expensive houses straight out of *Architectural Digest*. The lots they sat on were tiny so people added large windows and extra stories to remodel them. Some had small wooden rowboats tied up in front.

She turned toward a modest house, brown and drab, that was probably once a middle-class bungalow, but was now shabby and decrepit. She shuffled inside pushing her shopping cart. Finn decided that she probably needed the cart for balance and stability, not just as a receptacle for her newfound treasures.

He stood for a few minutes taking in the incongruity. This run-down house with garbage and debris strewn across the lawn, sat in the middle of one of the most desirable and expensive residential neighborhoods in Los Angeles. The Venice Beach canals were even listed on the National Register of Historic Places. Just then the door of the house next door opened and a gorgeous woman who looked like she just stepped off the cover of *Vogue* came out. She smiled at Finn and walked quickly past him. She was more the type he expected to be living here. He turned to leave and was startled by a loud quack. A family of ducks floated by to complete the picture of absurdity.

When he got home he made a new pot of coffee and sat down at his computer. He had a lot of Googling to do. He spiked his coffee periodically as he spent the rest of the afternoon looking things up. He added recycling and environmental issues, as well as hoarding, to homelessness and the history of Venice Beach. His Google history was growing quite long.

6

FINN WAS ABSORBED IN HIS RESEARCH when Kate called from the kitchen that dinner was ready. "I'm not hungry!" Finn shouted back.

"You have to eat something," Kate said as she entered his office.

"I don't want your rabbit food. I'll cook something later."

"It wouldn't kill you to eat something with more colors than brown and white. You may be Irish, but that doesn't mean you can't try food that's not overcooked meat and boiled potatoes."

"California cuisine doesn't suit me." He continued typing and reading, ignoring Kate.

"Oh, Dad, you're so pigheaded." She looked over his shoulder at the computer screen. "So you're finally writing."

"Researching."

She placed a couple of envelopes on top of a stack of mail and straightened out the pile. "By the way, some more letters came for you. Are you ever going to open any of these?"

"There's no reason to."

She shook her head and called over her shoulder as she left the room, "Your food's getting cold."

Finn took the top envelope off the pile and looked at the return address. It was another collection agency. He tore it up and threw it away without opening it. He picked up the next one and looked at the return address. "Antoinette Delon. She must be looking for a job recommendation," he said aloud.

Maggie had resisted having any caregivers come to the house but she had seen the toll it was taking on Finn and finally gave in. She was still lucid then, but the doctors had given that dreaded yet expected recommendation for hospice care to begin. When the pain got unbearable and the nosebleeds and breathing difficulties became a daily occurrence, she finally relented. She had already surrendered her daily insulin injections to Finn who had not warmed to the prospect easily, but had risen to the occasion. At least she could still walk to the bathroom with help, but he knew pretty soon that too would be impossible.

He remembered the first day Antoinette arrived. She had been recommended highly by the agency and both he and Maggie had been impressed by her warmth and knowledge. Although she was

61

originally from Jamaica, she had gone to nursing school in San Francisco and had lived in South America before coming to New York. Maggie had enjoyed talking to her. When Maggie slipped into a coma, Antoinette sensed Finn's reluctance to engage in conversation and left him alone. That was a huge relief to him.

He opened it and his jaw dropped. "What the hell?" He finished reading the letter and threw it across the desk in disgust. "What a bitch!"

He went straight to the cabinet for his whiskey bottle. He held it up and saw there was only a small amount left. "Fuck!" He swigged what was there and started looking frantically through a stack of cardboard boxes. He threw things helter-skelter as he emptied them. The floor became a jumble of papers, pictures and books.

Kate entered with a plate of food and set it on the table next to the computer. "What are you doing? It looks like a tornado hit!"

"I'm looking for something."

"Well here's some food, in case you change your mind about eating." She watched him suspiciously. "I hope you're going to take this opportunity to put things away."

"Maybe later."

"Let me help you look."

"No! I'll do it myself."

"Oh Dad, why must you be like this."

"Just leave me alone, please!"

"Fine!" She stomped out.

Finn continued looking through the boxes. He finally found what he wanted. He removed a manila envelope from the bottom of one of the boxes and opened it. He took out a small plastic bag, half-filled with a white powder. He looked at it for a minute and turned it over and over in his hand, contemplating the reality of what he was about to do. He opened the bag apprehensively, and after a nanosecond of wavering, stuck his finger in the bag and brought the powder to his nose and snorted. He sat back in his chair and savored the sensation.

7

NIGHTTIME ON THE VENICE BEACH BOARDWALK is a totally different ballgame. The tourists go back to their hotel rooms, the vendors and street performers pack up their tables and instruments, the stores and restaurants lock their doors, and the skateboarders and bicyclers can zigzag up and down the boardwalk with abandon. There is usually at least one drum circle on the beach, but the police are pretty vigilant about dispersing them at 9:30 or 10. Couples walk hand-in-hand, so enchanted with each other that they are unaware of the cold wind coming off the ocean. They are also oblivious to the danger of a rogue wave when they are walking on the beach, or a rogue criminal when they are walking on the boardwalk. The benches are filled with teenage runaways panhandling the few visitors that remain. The police make another sweep at midnight when the supposed curfew goes into effect, but they are rather lenient and don't bother any of the familiar vagrants. When the police have cleared the boardwalk, the homeless begin the search for where to bed for the night.

Jed walked through an alley lined with dumpsters, opening and closing them until he located one filled with pieces of cardboard. He sorted through them carefully until he finally found some large pieces that would be suitable. With Mother curled around his shoulders, he walked down the street to the boardwalk, dragging the cardboard behind him. He stopped at an alcove between two stores and set up his makeshift bed, placing the cardboard down neatly and brushing it off with the sleeve of his jacket. He took Mother off his shoulders and set her down gently. He curled up next to her and put one of the pieces of cardboard over both of them.

He never fell asleep quickly, but he had started using a breathing technique that seemed to help speed up the process. One of the other boardwalk regulars had brought him to a Buddhist temple and although he didn't want to follow a formal spiritual path, he found that the breathing techniques he had learned were beneficial. When he slept with Mother, he used her purrs as his guiding rhythm and soon they both drifted off.

Matt and Luke sauntered down the boardwalk, poking those who had scored a bench to sleep on and kicking those who had been too drunk or high to care that they were lying in the middle of the walkway.

Both young men were agitated, high on meth and looking for trouble.

"There's that nigger with the cat," Matt whispered. Luke shushed his friend as he tiptoed toward Jed and Mother. He carefully lifted the cardboard off the sleeping pair and tried to grab the cat.

Mother bit and scratched Luke until his arm bled. "Fucking cat!" he yelled as he tried to throw her down. Her claws reached out again and tore into his pant legs and flesh as she slipped to the ground. Jed awoke and was quick to respond with a punch. He fought with blind intensity even though it was two against one. When a slow-moving police jeep drove down the boardwalk, Matt and Luke fled.

Mother jumped onto Jed's lap. "Are you okay, Mother?" She purred her answer. He was in too much pain to run after them, so he sat petting Mother and breathing in time with her purrs until he composed himself. He got up slowly, wincing as he gathered up the cardboard. He folded it carefully and leaned it against the side of one of the stores. He gathered Mother up into his arms and limped into one of the public restroom buildings.

As he washed the blood off his face and arms, a man came out of one of the stalls. He was black and about Jed's age but looked about twenty years older. Being out in the elements had not been good to him. Earl was a cop gone bad. He had taken bribes and was unlucky enough to have been caught. While on administrative leave during the investigation, he had shot and killed a man in a bar. The man was a known gang member and other than a couple of his family members, no one in the police department or the general public was too sad to see his demise. But the media had a field day with the story. Although Earl was exonerated because he claimed it was in self-defense, it was the last straw and he was stripped of his badge and gun. He was eventually given a desk job, but he wasn't interested. He ultimately drank himself into getting fired and now made his home under the Santa Monica pier. He liked to think of himself as too classy for Venice.

He would guard the pier and monitor any activity at night. He, more than anyone, knew the nighttime troublemakers. He still fancied himself a policeman, even if a corrupt one, and he actually did keep Santa Monica somewhat free of the meth-addicted dirtbags that frequented Venice. But he knew them all and that's how he kept them away. He would solicit money in exchange for promising not to report them to the authorities, which in some cases were not the police but their parents. Part of the shakedown was that they had to stay on the Venice side of Rose Avenue. "What happened to you?" he asked Jed.

"A couple of Beverly Hills thugs caught me off guard while I was asleep."

"Got to watch your back around here, Jed. Venice ain't no place for a smart man like you."

"Not all of us can afford your fancy digs in Santa Monica."

Earl laughed and lit a cigarette. "You want me to talk to my friends and teach those creeps a lesson they won't forget?"

"No thanks. I can take care of them myself."

"Well, you know I still have some pull in high places," Earl said as he left.

By the time Jed finished cleaning up, the sun was bright and the boardwalk had started to come alive with the early morning exercise fanatics. The only table set up for business was Charlie's. He was there, rain or shine, always with coffee and donuts at the very least, and sometimes a full breakfast if a church or school group decided to make the boardwalk homeless their charity of the week. Jed got coffee and a donut for himself and a cup with half and half for Mother. After politely answering Charlie's queries about what happened to him and declining the offer to drive him to the hospital, Jed went to sit on a bench in front of the paddleball courts.

He sipped his coffee slowly and watched the game. A young black boy, about fourteen years old, sat on the other end of the bench. He looked lost and scared yet he was dressed in a top-of-the-line Nike outfit from head to toe. Someone had obviously spent money on those clothes, but they were now rumpled and soiled.

"You got any more donuts?" the boy asked.

"They're over at the Homeless Services table," Jed answered.

"Are they free?"

Jed smiled. "At the Homeless table? What do you think?"

The boy smiled back. "Yeah. I guess they would be." He got up and strolled over to Charlie's table, trying to hide that he was lonesome and afraid with a cool saunter. He came back with two donuts and sat on the bench, this time right next to Jed.

"The guy gave me two. He said he gives two to kids who are still growing."

"Nothing like a donut to help build strong bodies twelve ways."

"Huh?"

Jed smiled. "Old Wonder Bread commercial. Never mind."

They sat in silence and ate their donuts. Finally the boy spoke. "What happened to you?"

"What do you mean?"

"You're all banged up."

"Comes with the territory," Jed answered.

The boy shrugged his shoulders and they watched the paddle tennis for a few minutes until Jed stood and put Mother on his shoulders. "Cool cat," the boy added.

"That she is." Jed started to walk away and then turned toward the boy. "Shouldn't you be in school?"

The boy's expression turned sullen and suspicious. "Are you a cop?"

"No need to get bent out of shape. I was just asking." Jed turned and walked toward the trashcan and threw out his and Mother's cups. The boy hurried over to him.

"Where are you going?"

Jed looked at him skeptically. "Now who's acting like the fuzz?"

The boy looked crestfallen, although he again shrugged his shoulders as if he didn't care. "I just wondered." Jed started to walk away again when the boy called out. "What's your cat's name?"

Jed stopped and turned around. "Mother."

"Mother. That's a cool name for a cool cat. My name is Malcolm."

"You live around here Malcolm?"

"Kinda."

"What do you mean, kinda? Either you do or you don't."

"Okay. Yeah. I live around here."

"Well then. Maybe I'll see you around."

"What's your name?"

"Jed."

"Can I come with you?"

"No," Jed answered a little too quickly.

"Sorry. I just—" Malcolm stared at the ground.

"Uh, not today." Jed interrupted. He hoped he hadn't hurt Malcolm's feelings. "Another time." Malcolm watched Jed walk onto the beach, and then turn toward the Santa Monica Mountains. He kept his eyes on him as he got smaller and smaller until he couldn't distinguish the man with the cat on his shoulders.

Malcolm walked back to Charlie's table. "Got any more donuts?"

Charlie reached in his pocket and took out a coupon for a free slice of pizza at one of the boardwalk eateries and handed it to Malcolm. "It opens at nine. At least it's a little more nutritious than donuts."

Malcolm took it eagerly. "Thanks!" He ran over to the pizza place. It had just opened. He gobbled down his slice as he walked past Muscle Beach and the basketball courts. He stopped when he arrived at the skateboard park. There were a couple of teenagers there, but it was mostly filled with the unemployed, twenty-something hotshots who used school day hours to do their more dangerous tricks. The mornings were safe from the dads egging on their kids to be the athletes they never were. Malcolm could watch those hotdoggers for hours. They were as good as those guys on the Extreme Sports channel. In fact, he overheard one guy say that he had once been in the X Games.

Venice Beach was better than television sometimes. You could spend a whole day watching a myriad of sports: weightlifters at Muscle Beach, skateboarders in the Skate Park, surfers by the pier, paddle tennis, basketball, and beach volleyball. The musicians, dancers, magicians and acrobats were exceptionally talented and their banter with the public made for great entertainment. All of that plus the people watching made the days go pretty quickly for those who had nothing else to do and nowhere else to go. The bathrooms were always open, the weather was warm, and there were tourists to panhandle. That's why Venice Beach was a mecca for the homeless of any age. Malcolm could pass the time quickly and painlessly as he avoided thinking about his dilemma.

Malcolm and his mother had been living in the Venice area for about a year. They had been on the run for several years, trying to escape the violent abusive man who Malcolm refused to acknowledge was his father. It seemed he would always find them when they stayed in Texas, where Malcolm had been born, so they fled to California and so far had been successful in eluding him. His school history had been spotty, but his mother had always made sure he had literature to read, pads to write on and math texts to work in. She had always managed to find jobs and he had always had somewhere to sleep and nice clothes to wear. Until now.

His mother had been diagnosed with cancer and her decline had been rapid. She tried to stay home as long as she could, even though she had been bedridden for several months. She signed the welfare checks so Malcolm could cash them and pay the rent and buy food, but her medical expenses became exorbitant. They hadn't paid rent for a couple of

72

months and then one morning he couldn't wake her up. He called an ambulance and she had been in the hospital ever since. He had stayed in the apartment until the landlord found out and changed the locks. He was afraid to tell anyone for fear they would send him back to his father in Texas. He had never known any of his mother's family. She never spoke of them and he never asked. His childhood had not been one full of candor and trust.

Since he hadn't gone to school and spent most days holed up in his apartment with his mother, he didn't know the city or any people in it other than the neighbors, shopkeepers and hospital personnel he had encountered. He had no idea what to do. He just hoped his mother would wake up and the doctors would say it had all been a big mistake.

8

FINN STROLLED DOWN THE BOARDWALK and saw Davion and Ty playing steel drums and break dancing with a group of other Jamaican performers. Usually he was mesmerized watching them, in awe of their athleticism and musical talent. But today he waited impatiently for them to finish their song. Davion saw him and danced over with a wide grin.

"Hey, wa'ppun, mon? How you feel today?" He peered at the scab on the side of Finn's head.

"Have you seen Jed?" Finn asked, ignoring Davion's question.

"Not lately. I think he on another trip."

"Trip?" Finn was puzzled.

"No one know where he go or what he do," Ty answered as he joined them.

"He on a trip all right. A mind trip," Davion added.

"You mean like LSD?" Finn asked.

"No, mon. He don't need drugs to take him anywhere," Davion chuckled. "He jus' trippin' in his head all by himself."

"Oh." Finn tried to understand.

"He be back. He always come back." Ty patted Finn's shoulder.

"If you see him, tell him I may know where his backpack is." Finn turned abruptly to leave.

"Try the Mexican restaurant over there," Davion called to him.

Finn looked back at him. "Where?"

"There." Davion pointed up the street. "Sometime he work there washing dishes."

Finn nodded a thank you and walked toward the restaurant. He looked through the window of Luis' and stepped inside. The room was dark and empty of customers, as it was still too early for the lunch crowd. It was your usual Mexican family restaurant: Naugahyde bench seats and Formica tables, old Corona beer posters on the walls, that familiar picture of a senorita wearing a shawl and holding a basket of flowers, a mural of the stereotypical Mexican town plaza with a fountain and people milling around in colorful costumes, paper flowers and maracas hanging from the ceiling. Mercedes, an attractive young woman about twenty, was refilling the sugar containers and saltshakers.

Finn approached her. "Hello. I'm looking for Jed. Is he here?"

She pointed to Luis. "Talk to my dad."

Finn walked over to the cash register where Luis was counting money. "Excuse me. I'm looking for Jed. I believe he works here?"

Luis looked up guardedly. "He washes dishes sometimes at night."

"Will he be here tonight?"

"I don't know if he'll show up. He had one of his fits."

"What do you mean, fits?"

"He gets really mad sometimes, like he's out of control. But he always calms down and apologizes."

"What sets him off?"

Luis shrugged his shoulders. "I never know. Sometimes it's just the smallest thing. All I know is he can be pretty scary when he gets like that."

"Are you afraid he'd hurt you?"

"Oh no. Jed's a good, kind man. He just gets so angry, so upset."

"I'll check back tonight. What time does he get here?"

"He comes at six but he has a job to do when he's here."

"Okay. I'll come toward the end of his shift. Thanks." Finn walked out and nodded to Mercedes as he left the restaurant.

He walked back to Kate's along Main Street, one of the busier north-south thoroughfares that connect Venice and Santa Monica. It runs parallel to the boardwalk, a few blocks east of the beach. In Venice, Main Street is a mix of drug stores, banks, and hair salons: stores that cater to the needs of its local residents. As you walk north toward Santa Monica, the shops resemble the same type of high-end boutiques, art galleries and restaurants that you'd find on Abbot Kinney Boulevard, catering to the wealthier tourists.

Kate's house was in the more nondescript area of Venice on the east side of Main Street—close enough to the beach to be easily walkable, but far enough from the beach to be halfway affordable. Her neighborhood was a microcosm of Venice, an eclectic mix of hipsters, middle class families and elderly pensioners who had lived in their apartments for years. It reminded Finn of his old Manhattan neighborhood. It was not the car-oriented, suburban lifestyle that typically comes to mind when you think of Los Angeles.

When he got to Kate's, he went to his office to brood about Antoinette's letter, Jed's moodiness, his persistent writer's block, and the sorry state of his finances. At least it took his mind off Maggie's death and his loneliness and sorrow.

9

KATE DROVE FINN TO LUIS' RESTAURANT that night, much to his dismay. "You didn't need to drive me! I'm not a child!"

"Dad, I can't let you walk around here at night by yourself. It's too dangerous."

"I used to walk around New York at night all the time."

"That's different."

"Different? You want to tell me New York is safer than Venice?"

"Your neighborhood in New York was. And anyway, there are always people around in New York. Venice gets deserted at night except near the restaurants."

"Then what's the problem, Kate? This is a restaurant, isn't it? Jesus Christ! Look for yourself. Don't you see people all around?"

"Yes, there are people, but what sort of people."

"What kind of thing is that to say? I'm surprised at you."

"I'm just being realistic. And what is it with this Jed character, anyway? Why is it so imperative that you see him tonight?"

"What do you mean?"

"This interest you have in him. It's weird and doesn't make sense."

Finn got out of the car without answering and went inside. A couple of the tables still had customers and Luis sat at one with his daughter. They were counting money while a busboy cleared off the remaining empty tables. Luis looked up when Finn entered. "Did Jed show up?" Finn asked.

"He's in the kitchen, but don't take too long. He's got work to do."

Luis pointed to swinging doors and Finn walked through them. Jed's back was to Finn and he seemed engrossed in his dishwashing duties. "Jed?" Finn said tentatively. Jed turned around and Finn gasped when he saw Jed's cut and bruised face. His eyes were swollen and bloodshot. "What happened?"

"What do you want?" Jed snapped back.

Finn took Jed's handkerchief out of his pocket and handed it to him. "I washed your handkerchief."

Jed stuffed it in his pocket. "Thanks." He turned his back to Finn and resumed washing dishes.

"Did you get Mother back?"

"Yes. She always finds me."

"How "bout your stuff? Did you find it?"

Jed turned around angrily to face Finn. "Why do you care?"

Finn stepped backward. "I was concerned."

"Why? I don't even know you."

"You helped me on the boardwalk when—"

Jed interrupted him. "I remember."

"A bag lady found your backpack in a trash can. I followed her and I think I know where she lives."

Luis entered the kitchen and spoke before Jed had a chance to respond. "Sorry mister but Jed needs to get back to work."

"Take my phone number and address." Finn wrote on a scrap of paper and handed it to Jed. "Please." Jed took it and stuffed it in his pocket, but said nothing.

When Finn got back in the car, he saw Mother sitting on Kate's lap. "Where'd you find that cat?"

"He was sitting so patiently outside the restaurant. Isn't he sweet? I wonder if he has a home."

"It's a she and yes she has a—" Finn stopped and Kate looked at him expectantly. "She has an owner," he finished.

"You know who owns this cat?"

"It's Jed's cat, Mother."

"That's her name? Mother?"

"You need to leave her here. She's waiting for Jed."

Kate opened the door to let her out and started the car. "What do you know about this Jed guy? Why is he homeless if he has a job here at this restaurant?"

"I don't know. Let's just go."

She shrugged her shoulders and pulled away from the curb. Just then Luke and Matt walked by the restaurant and saw Mother sitting patiently at the door. "Hey, there's that nigger's cat."

"Where's the guy?"

"I don't see him."

"Let's get this fucking cat once and for all." They lunged for Mother. She arched her back and hissed, clawing at Luke as he grabbed her. He was able to keep her at bay, though, as she squirmed and scratched at him. They took her into the alley behind the restaurant. Luke held her down while Matt slit her side with a knife. She fought back hard and finally wriggled out of his grip. She was bleeding but managed to run away.

Kate and Finn arrived home and went their separate ways: Kate to the kitchen and Finn to his office. He stepped around the mess of books and papers on the floor and sat at his computer. He tried looking up the causes and effects of homelessness but couldn't muster up much enthusiasm. He stared at the screen for a while and then started a game of solitaire.

Kate entered with a scowl on her face. "Your office is a pigsty."

"You said I could use the dining room for my office when I moved in, did you not?"

"I know but I didn't know you had turned into such a slob."

Finn frowned at her. "What do you want?" he grumbled at her.

"There's a message on the answering machine for you."

"Who is it?"

"It's Judith and I think you'd better listen to it." Finn reluctantly followed her to the kitchen and pressed the button.

Judith's booming voice came on. "Finn! I spoke to the publishers like you asked and they're not going to give you anything without some chapters written. Too much time has passed since your last bestseller and frankly, Finn, they're not convinced that you can deliver. You'd better call me back. I don't know if I can keep stalling them."

Finn looked at Kate standing in the doorway and brushed past her. She yelled after him, "Aren't you going to call her back?"

"It's late in New York, for God's sake. I'll call her tomorrow."

Finn went to his office and filled a tall glass with whiskey. Kate entered and grabbed the bottle away from him. "This isn't the way to get anything written."

Finn shouted at her, "What are you doing? Give me that!"

"No!" She held the bottle close to her chest.

"Don't tell me how much I can drink!"

"Someone has to! You're going to drink yourself to death at this rate!" They struggled over the bottle and it fell to the floor and broke, whiskey flowing everywhere.

"Now, look what you've done!" He, of course, was referring to the fact that he now had no whiskey left. Kate was more upset that the hardwood floor would be ruined.

"What I've done? No, Dad. You're doing this to yourself." Finn scrambled to pick up books and papers from the floor before they got saturated. Kate stomped off and came back with a bucket and a mop. She shoved him out of the way. "Move so I can clean this up!"

He grabbed his glass and took it to the kitchen. He paced back and forth, debating about whether he should leave a message on Judith's voicemail. He finally picked up the phone and dialed. "Judith? Please! Talk to them. I need that advance. Can't you sweet-talk them into giving me something? I'll have a couple of chapters for them this week." He hung up knowing full well that there was little chance he would write a word.

10

JED CAME OUT THE BACK DOOR of the restaurant and looked around for Mother. He walked around the block, searching in bushes and between buildings. When he got back to the alley, he heard faint meowing and frantically knocked over crates and garbage cans until he found Mother lying under the dumpster. He picked her up and felt how limp she was. "Mother? What's wrong?" She meowed weakly and then he saw the large bloody gash on her side. "Mother!" He took off running down the street.

He sprinted for several blocks until he got to a small building housing a 24-hour veterinary clinic. He rushed inside to the receptionist. "I need the doctor. Now!" When the receptionist saw Mother's bloody fur, she rushed out and came back with the doctor. He looked at the gash on Mother's side, took Mother in his arms, and hurried through a rear door.

Jed tried to follow the vet, but the receptionist stopped him. "You need to stay in the waiting room so the doctor can help your cat. And you need to fill out some papers." Jed reluctantly took the papers and pen from her and sat down. He went through the questions quickly and handed them back to the receptionist.

She looked over the papers. "I'll need an address and phone."

"Don't have any."

She looked at him suspiciously. "Well, is there anything at all you can write down?"

"No."

"How about a friend or relative?"

Jed glared at her without saying a word. She squirmed in her seat and put the papers in a folder. Jed turned away and paced the floor, fidgeting and breathing heavily. He finally sat down and tried to calm himself. After about an hour the doctor came back out to the waiting area and Jed jumped up. "She'll be okay. I stitched her up but she needs to stay overnight so we can watch her. That was a very deep wound. How did it happen?"

"I don't know. I found her like that in an alley."

"Oh, so she's not your cat?"

"Yes, she is my cat!" Jed shouted.

"Okay, calm down."

"Can I see her?"

"She's sleeping. She's heavily sedated."

"I'd still like to see her."

"I can't let you back there right now. Come back tomorrow and we'll see how she's doing."

Jed sighed with resignation. "How much is this going to cost?"

"We will go over that with you tomorrow."

"Can't you tell me now?"

"No, you need to talk to the office manager and she won't be in until tomorrow morning."

"I really need to know." Jed punched the counter, his eyes blazing.

The vet took a few steps backwards. "I'm going to have to ask you to leave, sir." Jed took a deep breath and stomped off, slamming the door behind him.

He walked down to the beach, determined to walk off his anger, but stopped at the boardwalk when he saw a familiar figure lying on a bench. Malcolm had no blanket or sleeping bag and was curled up in a fetal position, evidently trying to get warm. He approached the bench and gently shook the boy's shoulders. Malcolm sat up abruptly; his eyes ablaze and darting from side to side like a frightened animal. He jumped off the bench and started to run.

"Malcolm!" Jed called after him. "It's me. Jed."

Malcolm turned around. "Oh." He walked back to the bench and sat down.

"It's kind of late for a kid your age to be out here."

Malcolm looked down at the ground and didn't answer. Jed sat quietly waiting for him to speak. He finally did. "I ain't got no place to go."

"I thought you said you lived around here."

"I said I kinda did. I used to."

"Then where do you live now?"

Malcolm stared at Jed, frightened to answer, but also wanting desperately to share his predicament with someone he could trust. "I, uh, don't really live anywhere. We got kicked out of the apartment."

"Who did? Your family? Where are they?"

"It's just my mom. She's in the hospital."

Jed looked closely at Malcolm and realized from the look of his clothes, that it had been awhile since he'd slept in a bed. "How long has your mother been in the hospital?"

Malcolm shrugged his shoulders. "I don't know. A week I think?"

Jed took off his jacket and put it around Malcolm's shoulders. Malcolm finally let the tears come, the tears he'd kept inside for months. Jed put his arm around him and he nestled into Jed's shoulder and wept. Jed took out the handkerchief Finn had given him and handed it to Malcolm. They sat like that for several minutes until Malcolm's sobs turned into sniffles.

"The landlord kicked you out knowing your mother was in the hospital?" Jed asked.

"He didn't know. He would have called Welfare."

"What's wrong with your mother?"

Malcolm stared at his feet and blew his nose into the handkerchief. Again Jed waited for him to answer. "Cancer," he finally said. "She's dying. They don't tell me that but I know."

"Is she awake? Does she know you're on the streets?"

"No. I go see her every day but she don't know nothing, not even that I'm there."

Jed pulled him tighter to him and they sat on the bench silently. Malcolm finally fell asleep on Jed's shoulder, but Jed stayed awake and held him until the sun came up.

11

THE MORNING SUN STREAKED ACROSS FINN'S FACE as he slept in his chair in front of the computer. Kate entered and stared at him with both disdain and concern. She listened to his breathing to see if it was steady. When she was sure he was asleep, she started reading what was on the computer screen. Finn woke with a start. "What are you doing?"

"Just looking. I see you finally got some writing done."

"It's crap," he said stretching his arms in the air and yawning. "What time is it, anyway?"

"Way past your usual waking hour. Were you here all night?"

He looked down at his clothes. "I guess I was."

Kate shook her head in disgust and left the room. Finn read over what he had written the night before. "What a bunch of trite garbage!" He pressed

EDIT, SELECT ALL and DELETE and strode defiantly into the kitchen expecting another argument with Kate. She was pouring two cups of coffee and looked up at him as he entered. She handed him one of the cups silently along with the *NY Times* and sat down with her own coffee and the *LA Times*.

"Thanks," Finn said. "Aren't you going to be late for work?"

"It's Saturday, Dad," Kate muttered without glancing up from the newspaper.

"Is it really? My, my, how time flies," Finn replied.

"I didn't know we were having fun," Kate grumbled.

"Aren't we the picture of sunshine and lollipops?"

Kate finally looked up with piercing eyes. Finn got the message and went back to his office where he spiked his coffee and settled into his chair to read the paper.

When Malcolm awoke, Jed took him to Charlie's table. At first Malcolm protested vehemently, afraid that Charlie would report him to Child Protective Services. Jed assured him that Charlie's intentions were purely altruistic and that he never reported anyone. Malcolm finally acquiesced. "The kid needs a shower and some clean clothes," Jed told Charlie.

Charlie nodded and gave Malcolm a card. "Go to this address and they'll help you out."

"I don't want to." Malcolm had changed his mind.

Jed took him aside. "No one's going to ask you questions or make any phone calls unless Charlie tells them and he won't say anything without your permission. They'll just let you shower and give you some clothes and breakfast."

"But I want to stay with you."

"I've got things to do. I'll find you later. I promise."

Malcolm nodded and Jed started to leave. "Hey Jed! Where's Mother?"

"I'm going to get her now." Jed walked away.

Jed paced back and forth inside the waiting room of the emergency veterinary clinic building. He kept glancing at the clock over the counter.

"The office manager should be here any minute," the receptionist finally said after she tried to ignore him for several minutes. A woman arrived with keys and unlocked the door to a back office.

"Is that her?" Jed asked the receptionist.

"Yes, but—"

Jed didn't wait for the rest of the sentence and followed the woman into her office.

"Yes? How may I help you?" the woman asked cautiously.

"I brought my cat in last night. I need to find out how much it will cost to get her out."

"Okay. What's the cat's name?"

"Mother."

"Cute name." She smiled as she leafed through some folders and turned on her computer. "I need some time to sort it out."

"Okay." Jed sat down at her desk.

"Would you mind waiting outside, please?"

Jed nodded and went back to the reception area. He sat for a minute and then got up to look at the Dog Heartworm Chart that graces the wall of every veterinary clinic.

The woman came back a few minutes later and called him to the counter. She handed him a piece of paper. "That's for the stitches, the medication, and for keeping her overnight. But she won't be ready to leave for another few hours."

He took the bill but didn't look at it. "Can I see her?"

"No. You need to pay the bill first."

"I'll have to come back with the money. Can I just see her for a minute?"

"I'm sorry, but that's not our policy. And if we keep her an extra day, it'll cost more."

Jed took some deep breaths and didn't argue. He kept his cool. He left without responding and stood outside the vet's office for a minute, looking at the bill. He shook his head and started walking, slowly at first, trying to figure out what he was going to do.

He quickened his pace as he got closer to Luis' restaurant.

He went inside and nodded to Mercedes at the cash register. "My father's in the kitchen," she said.

"Thanks."

Luis hummed as he stood at the stove preparing for today's lunch. He did a double take when he looked up and saw Jed coming through the door. "Jed!"

"I need an advance, Luis."

"An advance?" Luis shook his head. "I'm sorry. I don't have any extra money."

"I promise I'll work it off."

"I just paid my taxes, Jed, and I'm living hand to mouth myself. I wish I could help you."

Jed turned abruptly and stalked out without responding. As he passed the cash register, he stopped suddenly and took a crumpled piece of paper out of his pocket. He turned to Mercedes. "Can I use your phone?"

"I guess so." She took the receiver off the cradle and handed it to him. He dialed the number off the paper and strummed his fingers on the counter as he waited.

Finn stared at the blank computer screen when the phone rang. Kate answered it and called from the kitchen, "It's for you."

"Is it Judith?"

"No."

"Who is it?"

"I don't know."

"Would you ask?"

"Just get the phone, Dad." Finn didn't answer or make a move to get up and waited until he heard her sigh with exasperation, "Oh, all right, I'll ask." A minute later she entered. "It's Jed."

"Jed?" He looked at her incredulously. "Really?" Finn practically ran to the kitchen. Kate followed him and stood at the sink, watching him apprehensively. "Hello? Sure. Come on over. The address is on the paper I gave you." He hung up and smiled at Kate.

"You gave a homeless person my address? Are you nuts?"

"I trust him."

"How can you trust him? You don't even know him! And why is he coming? What does he want?"

"I don't know. He just said he wants to talk to me."

"You are a real piece of work!"

"What are you afraid of? That he'll steal something?"

"Perhaps. Or maybe he's a psychopath."

"A psychopath? Oh Kate, he's not going to hurt you." She hurried out and Finn followed, mumbling to himself, "More likely he'd hurt himself."

He entered his office and found Kate picking up the books and papers strewn around the floor. "What are you doing?"

"We have company coming," she replied indignantly.

"Oh, so now he's a guest instead of a murderer?"

"Apparently."

"Where are you putting my stuff?"

"Back in the boxes."

"I'll do it." He grabbed the books out of her hand as the doorbell rang.

Kate glared at him and left to answer the door. She came back in with Jed and eyed him warily as he entered the room.

"Hello, Jed." Finn stretched out his hand. "I see you've met my daughter, Kate."

He shook Finn's hand. "Yes. We met at the door." Kate left the room without a word.

"I'm glad you came, Jed."

"You said you know where my backpack is?"

"Yes. I saw this woman take it out of a trashcan. I followed her to a house on the canals."

"The canals? What would a woman who lives on the canals want with my backpack?"

"I wondered the same thing."

Jed walked to the window and gazed out silently for a moment before he asked in a barely audible voice, "What do you want from me?"

"I'd like to interview you."

"What for?"

"For my book."

Jed turned around and faced Finn. "You're a writer?"

"Yes."

"What kind of a book?"

"I'm not exactly sure, something about homelessness."

Jed wandered the room and looked around for a few minutes before speaking. "What kind of questions would you ask?"

"The usual ones: who, what, where, when, why, and how."

"Sounds like a newspaper article, not a book."

"I'm hoping that a book will present itself from our interview. I'm not sure exactly what I want to do." Finn smiled and added, "I've had a bit of writer's block lately." Jed paced up and down as Finn watched him. "I can change your name and you don't have to talk about anything that might make you uncomfortable."

Jed sat down at the table and looked directly into Finn's eyes. "How much?"

Finn was startled. "What do you mean how much?"

"How much will you pay me?"

"Pay you? Uh, I don't know. I hadn't thought about paying you."

"Did you think I'd be so flattered that you wanted to write a book about me that I would just jump at the opportunity?"

"I just hadn't thought about it one way or the other. I'll have to see what I can do. I don't have any money right now."

"How can you live in this place and not have any money?"

"It's not my house, it's my daughter's."

Jed stood up and gazed out the window again. "Mother's in the hospital."

"What happened?"

"She was stabbed."

"Stabbed? A cat? Who would stab a cat?"

"It doesn't matter who did it, but I need to pay the vet before they'll give her back to me."

"Is she going to be okay?" Finn asked.

"Yes. She had stitches."

"I can't get any money until I write something. The publishers will send me some of the advance after I send them a few chapters."

"You already have a publisher?"

"Yes, the same one I've always used."

"You've already written a book?"

"Actually, I've written more than one." Finn took his book off the table and handed it to Jed.

"*Ode to Forgiveness: A Memoir* by Finn McGee," Jed read. "So you're Finn McGee?"

"One and the same."

"I've heard of you."

97

"Yeah. This book was a bestseller."

"I'd like to read it."

"Take it. I have other copies."

"How come you have no money if you had a best-selling book?"

"That was a long time ago."

Jed flipped through some pages and closed the book. "The longer Mother stays in the hospital, the more they'll charge."

"So you'll let me interview you?"

Jed didn't answer right away. He finally spoke. "They take Visa or MasterCard."

Finn stood up and reached in his pocket. He took out his wallet and checked for his credit cards. "I think I still have some room on one of them. Let's go get Mother."

Most of the performers and merchants had closed up shop for the day by the time Jed had picked up Mother and gone back to the boardwalk to look for Malcolm. He found him on the same bench, clean and neatly dressed, eating a hamburger. He sat down and lay Mother on his lap. "Where'd you get the burger?"

"Charlie gave me a coupon," Malcolm answered.

"He's a good guy, Charlie. Got any extras for Mother?"

"I'm sorry. I used them all." Malcolm looked genuinely distressed.

"That's okay. She'll probably just sleep tonight. I'll get her food tomorrow."

"What happened to her? Why's she all bandaged up?"

"Had some stitches. Did you go see your mom today at the hospital?"

"Yeah. I stayed for a couple of hours."

"How's she doing?"

Malcolm shrugged his shoulders. "They don't tell me anything. They just keep asking me if there's some other relative."

"Is there?"

"No."

"You know that guy, Charlie, can help you. He knows lots of people and places for kids like you to stay. You can't live on the streets."

"Why not? You do."

Jed looked at Mother on his lap and petted her. "That's why I know you can't."

"I'm okay."

Jed focused his attention on Mother as Malcolm fidgeted next to him. Jed finally broke the silence. "You have no one else you can call? A grandmother? An aunt?"

Malcolm stood up angrily. "I got nobody but my momma. And I'm not going into no foster home."

"Okay. Sit down and relax. Do you want to pet Mother? She'd like that." Malcolm shrugged his shoulders and sat back down. Jed put Mother on Malcolm's lap and Malcolm smiled as he petted her. They sat in silence for a while; the only sound was Mother's purring. Jed finally stood and picked up Mother. "Let's go find Charlie. You can trust him. He'll find you a good situation."

Malcolm sighed and stood up. Jed put one arm around Malcolm's shoulders and cradled Mother in his other one and they walked down the boardwalk.

12

FINN SPENT THE REST OF THE DAY AND INTO THE EVENING trying to come up with a list of interview questions for Jed. It wasn't easy though, because he really hadn't figured out what he wanted to write about homelessness. Every time he tried to research the topic online, he would get sidetracked into some other site that would pique his interest for a while. He finally gave up and played a gazillion games of solitaire until he was tired enough to go to bed.

He left the house early the next morning. He walked along the canals until he got to the front of what he thought was the bag lady's house. He wanted to catch her before she started making her rounds. Hers stood out among the expensive, well-maintained houses. It was dilapidated and in dire need of paint and repairs. The front yard was littered with broken garden equipment, lumber, old toys and furniture. The curtains were closed and it looked deserted. He walked up to the front door and knocked. No one answered so he walked around the house, trying to look in the windows. Stacks of boxes and newspapers were piled up inside, blocking the view.

He walked down the sidewalk, crossed a couple of bridges out of the canals and went down the street toward the beach. When he got to the boardwalk he sat on a bench in front of Muscle Beach and looked around until he saw her rummaging through a trashcan. He got up, but she had already finished digging and was approaching the bench, leaning heavily on her shopping cart as she pushed it. She grimaced as she sat down slowly and Finn took her arm to help her down. "Thank you, young fella," she said in a thick New York accent.

Finn pretended to tip a hat. "Top of the morning to you, dearie."

They sat in silence a few minutes watching the body builders and the street performers. She finally spoke again. "Come here often?"

"Are you trying to pick me up?" Finn answered with a twinkle in his eye.

She laughed. "Sorry sonny, but you don't hold a candle to the hot specimens here."

Finn feigned disappointment. "I'll try not to take that personally." He scanned her shopping cart. "Looks like you're going to make a killing at the recycling center."

"What?"

"That's a lot of cans and bottles."

She ignored his last statement. "So sonny boy, you're an Irish lad?"

"Last time I checked."

"Sean? Seamus? Brian? Kelly?"

"Are we playing Rumplestiltskin?"

"Hah! There's no gold to be spun on this boardwalk."

He laughed. "My name's Finn. It's short for Finnegan."

"Your parents must have had a thing for Broadway shows."

"I believe you're thinking of one called *Finnian's Rainbow*."

"I know the name of the show. I figured your parents had it wrong."

"I think the show came out a few years after I was born," Finn added with a smile.

"I always liked *Brigadoon* better."

"That takes place in Scotland, not Ireland."

"All the same as far as I'm concerned."

"I doubt the Scots would agree."

"You'd know better than me. It doesn't matter. I guess your parents were more the bookish type, anyway."

"What makes you say that?"

"James Joyce? *Finnegan's Wake*? You don't have to be Irish to know the difference between Finnian and Finnegan."

"Well, aren't you the literary scholar," Finn smiled.

"I've had my share of academic pursuits."

"And what name did your parents pick out for you on the fateful day of your birth?"

"Do I detect a tiny bit of sarcasm there?" she asked.

"I've been known to use it."

"Bella. I think they made use of some irony as well."

"Now, Bella. You mustn't beat up on yourself. You must have been a beautiful baby."

She laughed and sang, "I must have been a beautiful child."

"'Cause baby, look at you now," Finn finished the line.

"Well, the name has served me well even if I don't fit the definition."

"Do you wear a large hat like your namesake?"

"So you're a New Yorker?" Bella asked.

"I'm sure people have heard of Bella Abzug outside of New York, but yes, I am."

"So is half of Los Angeles."

"And which half are you in?" he asked.

"The half that voted for her three times."

"As if I couldn't tell."

"You'd think by now I would have lost some of the accent."

"Well we are certainly representing a good portion of the lower East Side of New York."

"You mean Irish and Jewish?"

"All we need is an Italian and a Chinese and we could have our own south of 14th Street caucus."

They laughed and watched the bodybuilders grease themselves and huff and puff through their routines.

"Why do they need all that suntan lotion?" Bella asked.

"I don't think they're trying to get a tan. I think it's part of their look."

"So why do they need to look like French fried onion rings? Don't they lose their grip with such greasy hands?" she asked.

"I think they powder their hands so they don't lose their grip."

"How do you know so much? Are you a weightlifter?"

Finn chuckled. "Shall I take that as a compliment?"

"Sure, but that and a nickel won't get you a cup of coffee."

"You're quite the comedian, Miss Belle of the ball."

"So when did you leave New York, Mr. Irish eyes are smiling?"

"About a month ago. And you?"

"Oh, a newbie. I've lived here for thirty years. My husband, rest his soul, was a talent agent. Hollywood was where the money was. Broadway was dying."

"Now I understand why you know your Broadway shows so well."

"And what's your excuse?"

"I guess I just like the music." They were quiet awhile, lost in their own thoughts. Finn finally broke the silence. "Thirty years is a long time."

"It seems like yesterday."

Finn smiled. "I don't like to dwell on the past."

"What are you, one of those Buddhist types? Be here now, one day at a time, or whatever that crap is."

Finn laughed. "Not a spiritual person, eh Bella?"

Bella pretended to spit. "What has religion gotten us other than war and carnage."

"I can't argue with you there."

"So what misery are you trying to escape from?" Bella asked.

"Nothing specific. Like Karl Marx said, 'The past lies like a nightmare upon the present.'"

"You are quite the depressing erudite."

"That's a big word for a little lady."

"Is that a putdown?"

"No, ma'am, not at all."

"It better not be."

Finn decided it was time to ask the question. "A friend of mine lost his yellow backpack. I thought perhaps you'd seen it."

Bella stiffened and looked at him suspiciously. "I may have."

106

"He'd like it back."

Bella was silent for a minute and then got up with difficulty. Finn stood and helped her up. "I suppose I can look for it," she finally said.

"I'll walk you home."

"No need. If I have the backpack, I'll get it to you."

"I don't mind."

"Suit yourself," Bella shrugged. She leaned on her shopping cart and pushed it as Finn walked alongside her.

Finn wanted to keep the conversation light. He was afraid he may have alienated her and he wanted to get Jed's backpack so he tried small talk. "Do you get to the theater here in Los Angeles?"

"Not so much anymore. I don't get out much." They continued walking in silence until they arrived at the canals. She turned to Finn and tried to brush him off. "Thanks for the company, but I'm quite capable of making it home."

"A gentleman always brings a lady to her door."

"Oh fine." Bella gave up and continued pushing her cart.

"Have you always lived here in Venice?" Finn kept up the chatter.

"No. We lived in Beverly Hills for many years and then moved here a couple of years before Morty died." Finn followed her as she approached the front door of her house. She took out her key and turned toward him. "Thanks for renewing my faith in the male species."

He cut right to the chase. "Can I have the backpack?"

"I'll look for it tomorrow."

"I can wait for you to find it."

"I don't know where it is exactly." Bella was getting quite annoyed with Finn's persistence.

She opened the door and Finn peered inside. The foyer was piled from floor to ceiling along both walls with boxes, large garbage bags, and furniture. There was a narrow pathway going through it toward the other rooms. When Bella saw him inspecting the inside of her house, she closed the door so it was only open a crack and frowned at him. "Okay. I'll look. I'll be right back," she said as she shut the door.

Finn didn't have to wait very long before she opened the door and handed him the backpack. "Thanks, Bubba," he said.

Bella couldn't help but smile. "You're welcome, Zeyde. So you know your Yiddish, I see."

"You know what Lenny Bruce said, 'If you're from New York and you're Catholic, you're still Jewish.'" He winked and tipped his hat.

"Such a comedian you are." She shut the door.

He was excited to have gotten the backpack from her. He knew that hoarders were usually reluctant to let go of their possessions. He started to unzip one of the compartments but then decided to wait until he got home to examine the contents. It

108

would be better to be able to spread things out and take time. He was curious to see what Jed carried with him. What would a homeless person need and treasure? He knew it wasn't appropriate to search through Jed's things, but rationalized away any guilt he felt. After all, if he had just found the backpack in the trashcan and hadn't known that it belonged to Jed, he would have looked through it to find the identity of the owner.

When he got home, he made himself a cup of coffee and spiked it with his usual flavoring. He sat at his desk/table and unzipped the backpack carefully. He peered inside and started removing things. He took out a pair of socks, a couple of shirts, and some underwear. There was a book about Pranayama, a bottle of water . . . nothing very significant or interesting. He leafed through the book, curious what Pranayama was. It was some kind of breathing thing. Finn chuckled to himself. It was hard to imagine Jed as the yoga type. Then he reached in and removed a framed picture. He put it down on the table and examined it. A young black woman held a young black boy in her arms. His fingers grasped a locket dangling from a chain hanging around her neck. They were smiling as they stood in front of a sign that said, 'Those who do not remember the past are condemned to repeat it. Welcome to Jonestown.' Finn sat back in his chair and sipped his Irish coffee. "Wow! Jed was in Jonestown!"

After the initial shock wore off, and after he finished his coffee, he turned on his computer and started searching for information on Jonestown. Finn hadn't thought about the massacre since the media had lost interest in plastering it all over the television and newspapers. He remembered reading something about a memorial being erected at a cemetery in Oakland a few years ago, but that had been a small story and he hadn't given it much more than a passing glance. It wasn't long before he became engrossed in his research. He found several YouTube clips and a website called "Alternative Considerations of Jonestown and People's Temple" sponsored by the Department of Religious Studies at San Diego State University. As he read, he forgot to eat and he even forgot to refill his cup.

Jim Jones had started the People's Temple in Indiana in 1956 as an integrated church with socialist overtones. He moved it to northern California ten years later and both he and the church were well respected by San Francisco progressive politicos. Their message of peace, love and equality resonated in the culture of the sixties and the recruitment numbers were high. As his power and influence grew, however, Jim Jones became somewhat delusional and paranoid. He thought the United States government was after them and that they needed to move out of the country. He bought the land in Guyana in the early seventies, but only a handful of people lived there at first. In 1977 the *San Francisco Chronicle* interviewed several

People's Temple members and was about to print an article exposing Jim Jones and the People's Temple. These members had talked of beatings and fake healings and how they had been forced to turn over millions of dollars from savings accounts and sales of their homes.

Things got worse and worse as Jim Jones slipped further and further into drugs and insanity. The utopian vision that had been the essence of the People's Temple had morphed into a horrific nightmare. And then the unthinkable happened.

The Jonestown massacre was the most deadly disaster in American history until 9/11. Over nine hundred people died, a third of them children. Only a handful escaped. Finn wondered if Jed had actually fled or had left before the massacre. He was glued to his computer for the rest of the day.

13

FINN WAS STILL SITTING AT HIS COMPUTER, excitedly Googling and YouTubing, when Kate got home and entered his office. Her scowl turned into a smile when she noticed he was working. "It looks like you're finally getting some writing done."

"Just researching."

She looked over his shoulder. "Now you're going to write a book about Jonestown?"

"Maybe."

"What happened to homelessness?"

"I like this idea better."

"Why are you so interested in something that happened forty years ago?"

"It's important for people to know about it. It was an amazing story and a significant part of history," he answered with his eyes still focused on the computer screen. He stopped typing and turned toward his daughter. "Do you know what happened?"

She shrugged. "Wasn't that the place where they committed suicide by drinking spiked Kool-Aid?"

"That's part of it, but there was much more. Is that all you know?"

"I don't know. I think it was some kind of religious cult, wasn't it?"

"Sort of, but it didn't start out to be a cult. The People's Temple began as a religious group in Indiana that was interdenominational. It was unique because it sought out an interracial congregation."

"Was Indiana such a bastion of racism? I thought being a northern state it would have been more tolerant."

"It was the fifties. Before Martin Luther King and the Civil Rights Act. It was pretty bad everywhere for blacks and remember, Indiana is just north of Kentucky so it's pretty close to the South. I'm not sure you can categorize it as northern like you would New York."

Kate sat down, her curiosity piqued. "I guess you end up taking things for granted, growing up in New York City and living in California."

Finn looked at his computer screen and typed a few words. "You know, the People's Temple actually had its roots in communism."

Kate got up and looked over Finn's shoulder. She read aloud from the screen. "*Jim Jones was a long-time dedicated Marxist communist who admired totalitarian communist dictatorships such as the Soviet Union and Cuba so much that he built one of his own in Guyana.*"

"That explains things," Finn said.

"It was a totalitarian dictatorship? Is that a well-known fact?" Kate asked.

"I don't think so. Most of us knew that some people were being held there against their will, but we didn't think of it in those terms."

"How large was it?"

"It started out pretty small when they were in Indiana. Folks joined who were looking for an integrated place to worship where everyone was treated equally. But they didn't like Stalin's policies so Jones moved away from communism and made the People's Temple more religious-oriented."

"I would imagine that being involved with communists in the fifties was not looked upon very favorably. Isn't that when the McCarthy hearings were going on?"

"Yea. It was the spring of 1954."

"He probably made quite a few enemies. If I remember my history classes, this country was pretty scared then of the cold war."

"In some ways it was worse than the fears of terrorism Americans have now. People had fallout shelters in their basements. We had duck and cover drills in school like you have fire drills now." He laughed. "As if lying prone and putting your coat over your head would really do anything against radioactivity from a nuclear bomb."

"That's how I feel about the safety drills we do now in school since Columbine and 9/11," Kate replied. "They are kind of pointless. If someone wants to shoot up or bomb a school, they're going to do it no matter what we do. We are pretty helpless in the situation. And if there is something that can be done, it will be instinctual, not because we've rehearsed it."

"Sadly you've been proven right too many times. There are an awful lot of school bloodbaths."

She read more from the computer screen. *"When Jones was accidentally placed in the black ward of a hospital after a collapse in 1961, he refused to be moved and began to make the beds, and empty the bedpans of black patients. Political pressures resulting from Jones' actions caused hospital officials to desegregate the wards."*

"You and I may think he was doing good work, but a lot of people there didn't, especially after he and his wife adopted Korean and black children. They only had one child of their own," Finn explained.

"They were really ahead of their time, weren't they?"

"I guess." He glanced down at the screen. "Look at this. He moved his family to Brazil in 1962 because he was so afraid of a nuclear Holocaust. That I didn't know." He read some more. "That's when he first went to Guyana. Hmmm. And after that was when he moved the church to northern California."

"So he moved to California because he thought it was safe in case of a nuclear war? Not because they were more tolerant of his integrationist views?" Kate asked.

"Probably both."

"Where did they go?"

"Ukiah."

"That's north of San Francisco, isn't it?"

"Yes. About sixty miles east of Mendocino."

"Did he think they'd be somehow spared from nuclear war in California?"

"I doubt it. I'm sure it was because his communist ideas would be more accepted in northern California than in Indiana. He was just looking for new followers. Folks at that time were looking for a kind of socialist paradise where they could escape the violence and hatred that had become so prevalent."

"He probably attracted a lot of hippies."

"Yeah, not that hippies were particularly religious, but they were fascinated by mysticism and spirituality so his philosophy fit into their own beliefs."

"How sixties, all peace and love and freedom," Kate teased.

Finn ignored his daughter's mockery as he mused about those days that had been so carefree on the one hand and intense on the other. He and Kate's mother had lived on its periphery. They believed in it all, but they also wanted to finish college and have jobs. They partook of the music, the politics and the drugs, but not to the extent of revolution or denouncing a comfortable lifestyle.

He finally spoke. "I guess that's how it looked to people. For a time, though, the leader Jim Jones was admired and respected by the local politicians for all the good the People's Temple was doing for the

116

community. He was even appointed as a commissioner in San Francisco and hobnobbed with extremely influential people in local and national politics. He was a prominent figure and a spokesperson at rallies and in newspapers and magazines."

"Jeez, didn't they know better?"

"I don't think he showed his true craziness until later."

"I guess most people in power are insane. At any rate, they have to have big egos."

"Maybe so," Finn agreed. "But they are also usually charismatic and persuasive speakers."

"And smart. I look at the gang leaders in my school and they are usually some of the most intelligent students. If only they would direct their energy into academics instead of bullying . . ." Kate's voice trailed off.

"I remember that being true when I was teaching too."

"How could he be so admired if what he was really doing was manipulating and coercing people into his cult?" Kate asked.

"The ones who followed him thought it was going to be utopia. They didn't view themselves as joining a cult. I think everyone had their own personal reasons for joining."

"When did they leave and go to that South American country, what was the name of it?"

"Guyana. That was in the seventies. He wanted to build a perfect communist, agricultural sanctuary."

"But why would they be so stupid as to follow him into the jungle? How could they not know they were joining a cult?"

"They weren't stupid at all. In fact, they were intelligent people searching for answers and a better life. Once they were in Guyana is when things got weird. Before that, they were passionate and devoted to creating a better world. It didn't seem radical to them."

"So it was like a hippie commune?"

"In some ways, I guess."

"But he was a dictator. That doesn't sound all peace and love."

"He did let his lust for control go to his head, like most people who are obsessed with power. But the majority of the members were black. They saw it as a chance for racial equality and a place free from prejudice."

Kate sat hugging her knees, trying to take in all that her father had told her. Finn stared at his computer screen, actually excited to continue his research. His daughter's eager questions had reinforced his belief that Jonestown would make a good read and would be marketable. He, too, wanted to know what motivated people to follow someone into the jungle, abandoning family and friends and their whole way of life.

Kate broke the silence. "I also heard that Jim Jones was a heavy drug user."

Finn stiffened. Kate didn't know about his drug use and he aimed to keep it that way. It was enough to have to listen to her barrage of criticism about his alcohol consumption. "Yes. Eventually the drugs took over and he basically lost his mind."

"Didn't some congressman go there to bring people back home and then get himself killed?"

"Yes, Congressman Ryan was killed along with some reporters and photographers. But most of the Jonestown residents were not murderers. They were good people . . . gentle souls who had been starved and deprived of sleep, even tortured. I don't think many of them had the energy and clear thinking to know what was going on at the end."

"But he had gone there to help them?"

"We can't know what goes through people's minds when they're in that kind of situation. Have you ever heard of the Stockholm Syndrome?"

"I don't know. What is it?"

Finn Googled and read aloud, "*Stockholm syndrome, or capture-bonding, is a psychological phenomenon in which hostages express empathy and sympathy and have positive feelings toward their captors, sometimes to the point of defending and identifying with them. These feelings are generally considered irrational in light of the danger or risk endured by the victims, who essentially mistake a lack of abuse from their captors for an act of kindness.*"

"But that's not really the same thing. They weren't exactly prisoners or hostages," said Kate.

"It goes on to say, though, that it doesn't always have to be a hostage scenario. Sometimes they are just victims of abuse and it's a way to defend oneself against trauma."

She shuddered. "What a tragedy." She stood up abruptly and said over her shoulder as she left, "I'm glad you found something you want to write about. Dinner will be ready in an hour. Will you be eating?"

"Yes," Finn called after her. He could see the smile on her face even though she was in another room.

That evening Finn washed dishes while Kate dried and put them away. "Why won't you use the dishwasher? It's so much easier and faster." She smiled. "You're beyond old-fashioned, Dad. You're prehistoric."

"I don't like dishwashers."

"Why?"

"They use up precious resources."

Kate laughed. "When did you start caring about precious resources?"

"Our planet is in trouble."

"Living in California is turning you into an environmentalist?"

"Maybe . . . but besides that, I like washing dishes. It's mindless. You can meditate while you're doing it."

"Meditate? You really are becoming a Californian. Next thing you know, you'll be going to yoga classes!"

14

FINN SPENT THE NEXT MORNING exploring Jim Jones' biography. When the afternoon rolled around, he thought he might be ready to write something, but he wanted to wait for Jed. He had easily formulated a long list of questions for him. Jonestown was much more interesting to him than homelessness. He felt like he actually understood the mind of Jim Jones after reading about his admiration for Marxist communism. It was Jed's mind that he was having trouble understanding.

He sat at his computer, staring blankly at the screen. He played a little solitaire but even that didn't keep his interest very long. He picked up the envelope from Antoinette, turning it over and over, but he decided not to reread it and put it back on the pile of papers. He didn't want to be distracted from his upcoming meeting with Jed.

He looked at the mess on the floor and decided to put the books and papers away in the cabinet. Kate entered and happily joined in. "I'm glad you're finally cleaning up and moving in," she said.

"Jed's coming over."

"What for?"

"I'm interviewing him."

"Is there anything valuable here?"

"Are you afraid he's going to steal something? Or is it that, heaven forbid, he'll see a messy room?"

Kate gave him one of those teenage girl eye-rolls and took one of the empty boxes and flattened it. "You don't need the boxes for anything, do you?"

"No."

"Then I'll put them in the recycling bin. Like you say, got to do what's right for the environment."

"Your sarcasm is unattractive, my dear."

Kate exited with the flattened boxes just as the doorbell rang. She answered the door and brought Jed and Mother into the room. She gave Finn a cautionary look as she left and Finn waved her off.

"Thanks for coming, Jed. Glad to see Mother is better. I have your backpack."

He handed it to Jed, waiting for a reaction, but Jed just put it on the floor next to him. "Thanks."

"Aren't you going to look inside and make sure everything is there?"

"Nope."

Finn needed another way to segue into asking Jed about Jonestown, but he didn't want to tell him that he had looked inside and found the picture. "I spoke to the lady who found your backpack. She's

122

quite an interesting character. She's actually a hoarder, not a bag lady." Jed raised his eyebrows showing a semblance of interest. Finn decided to lie. "She said there was a picture inside of a woman and a young boy at Jonestown." Jed blinked and the corner of his mouth twitched but he still said nothing. "Are you the boy? Is that your mother?"

"I don't think that's any of your business."

Finn racked his brain trying to figure out how to get Jed to talk. He finally decided to jump right in. "Well, that picture piqued my interest. Anyway, are you ready for the interview?"

Jed looked out the window and stayed silent for quite awhile. Finn waited patiently for Jed to speak first. He finally did. "Yes."

Finn breathed a sigh of relief and took out a yellow legal pad and pen. He had written down a bunch of questions. "Would you answer my first question now?"

"What question is that?"

"Is the picture of you and your mother?"

Jed sat down again across the table from Finn, petting Mother on his lap. Several moments passed before he finally answered. "Yes."

"I think I'd like to write the book about Jonestown instead of homelessness. Are you willing to let me interview you about that?"

"I guess I owe you for getting Mother out of the hospital."

Finn turned a few pages of his pad until he found his list. "I jotted down a few questions." He sat upright and his expression changed from sympathetic curiosity to serious journalist mode. "Were you there during the massacre?" Jed stiffened and stared at Finn with narrowed eyes, pursed lips, flared nostrils, and tensed muscles. It looked like he might explode out of his skin. "I know this is hard for you," Finn added, trying to diffuse the heaviness in the air.

Jed finally spoke. "Yes, I was there during the massacre."

"You must have been very young. That was November 1978."

"I was old enough to know what was going on."

"How frightening for you." Finn immediately felt stupid for commenting on the obvious and jumped into the next question. "What did you do?"

Jed answered every question slowly and thoughtfully, but sharply, and with as few words as he could get away with. "I ran away."

Finn, on the other hand, snapped back with the next question as quickly as he could, afraid that Jed was going to stop the conversation. "Were you there with your whole family?"

Jed walked to the window and gazed out, opening and closing the blinds. "My family died there."

Finn waited to ask the next question when he saw how distressed Jed had become. "How many

124

members of your family were at Jonestown?" Finn said quietly.

Jed took a while to answer. "My mother, my sister and me." He walked slowly back to the table as Finn typed the responses.

"How long were you there?"

"In Jonestown? Or with the People's Temple?"

"Both, I guess."

"We belonged to the People's Temple in San Francisco for a couple of years before going to Guyana."

Finn finally got to the question he was most anxious to get answered. This, he felt, would be the heart of the book. "Why did your mother join?"

Jed shook his head sardonically; irritated that Finn would even bother to ask. "Why do you *think* a poor, black, single mother in Oakland would join the People's Temple?"

"Is that a rhetorical question?"

"I think you probably know the answer."

"There are other things she could have done to escape the mean streets."

"Not in her view. She was a proud woman, not willing to take welfare without giving something back. But she didn't have education or skills. She was religious and socially conscious, though, and when she found the People's Temple, she felt she had found the perfect solution."

"How did you feel about going to Guyana?"

"I was a kid. I liked the idea of living in the jungle."

Finn smiled. "Did you think you would be living with lions and tigers?"

Jed smiled back. "Actually, in the South American rainforest there are jaguars and mountain lions."

"Seriously, you saw them?"

"Sure. I had to learn how to fend for myself. You know, like Mowgli in *The Jungle Book*."

"You read Rudyard Kipling?"

Jed stared hard at Finn and shook his head. "Just because we were poor and black doesn't mean we were illiterate."

"I'm sorry. I didn't mean -"

Jed interrupted. "Just let it go." Finn felt like an idiot, but then Jed lightened the mood. "I had seen the Disney movie before we left." They both relaxed and even smiled at each other.

"Do you mind if I type some of this before I forget your answers?"

"Doesn't matter to me."

Kate knocked softly on the door while Finn typed. "What?" Finn asked brusquely.

Kate opened the door tentatively. "Is your cat hungry?"

Jed smiled at her. "I'm sure she is."

"I don't have cat food but I can probably find something to give her. May I take her to the kitchen with me?"

126

Kate took Mother from Jed's outstretched hands and carried her out. "Thanks, Kate!" Finn called after her as she shut the door. He then turned back to Jed. "What was it like? Did you go to school there?"

Jed took a deep breath and stared into Finn's eyes with a look that was intense yet distracted. "It was hell."

Finn sat back and pondered what to do next. Was this a sign that Jed was done talking, or just a statement of fact? He decided to press on.

"How did you escape?"

"Some people helped me."

"How?"

Jed closed his eyes and took so long to answer that Finn was again afraid he was going to stop the interview. "I was in the pavilion. Jim was ranting and raving that it was time. It was chaotic."

"Time for what?"

"White night."

"White night?"

"That's what Jim called it when there was a crisis and we all had to go to the pavilion for an all-night suicide drill."

"Even the kids?"

"Everyone."

"So there was more than one white night?"

"Yes. But this one was different. This wasn't just Jim's delusion. The congressman and the reporters were there and some people wanted to leave with them."

"What happened at these white nights?"

Jed breathed deeply and started pacing again. "He told us that the CIA was out to get us."

"So the only solution was to commit suicide?"

"Not at first. He said we could try to escape to the Soviet Union but obviously that wasn't feasible."

"Did people believe him?"

"Let me explain something, Finn. We were starved and sleep-deprived. He'd keep us up all night, sometimes more than one, talking at us, trying to make us paranoid. Before the final white night, there were rehearsals."

"What do you mean rehearsals?"

"For the mass suicide."

Finn gasped out loud. "Jesus!"

Jed smiled. "Yeah, he was involved too."

Finn smiled back. "So what was the final one like?"

"There were armed guards running around. And then people started drinking the concoction. It was crazy."

"Did you ever find your mother and sister that night?"

Jed exhaled a long breath. "They died there."

Finn stayed quiet for a few minutes, for both of their sakes. He finally spoke. "So that's when you ran?"

"I raced outside and then I saw all the shooting going on around the plane. People were lying dead on the tarmac. Someone took my hand and pulled me with him."

Finn stopped typing and sighed deeply. "You must have been petrified. You were just a child. Did you realize what was happening?"

"I realized that I needed to leave and luckily I was a fast runner."

"Do you know who helped you escape?"

"I knew who he was, but I didn't know him well."

"How many were with you?"

Jed's irritation was starting to show. "I don't know," he scowled at Finn.

Finn continued typing. "Did people try to catch you?"

"It wasn't like that. There was such turmoil. No one knew what to do. I doubt the armed guards cared about me at that point since I was just a child. They were more concerned with the reporters and the congressman and those that were trying to leave."

Finn typed feverishly as Jed watched. Kate opened the door a crack and Mother entered and leaped onto the table. After a few minutes Finn stopped typing and turned to Jed. "So why, then, did people willingly drink the Kool-Aid?"

Jed stood with eyes blazing and lashed out at Finn. "No! As I said, it wasn't like that! Not everyone wanted to drink it. Some people were forced." Jed took a couple of breaths and sat down to compose himself. He folded his hands in his lap and continued.

"I think they drank it because they thought it was the only way out." Jed glared at Finn.

"Is this the first time you've been interviewed about it?" Finn desperately wanted Jed to stay.

"The FBI questioned me."

"You mean after you were rescued?"

"When I got to Georgetown. That was about a week after I fled."

They talked through the afternoon to Finn's surprise and delight. Finn asked many questions and Jed answered them with resigned irritation. Finally Jed took Mother in his arms and stood. "Are you leaving?" Finn asked.

"Yes, I need to go," Jed said as he walked out.

He hiked along the beach and into the mountains. He had only walked a couple of miles when he felt his body relax a bit. He had been thinking about Malcolm and how it felt holding him as he sobbed. It had worked not only to soothe the boy, but also himself. Maybe that's what he needed.

Finn sat motionless for a long time. He needed to mull over everything Jed had told him. He didn't know how to put it into words. Maybe he needed a little help. He went to the cabinet and searched through a stack of records. He put one on the turntable and Van Morrison's voice filled the room as he locked the door. He reached in his pocket for the baggie of white powder and placed it on the table. He carefully lined up the powder and snorted it, then leaned back and closed his eyes. He listened to "'Til we Get the Healing Done" as the powder did its work. It didn't take long before he was ready to write. He waited until the song was over and then went to work.

15

FINN WROTE THROUGH THE NIGHT, bolstered by his powdered friend. He alternated between writing and catnapping throughout the next day and night. Kate was so happy to see him working that she left him alone. He finished with a flourish when the room was fully bathed in sunlight. "Tada!" He strode into the kitchen and dialed the phone. "Judith? I have a few chapters done. Check your email."

He showered and dressed while the printer spewed out last night's work. He went to the kitchen to make a cup of coffee and brought it into his office. He found a full bottle of whiskey and spiked his coffee, this time in celebration rather than resignation. He gathered the chapters into a neat pile while he finished his coffee. He placed them under his arm and walked down the front steps with the liveliest gait he'd had in ages.

Harper sat at a table in the cafe typing on her laptop. Finn approached and set his pile of papers on the table in front of her. She looked up and grinned. "Finn! You're writing!"

"I brought these to impress you. I thought you might give me some feedback."

"You're asking me to read your manuscript? Really?"

"It's just the first few chapters, but yes. That's what I'm asking."

"I'd love to!"

"I read your story, Harper. You're very good. I can see why you won the contest."

She hugged him. "That means so much to me, coming from you."

He smiled at her. "I've sent this to my agent but I'd like another writer's opinion."

"I'd be honored."

She picked up the pile and looked through the first pages. "Jonestown? I'm trying to remember . . . was that some crazy dude who killed a whole bunch of people? Oh wait, didn't they commit suicide or something?"

"You young people know so little about it. My daughter didn't know much either and she's almost twice your age."

"I know it was kind of a cult like that group in Waco, Texas who got killed by the FBI or those crazies in San Diego looking for some comet to take them away."

"This was different. People joined the People's Temple for all the right reasons. They weren't hateful or crazy. And they certainly weren't bigots—quite the opposite."

"But aren't members of any cult just a little crazy?"

"No," Finn smiled at her. "It wasn't like they believed in UFOs and alien worlds. They truly wanted to create a peaceful, better world. We all did in those days."

"Were you a member?"

"No. It was a different environment then. There were many more of us who were idealistic and hopeful that we really could change the world. It seems that now young people are more materialistic." He shrugged his shoulders. "Maybe I'm wrong. Maybe there are still a lot of people who aren't jaded and disillusioned and whose sole interest isn't in accumulating money."

Harper's smile faded. "You shouldn't lump us all together."

"As I said, maybe I'm wrong. Read what I've given you, Harper, and you can learn more about it."

"I look forward to it." She put the chapters in her backpack. An envelope fell out of the middle of the pile and dropped to the floor. Harper picked it up and looked at it. "Is this important? It's from an Antoinette Delon."

Finn frowned. "She was my wife's nurse."

"Then you probably want to keep it."

134

"I suppose." Finn took the letter and stuffed it in his pocket. "So, when do you think you'll have time to read these chapters?"

"I can do it tonight. I don't have to work."

"Great. Same time same place tomorrow?" Finn asked.

"It's a date."

Finn pretended to tip his imaginary hat. "Take 'er handy."

"Huh?"

"It means see ya'." Finn winked as he left the cafe.

He walked down the boardwalk and noticed Jed sitting by the paddle tennis courts, watching the players intently. He sat down next to him on the bench. "Do you play?"

"Huh? Play what?"

"Paddle tennis."

"No. I wasn't really watching."

"You look so absorbed in the game."

"Oh . . . no . . . I was just thinking."

Mother leapt onto Finn's lap. "Why hello Mother." She purred as he petted her. "I sent a few chapters to my agent this morning. Now I'm just waiting to hear back whether the publishers will give the green-light to continue."

"That's good," Jed answered indifferently.

"You're okay with continuing, aren't you?" Finn asked tentatively.

135

"Yes, Finn. I'll be over to answer more of your questions."

Finn stood up and placed Mother gently on the bench. Jed was obviously in no mood for conversation. "Okay. Good. I look forward to it," Finn said and walked away.

"Hey, man." Malcolm slid onto the bench next to Jed, taking the seat Finn had just vacated. "Who's the old man you were talking to?"

Jed's face brightened a bit. "Hey, Malcolm. He's a friend. New shoes?"

"Yeah. Cool, huh?"

"Looks like a new backpack too. Did you win the lottery?"

Malcolm laughed. "I wish. Nah, that guy Charlie hooked me up with them."

"I thought he might."

"He got me into a real nice old lady's place, too."

"That's great."

"And he kept me out of the system. Ain't no social workers sticking their nose in my business."

"I told you Charlie was a good guy."

"Yeah."

"How's your mother, Malcolm?"

"Same."

"Have you been visiting her?"

"Yeah. I go after school."

"So you've been going to school, too?"

"Yeah. The old lady's kind of a tyrant about that. Makes me go to church too."

Jed smiled. "So where are the new digs?"

"Other side of Lincoln, near Rose. Want to come see it? I've even got my own room."

"Yes. I'd like to."

"I better go. I have to get to the hospital so I won't be late for dinner. The lady I live with gets really pissed if you ain't at the table at 6 p.m. sharp."

"It sounds like she runs a tight ship."

"She's got to. There are all those babies to take care of."

"Babies?"

"Yeah. That's who she takes care of mostly. Babies with AIDS or born from addicts so they got the drugs in them too. There's just me and one other kid living there besides the babies."

"How many babies are living with you?"

"There's three now. They cry a lot. Gotta rock them so they don't cry. That's what she do all day. Sit and rock them babies. Wanna come over on Sunday? I can ask Miss Ruthie if that's okay. I gotta go to church and then to the hospital, but I can come get you after I visit Mama."

"That would be nice, Malcolm. I'll meet you here on Sunday."

"I don't know what time though."

"I'll be here. Don't worry."

"Cool. Bye, Jed."

Malcolm ran off as Jed turned back to not watching the paddle tennis game.

16

FINN CONTINUED TO WRITE FEVERISHLY for the next few days, absorbed in his subject. By the time Saturday morning rolled around he had finished several more chapters. He decided to take a break and finish the crossword puzzle and was about to refill his cup of coffee and settle in with the magazine section when the doorbell rang. "

"I'll get it," Kate shouted from the kitchen. She brought Jed and Mother in and then exited quickly.

"Good to see you, Jed. I was wondering when you would show up."

"Well here I am," Jed replied.

"Good news. The publishers liked what I sent them. As soon as I have a couple more chapters done, they'll send some money."

"That's good."

"Can I get you a cup of coffee or something stronger?"

"Maybe some coffee."

"How about something to eat?"

"No, thanks."

Finn left and came back with two cups of coffee. He set them down on the table and went to the cabinet for the bottle of Jameson. He poured some into his own cup and started to pour some into Jed's.

"None for me, Finn. Really, I just want coffee. Do you ever drink yours plain?"

Finn stiffened. "I've been known to once in a while." He took out his yellow pad, searched for a particular page and settled into his chair. "So, tell me about Jim Jones."

Jed took a sip of coffee and waited his customary few moments before answering. "Jim Jones had enormous power over people. He changed them without their even knowing it was happening."

Finn shook his head. "It's hard for those of us who weren't there to understand that."

"It's hard for me to understand it and I was there."

"How come his magic didn't work on you?"

"I was a child. I hadn't chosen to go there. I never had any belief in him or what he and everyone else were trying to accomplish there. I just followed my mother. But more importantly, I wasn't afraid of him."

"Is that it? Everyone was afraid of him?"

"Sure. Many were. Some were already fearful of other things and he provided them a feeling of safety. You have to understand that for many, this was their family. It was a place where they felt comfortable, a place where they felt like they belonged and were loved. It's complicated."

"It's those damn family relationships. They're always complicated." Finn smiled.

Jed looked at him, puzzled at his response. "You find this amusing?"

"Oh no, it's not that at all. I'm just smiling about how much I've used the term 'it's complicated' lately to describe family relationships."

Jed looked at him, partly puzzled and partly irritated, but went on. "People had their own personal reasons for being there. Not all of them were global and altruistic reasons."

"You use the pronoun 'they.' How about you? Did the People's Temple serve any purpose for you?"

Jed was silent, not sure how to answer that. He finally spoke. "I was a kid. I don't know. I didn't have a choice. It was just where I was then. It's where I lived."

"What was it like living there? Did you fight those jaguars and mountain lions with your bare hands?" Finn asked with a twinkle in his eye. He wanted to diffuse any tension that might be arising with his barrage of questions.

Jed let his lips relax into a smile. "Absolutely."

Finn picked up Mother and looked into her eyes. "Did you hear that, Mother? That must be how he learned to take such good care of you!" Then he looked at Jed. "And himself."

"I actually did learn how to live in the wild and take care of myself at an early age. Jim thought it was a punishment to send us into the jungle to fend for ourselves. But it was in fact a good experience as I look back. That knowledge has served me well."

"But you probably didn't think so at the time."

"At least I got away from the insanity for a bit. And it was better than some of the other punishments he liked to dole out."

"What were those?"

Jed took a few minutes before answering, reflecting on all the horror. "Solitary confinement. Beatings. Starvation."

"And this was supposed to be utopia?"

"Hardly." Jed turned and faced Finn. "The worst thing, though, was how he would force the mothers to beat their own children."

"Seriously? How did he force them?"

Jed took a moment to answer. "He'd give the mothers a choice. Either they would or he would."

Finn shuddered and started to type. "Well, at least you learned those survival skills."

Kate entered with a tray. "I baked some cookies."

"You baked cookies?" Finn asked mockingly. "Didn't think you allowed that evil ingredient called sugar in the house."

"Not everyone drinks whiskey at ten in the morning."

"I love cookies. Thanks, Kate." Jed smiled at her as he took one and broke off a piece and gave it to Mother. "Mother loves cookies too."

"Who doesn't love cookies?" Finn teased.

Kate glared at her father and then turned to Jed. "Can I get her something else? I don't have cat food but maybe a can of tuna?"

"She'd like that. Thanks."

"I'll take Mother into the kitchen to eat."

"Heaven forbid a drop of food falls on the floor," Finn chided her. Kate rolled her eyes.

"That would be nice, Kate." Jed handed the cat over.

Mother melted into Kate's arms. "She's very affectionate," she gushed.

"She likes a woman's attention," Jed replied. "Everyone does. Even cats." Kate smiled and left. Jed then turned to Finn. "I'm not sure I'd use the word 'complicated.' Your relationship with your daughter seems more conflicted than that."

"You're probably right," Finn answered as he poured himself some more whiskey. Finn sat back at the computer. "What happened after you escaped? You were just a child. Where did you go?"

"I had family in California."

"So you returned to Oakland?"

"At first. Then I moved around."

"What have you been doing all these years since you left Jonestown?"

"A little of this . . . a little of that."

143

Finn smiled. "A bit of an evasive answer."

"That's a lot of years to cover, Finn."

"Well, have you been here at Venice Beach long?"

"I moved here for the weather when I got old and my joints started to ache." He grinned at Finn.

"That's what this is for." Finn held up the bottle. "Seriously, can't you give me a little more about where you went and what you did?"

"I bounced around some communes . . . lived in Alaska for a time . . . worked in the oil industry and on a fishing boat. I did construction work and worked for a landscaping company. I was also a fire lookout and a lighthouse keeper."

"Sounds like you tried it all: group living in small quarters and solitary jobs with no one around for miles."

"All part of the journey, I suppose."

Kate entered holding Mother in her arms. "She was very hungry. She ate the whole can of tuna and drank a saucer of milk." She handed her to Jed.

"I'm sure she is very appreciative. And so am I," Jed replied.

"She's a lovely cat."

Jed smiled broadly at Kate who smiled back shyly and left. Finn dove immediately back into his questioning the minute she closed the door. "Let's go back to Jonestown since you're not too interested in sharing the last forty years. You still haven't told me that much about what your life was like there."

144

Jed was getting more irritated. "Jim Jones was a drugged-out, narcissistic dictator. There were food shortages; people were emotionally, physically, and sexually abused."

"It sounds awful."

"That's an understatement."

Finn typed for a few more minutes and then sat back in his chair. "What about your own emotions? How did you react to all you went through?"

"You ask too many questions! Don't you have enough for your book, yet?"

Jed got up abruptly and Finn was taken aback by the sudden change in Jed's demeanor. "I was hoping you'd be willing to continue the interviews. I'm sorry."

"Look! I gave you facts about what Jonestown was like. You don't need my story, just read some of the other books."

"But your story is intriguing. And you actually escaped."

Jed picked up Mother and started to walk out. He turned and faced Finn. "You know, Finn, I've learned that you have to stop running or you'll never find peace."

"Have you stopped running, Jed?" Finn asked quietly.

"I'm working on it."

"Have you found peace?"

"I'm working on it." Jed added and walked out.

Finn sat back in his chair, reflecting on all Jed had told him. His mind soon wandered off into the dangerous direction of his own memories. He found himself comparing his own childhood with Jed's. They were both pretty awful. But he, somehow, had managed to come out of it and lead what looked on the outside like a conventional life. He'd married twice, had a child, worked at a regular job, and been a best-selling author. Yet there they both were, obviously damaged and traumatized. He had chosen alcohol and drugs as his elixir while Jed seemed to manage his by yoga breathing.

"Those who do not remember the past are condemned to repeat it," Finn said aloud.

17

SUNDAY MORNINGS THE BOARDWALK is filled with exercise fanatics: joggers, bicyclists, and rollerbladers, even a man who crawls on his hands and feet, like in a child's wheelbarrow game. On the beach there are yoga classes and environmentalists picking up trash. The tourists seem to stay away until the afternoon on Sundays. It gives the working residents of Venice Beach a chance to have their turn. Jed walked down from the mountains and headed for Charlie's table for some breakfast. He had spent the night in the shelter of the forest, a much-needed break from the pandemonium of the boardwalk.

"Hey, Jed," Charlie greeted him as he handed him a cup of coffee and a bagel. "Let me get Mother some milk." He found a cup and tore off the top to improvise a makeshift bowl.

"Thanks, Charlie. And thanks for helping Malcolm out."

"He's a good kid. He has every reason to be angry at the world, but he chooses to try to make the best of his circumstances. We could all learn from him."

Jed shook his head in agreement and continued down the boardwalk, stopping to chat with Davion and Ty and several other regulars. When he got to the appointed bench, he found Malcolm waiting for him. He didn't look happy.

"Am I late?" Jed asked.

"No. I've been here awhile. They wouldn't let me visit Mama. She was getting some tests and stuff. They said she had a bad night."

Jed sat down and put his arm around Malcolm. "I'm sorry."

"They won't tell me much and they keep asking for another relative. I told them my granny's coming but she lives far away. I said that just to shut them up."

"Do you think they believe you?"

"Probably not. But I'm afraid they'll call the social workers."

"Do they know you live with Miss Ruthie now?"

"I don't know."

"Well, have her call the hospital and tell them." Jed pulled him closer and let him cry on his shoulder until Malcolm's sobs turned into whimpers. "Is Miss Ruthie waiting for us? We don't want to be late."

"Yeah. She wants to meet you. I told her about how you got this cat named Mother. She likes cats. She said you could bring her."

Jed stood and put Mother on his shoulders. "We want to meet her, too. Let's go."

Miss Ruthie's house was in a less affluent area of Venice. She lived closer to Lincoln Boulevard, a main thoroughfare that went south to the airport and beyond, past the Los Angeles city limits. It was a far cry from the expensive real estate by the canals or near the beach. Her house was one of the few that hadn't been converted into apartments or rooms for rent. It was in need of paint and mowing, but it was tidy and clean inside. There were even some flowering bushes on either side of the front walk. The way Malcolm bounded up the steps to open the front door, Jed could tell he was proud and eager to show off his new home.

All you could hear was the sound of crying babies as Jed followed Malcolm inside. "Miss Ruthie's probably upstairs. C'mon." Malcolm tugged at Jed's sleeve.

They entered an upstairs bedroom with four cribs and two rocking chairs. Miss Ruthie stood at one of the cribs and turned to greet them. "So this is Jed and his pretty cat, Mother." Mother jumped off Jed's shoulders and rubbed against Miss Ruthie's legs, purring. "Can't pet you now, kitty. Gotta quiet my babies." She took one of the babies out of a crib and handed the baby to a stunned Jed. "Would you mind rocking her for a bit."

Jed sat down tentatively in one of the rockers with the baby in his arms. He held her awkwardly at first, but then relaxed into the chair and settled into a rocking rhythm. Malcolm picked up Mother. "Is she hungry? We got any food for the cat, Miss Ruthie?"

Miss Ruthie called over her shoulder as she picked up another baby and settled into the other rocking chair," Look in the pantry, Malcolm. I think there's some in there."

Malcolm left with Mother and Jed and Miss Ruthie rocked silently for a couple of minutes. The only sound was the wailing of the newborns. Miss Ruthie started humming "Amazing Grace" and the baby in her arms whimpered softly and then stopped crying. Jed looked down at the baby girl in his arms and saw the tension and redness in her face dissipate. Soon the babies fell asleep and the house took on an aura of serenity and comfort, the only sounds being Miss Ruthie's humming and the rhythmic squeaks and creaks of the ancient wooden rocking chairs.

Malcolm ran back in and started to speak but Miss Ruthie put her fingers to her lips to shush him. Malcolm nodded and tiptoed out. Jed closed his eyes and held the baby to his chest, synchronizing their breathing. He rocked for a long time like that, not even aware that Miss Ruthie had put her baby in the crib and left the room. Finally Malcolm came in and whispered in Jed's ear, "Miss Ruthie wants to know if you could have dinner with us?"

Jed opened his eyes and gazed out the window. The sun had started to set. Jed smiled at Malcolm. "I'd like that."

"Miss Ruthie said she didn't even get a chance to talk to you yet."

"I know. Where's Mother?"

"She's sleeping on the windowsill downstairs."

"Shall I bring the baby downstairs?"

"I guess so. Miss Ruthie usually feeds them at the same time."

"This is a nice home for you, Malcolm."

Malcolm shrugged his shoulders. "Sometimes the babies cry a lot. Especially the one you're holding. She cries all night long sometimes."

"She must be in pain."

Malcolm shrugged again. "I guess."

"Where's the other one? Didn't you say there were three babies?"

"I think he had to go back to the hospital. C'mon, dinner's ready."

Jed stood up and smiled at the baby who gurgled back at him. He carried the baby on one hip and squeezed Malcolm's shoulder. "Great. I'm starved."

The kitchen table was covered with plates and serving dishes filled with chicken, potatoes, biscuits, and greens. Two ancient, very used high chairs were pulled up to the table. They were filled with blankets and pillows to keep the infants sitting upright. The baby Miss Ruthie had rocked was sitting in one, sucking on a bottle that Miss Ruthie held with one hand. Her other hand was busy mixing a jar of baby food. Jed put his baby in the other highchair and Miss Ruthie slid a bottle and jar to Jed. "I'd get her started

151

before you serve yourself. She must be very hungry. She slept a long time in your arms, longer than I've ever seen her do." Jed took the bottle and held it for the baby to drink.

A white boy about Malcolm's age sat at the table. He had braces on his legs, thick glasses and buckteeth. He grinned at Jed but didn't speak. Malcolm sat down and started to serve himself. "Malcolm, aren't you forgetting something?" Miss Ruthie chided.

Malcolm stopped with the serving spoon in the air and looked puzzled. He glanced at Jed and then put the spoon down. "Grace?"

"Yes. Also, you haven't properly introduced your friend."

"You already met him."

"Not me. What about Henry, here?"

"But he don't know nothing anyway. He'll just grin and drool and stuff."

"Malcolm!" Miss Ruthie admonished.

"Okay, okay. Jed, this is Henry."

"Hello, Henry," Jed smiled at him. Henry waved his arms and laughed.

"Now can we say grace so we can eat?" Malcolm asked.

Miss Ruthie smiled. "Go ahead, Malcolm."

Malcolm bowed his head and Jed followed his lead. "For what we are about to receive, let us be thankful and ever mindful of those less fortunate than ourselves."

152

Jed smiled, a bit surprised at the lack of "God" or "Jesus" in Malcolm's words. "Do you know where that's from?"

"I don't know. Miss Ruthie taught it to me."

"Someone once told me it was from Shakespeare, but I'm not sure."

"I didn't know that," Miss Ruthie smiled.

"Can we eat now?" Malcolm whined.

"Go ahead," Miss Ruthie answered. Malcolm piled his plate up and glanced at Miss Ruthie who frowned at him. He groaned and put some food on Henry's plate before handing the serving spoon to Jed. Miss Ruthie managed to feed the baby and help Henry who dropped much of his food off his fork before it got to his mouth. She even snuck a few bites into her own mouth. Jed had it a little easier; one hand held the bottle for the baby while he ate with his other hand. Malcolm just shoveled it in.

When dinner was over Malcolm and Jed cleared the table while Miss Ruthie helped Henry into the living room. She sat him in front of the television and turned on a cartoon. She then took the two babies upstairs, one on each hip. When she returned to the kitchen, she found Jed washing dishes and Malcolm drying. "You don't have to, Jed. You're our guest."

Jed smiled at her. "Why don't you go sit down and take a much needed break?"

"Oh no, I'm used to being busy."

"I know you are, but please. The babies are quiet. Take advantage of the opportunity."

"Well, okay. I'll visit with Henry a bit." She left the kitchen.

When Jed and Malcolm were finished, they went into the living room. Henry sat on the couch, his eyes glued to the cartoon. Miss Ruthie sat next to him, her head back and her arm around Henry's shoulders. Her eyes were closed and she snored softly. Jed and Malcolm smiled at each other. "Please thank Miss Ruthie for a delicious dinner and tell her I'll be back tomorrow to help her rock the babies."

"Okay. Bye, Jed."

"Bye, Malcolm." They stood looking at each other for a minute and then simultaneously opened their arms for an affectionate hug. Jed scooped Mother off the windowsill and went out the front door.

18

FINN HAD SPENT HIS SUNDAY AFTERNOON drinking and listening to Van the Man. Kate was out with friends and said she wouldn't be home until after dinner. That made it easy for him to procrastinate and avoid his computer except to play his endless games of solitaire. By evening, the whiskey had obliterated all his coherent thoughts so writing became completely out of the question. The phone rang and he went to the kitchen to answer it.

"Hello?" He frowned and stiffened. "Yes," he said solemnly. "I got your letter." He sighed heavily through tightly pursed lips. "How did you get this number?" His eyes narrowed. "Why are you doing this?" He stood up and paced back and forth, getting more and more enraged. "You can't prove anything. Don't call me again!" He slammed the phone down and stomped back to his office.

He downed the bottle of whiskey and started rummaging through his boxes, looking frantically for something to dispel the alcohol's effect. But he found nothing. "Shit!" He went into the kitchen and opened all the cabinets until he found a bottle of Kahlua. He took it back to his office and emptied it into his glass.

His mind raced, going over and over the events of that day. He remembered that she had watched him give Maggie the insulin dose, but how did she know it was the second one of the morning? And anyway, he could have made a mistake. He was distraught; his wife was dying. He had only recently learned how to give her the shots. She had always done them herself until she had slipped into the coma. Maybe he had forgotten that he had given her one earlier that morning. And who was to know that he had researched it; that an overdose of insulin was comfortable and quick and fatal. Antoinette couldn't prove anything.

He finished the bottle of Kahlua and stumbled around the room indignantly. He knew in his heart he had done the right thing. His anger turned into tears; tears that he hadn't yet shed; tears that had been welling inside all these weeks since she had died. He stumbled into his bedroom where he fell into a deep sleep.

Finn woke up the next morning with a headache. He was going to need more than a cup of regular coffee to get out of this funk. He waited for Kate to leave for work before going into the kitchen.

He was in no mood to listen to her tirade about empty liquor bottles. He searched more cabinets and found a dusty bottle of red wine. Kate wasn't much of a drinker herself. She probably had wine and Kahlua for guests. He found a corkscrew and opened the wine. He took a swig straight from the bottle and made a face. Wine wasn't his drink of choice anyway, but this was old and had already turned a brownish color. She may have had this bottle for twenty years. Well, it did the trick for the moment. He took the bottle into his office and hid it. It could always be drunk in a pinch.

He checked his wallet to make sure he had money and left the house. He was still in the clothes he wore yesterday. He did remember to brush his teeth, but his hair and stubble were untouched.

He stopped at Charlie's table. Derek was playing his guitar nearby and came over.

"How are you doing, Finn? Are you okay?" Charlie asked.

"I'm fine. Why do you ask?"

"You look like you haven't slept in awhile," Derek answered.

"Actually I slept like a baby last night." Finn was irritated and knew that neither of them could provide him with what he wanted. "Have you seen Jed?"

"Not this morning," Charlie replied. Derek just shook his head.

"If you see him, would you let him know I'm looking for him?"

"Sure," they answered in unison. Derek and Charlie watched Finn walk away. They glanced at each other with shared concern.

On his way to Muscle Beach, Finn came upon a large crowd watching Davion and Ty dance to a Jamaican song. The jar on the ground in front of them overflowed with money and people kept adding more and more as they danced. A middle-aged man in a shiny polyester suit came up next to Finn and started swaying to the reggae. "These guys are incredible," the man said.

"Yes. Davion and Ty are great performers."

"Do you know them?"

"Sort of. Yes."

The man reached in his wallet and took out a business card. He handed it to Finn. "Would you give them my card and ask them to call me?"

Finn took the card. "Okay." The man thanked him and left.

When the music ended, the crowd clapped and cheered, and the money kept coming. Davion saw Finn and danced over to him. "Wa'ppun mi key?"

"How goes it, Davion?"

"Everything cook and curry."

Finn handed him the business card. "A man asked me to give you this."

Davion looked at the card. "Who is he?"

"He's an agent. He wants to make you rich and famous."

Davion laughed heartily. "Wa mek yu galaan so?" Ty asked, approaching them.

Davion handed Ty the card. "Dis Samfi gonna make us rich and famous." Ty joined in the merriment.

"You want to clue me in on what's so funny?" Finn asked.

"Samfi mean tricky man . . . con man," said Davion.

"How do you know he's a con man?"

"You think good agent needs to act like—how you call dem guys, Ty?"

"Ambulance chaser."

Finn smiled. "You two aren't going to let yourself get hustled, are you?"

Davion and Ty laughed. "We learned from bandulu in Times Square. He taught us three card monte."

"I don't know what a bandulu is but it sounds like you learned from the top dog if you played three-card monte in Times Square."

"Want to try and beat me? I find some cards," Davion winked.

"No, sir. I wouldn't stand a chance."

"You sure? I give you a clue."

Finn put his hands up in surrender. "No way."

"You chicken, mon."

"Yep, I am. So how long did you live in New York?"

"First place we went after we left Kingston. How long we live there Ty?"

Ty shrugged his shoulders. "I don't know. Maybe one year?"

"I'm from New York, too. So do you miss Jamaica?"

"Miss me pickneys," Ty said with a touch of wistfulness.

"Pickney?" Finn asked.

"My babies."

"You have children?"

"Yes, mon. Two."

"Are you married?"

"I have a dawta in Kingston."

"Yes, you said you had two children. But do you have a wife?"

Ty and Davion smiled at each other.

"Yes, mon. I have a dawta." They laughed again.

"Am I missing something?"

"Dawta mean woman, girlfriend," Davion explained.

"I see."

"Do you?"

"Do I what?"

"Have a dawta?"

"Well, I have a girl-child daughter. But no, I don't have a wife or girlfriend dawta."

"Where your daughter's mama?"

"She died when my daughter was a baby."

"Sorry."

"It was a long time ago."

160

"You never marry again?"

"I did, but she died also."

"You like a black widower?"

Ty and Davion laughed heartily, but Finn found it less than funny and snapped back at them. "Why would you say that?"

Davion gently patted Finn's back. "I just joking, my mon."

"You have grandbabies, Finn?" Ty asked, trying to smooth things over.

Finn settled down. "No, my daughter never had children."

"No need to marry to have babies."

"I know, but she didn't want children. Anyway, she wouldn't be able to stand the mess."

"She like things clean and orderly, eh?"

"You got that right; a place for everything and everything in its place. She's a very independent woman and probably wouldn't have made a good mother, or wife, for that matter. It would mean she'd have to be flexible and compromise. That's not her style."

"Or she have to find man who let her be the boss."

They all laughed. "You never know about these guys handing out business cards. I've heard of people being discovered in odd places. The story goes that Lana Turner was discovered working in a drug store."

"Who?"

161

"Lana Turner." Finn then realized that of course these two young men from Jamaica would never have heard of a movie star from the 1940s. "Never mind. I'm just saying, you might check out this guy."

Ty took out the card and read it. "Coo ya! It say he from American Talent Search."

Davion grabbed the card from Ty and looked at it again. "Cha!"

"You should call him," Finn said. He then got serious. "I'm looking for Jed. Have you seen him?"

Davion shook his head. "No, mon. Not today."

"Okay." Finn started to leave and then turned back to them. "Maybe you can help me."

"Sure, mon. What you need?"

"What have you got?"

Ty and Davion glanced at each other and then Ty looked deep into Finn's eyes. "You saying what I think you saying?"

"Yes, Ty. I think you know what I mean."

"I can get you ganja but why don't you just go to the Kush doc and get it."

"No, Ty. Not weed. I've got alcohol. I need something to counter that."

Davion whispered in Ty's ear. "Mos def. Wait here." Ty left for a few minutes and came back with a small paper bag. Finn took out his wallet but Ty held his hand up to stop him. "No problem, mon. It on me."

"Thanks, Ty. I really appreciate it." Finn hurried off.

When Finn arrived home he went straight to his office. He found a piece of paper and laid out the powder, took a taste, smiled, and snorted. He spent several hours at his computer, writing feverishly. By late afternoon, however, he had wound down from his "energy burst" and decided that whiskey would be an appropriate end to his creative day. First he went to the mailbox and found a check from the publishers. "Good. Now I really have a reason to celebrate." He left for the bank and the liquor store and arrived back home about three.

Kate got home from work and found him dozing in his chair. She took the empty glass off the table with a loud, exasperated sigh. Finn opened his eyes and watched her leave but said nothing, preferring to feign sleep. He contemplated writing, but found himself staring at the computer screen, his mind far away from Jonestown.

After a while Kate entered with a plate of food and set it on the table. "Have you eaten today?" she asked with undisguised contempt.

Finn thought for a minute and realized he hadn't. But he sure wasn't going to tell her that. "I had breakfast."

She shook her head and said sarcastically, "Sure you did. Is Jed coming tonight?"

"I hope so. I wrote quite a bit today but I need some more information." He knew it would appease her if she knew he had written a lot. He pointed to his computer screen. "Take a look."

It worked. She relaxed her shoulders and even showed a hint of a smile. "Well, you should eat. It's a long time since breakfast."

He took a bite of food but pushed the plate away after she left the room. Thoughts of the phone call from Antoinette flooded his mind. He couldn't believe she was actually blackmailing him.

Just then the doorbell rang. "I'll get it," Kate called from the kitchen. She returned with Jed and Mother riding on his shoulders. "Have you eaten dinner, Jed? We have plenty since my father is on a hunger strike." She glanced at the full plate of food.

"I never turn down a home-cooked meal. Nor does Mother."

"I'll take her to the kitchen with me."

Jed handed her the cat and she left, fawning over Mother with affectionate babble. Jed sat across from Finn eyeing the plate of food. "You don't like your daughter's cooking?"

"It's a little too 'crunchy granola' for me."

Jed smiled. "I heard you've been looking for me."

Finn handed him an envelope. "It's the first installment of the advance."

Jed looked inside and took out some cash. "Do I need to count it?"

Finn was astonished. "You think I'm going to cheat you? I thought we trusted each other."

"I'm just kidding, Finn. No need to get bent out of shape." Jed put the money in his pocket. "You don't look very happy for having just received a chunk of money."

"I'm not." Jed was about to ask him why, but decided to wait for Finn to speak. He finally did. "There's something I want to discuss with you."

"What's that?"

"I'll wait 'til Kate brings your food. It's confidential."

Kate entered with a plate and set it down in front of Jed. "It looks delicious. Thanks."

"Mother is eating hers in the kitchen."

"Keep her with you for awhile. I want to talk to Jed privately."

Kate eyed her father suspiciously and left, slamming the door just a tad too hard.

"I take it you're not sharing this information with her?"

"I'm not sharing this with anyone except you."

"Why me?"

"Because I trust you."

"You barely know me."

"It doesn't matter. I know you're an honorable man who will keep this to yourself." Jed ate his dinner, silently, while Finn paced and spoke. "I'm being blackmailed and I don't know what to do about it."

Jed put his fork down and settled back in his chair, watching Finn pace, waiting for him to continue. Finn got the bottle of whiskey out of the cupboard and continued talking as he poured some into a glass for Jed. "I'm not sure she really has a case, but it could be extremely serious for me." He filled his own glass and downed the whole thing.

"Are you asking me to do something about it?"

Finn looked at him incredulously. "Of course not."

"Then why are you telling me this?"

"I don't know. I guess I just need to talk to someone about it."

"Are you asking for advice?"

"I don't know." Finn took a deep breath and sat back down. He was silent for a moment, gathering his thoughts. Jed ate a few bites and waited patiently for Finn to continue. "My wife died a few months ago in New York. I spent everything I had on her care so I had to move in with Kate."

"That must have been hard."

"Yes. It was very hard. But at least she got to die at home. That's what she wanted. She was a woman with strong beliefs about everything she did."

"You and she had a lot in common."

Finn smiled. "Yes. Stubborn, independent, and passionate about what we believe in."

"Apparently your daughter inherited these genes, too."

"Kate's not Maggie's child. My first wife died when Kate was a baby."

"You raised her alone?"

"Yes. I was a high school English teacher; I gave Kate a conventional, middle-class childhood. Well, the best one I could manage as a single father."

"It seems you were successful."

"Yes. I am proud of her."

"So who's blackmailing you?"

"Maggie's hospice nurse." Finn handed Jed the letter from Antoinette. Jed read it and handed it back to Finn. The look on Jed's face was a mixture of shock and contemplation. "What is it, Jed? You look like you just saw a ghost."

Jed stood up and paced, still silent and brooding. Finn was afraid he might have an outburst, although he had no idea why he would be so angry.

After several minutes Jed asked, "Antoinette Delon?"

"Yes. That's her name. Do you know her?" Jed continued pacing and finally sat down, wringing his hands and breathing heavily, but not answering. "What's going on, Jed?"

"Nothing." Jed took a deep breath and exhaled slowly. He closed his eyes and seemed to be in a meditative state, breathing in and out rhythmically. Finn watched him with both curiosity and apprehension until Jed finally opened his eyes. He seemed to have composed himself.

"She also called here, and I don't have any idea how she got Kate's number." Jed finished his whiskey and Finn poured more for both of them. "Maggie was a diabetic and needed insulin," Finn continued. "She was also on other medications for pain. Antoinette saw me give Maggie an extra dose of insulin."

"How does she know it was extra?"

"She counted the vials. That was part of her job. Also, she had asked me if I'd given her any yet that day."

"And what did you answer?"

"Yes."

Jed stared at Finn. Jed's eyes were questioning but also sympathetic. Finn's eyes were pleading but also fearful. "And too much insulin for a diabetic means?"

"Just what you think it means." Finn bit his lip and looked away. "She was suffering so."

Jed pushed his plate away and twiddled his thumbs. He took a couple of minutes before speaking. "Had you and your wife discussed this?"

Finn shrugged his shoulders. He tried to think of what he should say. "In a way."

"How long were you married?"

"About twenty years. We married after Kate graduated from college and moved out to California."

Finn poured more whiskey into his glass and tried to pour some into Jed's but Jed put his hand over his glass. "No more, Finn. I'm good."

"Suit yourself."

"So what are you going to do about Antoinette?" Jed asked.

"I don't know."

"Do you think she can prove that you killed your wife?"

Finn walked to the window. "It had to have been one of us who gave her the extra dose since we were the only ones who had access. She had no motive, of course, since she would be out of a job when Maggie died."

Kate knocked on the door. "Mother wants to come in."

She opened the door and Mother scampered unto Jed's lap. He petted her and smiled at Kate. "Dinner was delicious, and I can tell Mother thought so too."

Kate smiled. "Thanks." She took the plates, Jed's empty one and Finn's full one, and left, but not before giving Finn another piercing look.

Jed stood and put Mother on his shoulders. He turned to Finn. "I'll give all this some thought. And Finn, maybe you ought to lay off the whiskey a little." He left before Finn had a chance to respond.

19

KATE ENTERED FINN'S OFFICE before leaving for her morning jog. She found him asleep with his head atop the keyboard of his computer. He had apparently been there all night once again. She grabbed the empty whiskey bottle and threw it angrily into the wastebasket. It made a loud clunk and startled Finn awake. She continued to clean up the room as Finn bellowed, "What are you doing?"

"What does it look like I'm doing? Your office is a mess." She made quite a racket as she threw things away in disgust.

"I like it just the way it is."

She stared at him. "Really? You like your life just the way it is? When are you going to stop drinking yourself into a stupor?"

He closed his eyes and held his head. "Leave it alone, Kate. And leave me alone."

"You're impossible!" She stomped out.

Finn reached in his pocket and took out the plastic bag from Ty and tore it open. It had traces of white powder, but not enough to make a difference. "Shit!" He stood up slowly and made his way to the bathroom. He looked in the mirror and grimaced. He looked like hell, but he didn't care. Brushing his teeth and smoothing down his hair with water was enough to make him presentable.

He left the house, kicking both newspapers out of the way and walked down the front porch steps. He heard the beep of a car horn and noticed a strange car parked in front of the house. The door opened and Antoinette got out. "Monsieur Finn, we need to talk."

Finn stepped backwards, his eyes ablaze. "What the hell are you doing here?"

Antoinette took his arm and asked, "Can we go inside?"

Finn brushed her arm off his. "No."

"Then we can talk out here."

"No. I don't want to talk at all. I told you. You can't prove anything. Now, get away from me."

He tried to walk away but she pulled on his arm. "I will go to the police. I have a log of the medications I gave her. I was also able to get a statement from the doctor who examined her when she was brought to the hospital. They know she had too much insulin in her body."

He brushed her hand off his arm and stiffened. "How did you get that kind of information from the doctor at the hospital?"

171

"I know people that work there."

"How will they know it was me? You could have given her another dose?"

"I have a perfect record as a nurse. My supervisors will back me up. They will believe me. And I saw you give her the second dose."

"But it's your word against mine."

"It was my job, Mr. Finn. Why would I want to kill off my livelihood? I have no motive."

"I loved my wife very much. Why would I kill her?"

Antoinette took a moment to answer and then looked deeply into Finn's eyes. "Because you loved your wife very much." His scowl turned into a frown and he took a deep breath.

"Why are you doing this to me?" Finn asked in a soft voice.

She looked away from him. "Murder is against the law."

He glared at her. "So is blackmail!"

She handed him a business card and said, "I am staying at this motel. Bring me the money there." He took the card and watched her get in the car and drive away.

He stood frozen for a moment and then took off down the street, walking with a newfound vengeance. He went into a liquor store and came out with a brown bag. He searched for an isolated bench on the boardwalk and found one away from the merchants and performers setting up for the day. He sipped from the pint bottle inside the bag, contemplating his predicament. Jed approached the bench and sat down next to him. "Kind of early to be out here drinking?"

Finn took a long swig. "She's here."

"Who?"

"Antoinette." He took the business card out of his pocket and showed it to Jed. "She's staying at this motel. She wants me to bring her the money."

Jed stared at the card. "Do you think she'll go to the police?"

"She says she will."

"How can she prove anything? Did they do an autopsy?"

"Apparently she spoke to the doctor at the hospital. The doctor told her there was extra insulin in her body."

"How could she get that information?"

"She has connections at the hospital."

"How would the police know it was your doing?"

"As I said yesterday, why would she do it? I'm the one with the motive."

"What motive is that?"

Finn took another swig of whiskey and looked out at the ocean. "Because I loved my wife. Her words."

Jed looked at Finn silently, watching his eyes well up with tears. Finn guzzled down more of the whiskey.

Jed handed the card back to Finn and stood up. "Whiskey's not the solution."

"Got any other ideas?"

Jed walked away without answering, leaving Finn to brood and imbibe.

Jed left the boardwalk and the beach. He walked through alleys and walk streets, crossed Pacific Avenue and Main Street, until he got to the corner of Rose Avenue and Lincoln Boulevard. He stood on the corner of the busy intersection and looked up at a sign advertising an old, dumpy motel called the Golden Star. Only one car was parked in the lot. It looked like an economy-sized rental car so he assumed it was Antoinette's. He found a pile of newspapers by the ice machine and placed Mother on it. "Wait for me here." He went to the room where the car was parked in front. He knocked, at first hesitantly, and then with more intensity.

"I'm glad you came to your senses, Monsieur Finn," Antoinette said as she opened the door. Her eyes narrowed suspiciously when she saw Jed. "Who are you?"

"A friend of Finn's. I have something from him."

"Do you have the money?"

"May I come in?"

Antoinette hesitated. "No. I don't think so. Where is Mr. Finn?"

"Those who forget the past are condemned to repeat it," Jed said, staring at her with eyes filled with vehemence and hostility.

Antoinette swallowed hard and closed the door to a narrow slit. "Who are you?"

"I'm Jedidiah, Cora Gibbons' son. You remember Cora, don't you?"

Antoinette froze and Jed pushed his way into the room. He closed the door and faced her. She walked slowly to the bed and sat. They stared at each other for a moment until she finally spoke. "What do you want?"

"You murdered my mother and my sister and now you're blackmailing Finn."

Antoinette sat up stiffly and gulped. "I don't know what you're talking about."

Jed glowered at her, barely able to contain his rage. "Yes, you do."

"I did not murder your mother and sister." Jed grabbed her arm and she tried to squirm out of his grasp. "They took it on their own," she yelled.

He tightened his grip, as he got angrier and more agitated. "They would never have taken it themselves! I saw you do it! I saw you kill many of them! Babies! Mothers with their dead babies in their arms!"

"Let go of me!" she shouted.

"You injected them with the poison. You're a murderer! You're no better than Jim Jones himself! How can you blackmail Finn when you did the same thing! And you had no excuse! No reason! Nothing but evil and hatred in your veins!"

"No! No! Stop!"

He clutched the necklace she was wearing and gasped. "Where did you get this?"

"Stop! You're hurting me."

"That was my mother's, you monster!" As Jed pulled the necklace off, the clasp broke and she fell backwards. He watched her head hit the radiator. She didn't move. Blood seeped out of her ears and her eyes were closed. Jed froze. He stared at her trying to tell if she was breathing. He waited a few seconds and then knelt down and put his fingers on her neck. He thought he felt a faint pulse. He ran to the phone and dialed 911. He gave them the address and room number and hung up before they could ask any questions. He bolted out the door, clutching the necklace tightly.

He grabbed Mother who was sleeping peacefully on the stack of papers and ran north toward the mountains clutching the necklace tightly. After several blocks, he stopped and caught his breath. He realized he was across the street from Miss Ruthie's house. He sat down on the curb and put Mother down next to him. He laid the necklace on his leg and stared at it. He couldn't believe he was actually holding the locket.

Mother made a beeline for Miss Ruthie's front door. Jed got up slowly, put the necklace in his pocket and followed Mother's lead. He knocked and waited for Miss Ruthie to hear it over the sound of the crying babies. She finally opened the door with one of the babies in her arms. He could hear the other one screaming in the background. "Hello, Jed." She smiled. He nodded and smiled back. He entered the house and placed Mother on the living room windowsill. He climbed the stairs, two at a time, and rushed into the babies' room. He picked up the wailing baby and sat down. Miss Ruthie entered and sat down in the other rocking chair. Neither of them said a word. Soon the house was quiet except for the creaking of the rocking chairs and Miss Ruthie's soft humming.

They sat in silence until the babies were asleep and then put them gently back in their cribs. "Thanks," Ruthie said as they tiptoed out of the room and went downstairs.

"Thank *you*," Jed answered.

"Would you like some lunch?" Miss Ruthie asked.

"No, thanks. When does Malcolm get home?"

"He's always home by six for dinner."

"Could you tell him I might be gone for awhile?"

"I will. Can I give you some food to take with you? Something for Mother too?"

"Thanks, but I'd better go now." He picked up Mother and hurriedly left.

He walked cautiously down the street, watching for unmarked cars and listening for sirens. He went several blocks until he got to Kate's street.

He glanced around to make sure he wasn't being followed and continued down the street to Kate's front porch. He kissed Mother and put her down. "It would be better for you here. I'll find you when I get back." Mother watched him walk down the street and started after him. Jed turned around and saw her coming toward him. He went back and scooped her into his arms. "You need to go back to Finn and Kate's house. It's best right now." He put her down and walked toward the mountains. This time she didn't follow.

20

THE AMBULANCE ARRIVED AT THE GOLDEN STAR MOTEL about 10 minutes after Jed called. A middle-aged Chinese man came out of the office as it pulled into the parking lot and approached the EMTs as they got out.

"We had a call from Room 105," one of the paramedics told him as the other one knocked on the door.

"I know nothing about that."

"No answer. Do you have a key?" the other paramedic asked him. The Chinese man took a key ring out of his pocket and opened the door. "She's unconscious!"

The two paramedics rushed in to work on Antoinette. The motel manager walked in behind them. "What's wrong with her?"

"Looks like she's been hit on the head. You'd better call the cops."

"I don't want no trouble here."

"I think it's too late for that."

"Is she dead?"

"Not yet."

The manager went back to his office and the police arrived just as the paramedics finished loading Antoinette into the ambulance. "What do you have?" one of the cops asked.

"Traumatic head injury. Looks like there was a struggle. Manager says he knows nothing but the dispatcher said the caller was a male."

"Is she still alive?"

"Barely."

The ambulance took off with its siren blaring while one cop went inside the room and the other one went to get the manager. He called the precinct house as he walked to the office and asked them to send over a detective for an investigation.

"I don't know nothing about this. She just quiet lady from New York," the manager said as the officer entered.

"What's her name?"

The manager looked at the computer screen. "Antoinette Delon."

"How long was she planning to stay?"

"She pay for three nights."

"When did she arrive?"

"Yesterday."

"And you did not call for an ambulance?"

"No. Like I say I don't know nothing."

"Did you see anyone go into her room?"

"No."

"The detective will be here shortly and he'll need to talk to you too." The policeman turned around to join his partner in Room 105.

"What did you find?" he said as he entered the room.

"Not much. Did you call it in?"

"Yeah." He glanced around the room. "Manager said she's from New York."

"There were some papers on the dresser. I didn't touch them but they were written to some guy named Finn McGee here in Venice."

"Could you read them?"

"Some. Looked a little threatening."

"This might be an easy case then."

"Open-and-shut."

Finn had taken his solitary drinking binge to the cafe. He sat at a table doing the crossword puzzle, sipping his cup of coffee, frequently enhancing it from the bottle in the brown bag. Harper joined him, apprehensively. "You hate the coffee here that much?"

"I told you I like the Irish kind."

She took a pile of papers out of her laptop case and put it on the table. "I think you have done a disservice to the literary world by taking so long to write your next book! It's fascinating and captivating."

"Thanks," Finn answered without a hint of enthusiasm.

"You're a remarkable writer, Finn. It's hard to believe you wrote your first book when you were so old. I mean, not that you're so old."

"I had a child to support. I couldn't be a struggling writer. I needed to teach to pay the bills."

"You didn't write anything until you retired?"

"I wrote a few magazine articles and short stories, but nothing much. You're lucky that you can devote time to writing."

"I wish you'd tell my parents that."

"Weren't they proud that you won the competition?"

"I didn't tell them."

"Why not?"

"They don't support my decision to be a writer. They had other plans for their daughter."

"That's not unusual. I'm sure they would still be excited that you were acknowledged as the best."

"I don't know if they would."

"You're still their child."

"Our relationship is complicated."

He took a long swallow of coffee. "There they are again."

"There what are again?" she asked.

"Those damn complicated parent-child relationships."

Harper nodded and sipped her coffee. "My parents think I'm wasting my life wanting to be a writer. They don't understand why I don't want to have a career where I'd make a lot of money or at least marry someone who does."

"Apparently they don't know you very well. You don't strike me as someone who cares that much about money."

"You got that right, Finn. Anyway, I'll never be good enough for them."

"Why do you say that?"

"They just wanted me to be like my brother was."

"Was?"

"He was a stockbroker. His office was in the World Trade Center."

"In 2001?"

"Yes."

Finn touched her arm. "I'm sorry, Harper. He must have been very young."

"It was his first job after graduating from college." She swallowed hard. "I can't make my parents' pain go away, no matter what profession I choose. Why don't they see that?"

"I think they do see that. Parents want what's best for their children. It's just that sometimes parents and children don't agree on what that is. You're entitled to do whatever you want, of course, but you could certainly have chosen something more fruitful."

"Waiting tables is not my profession."

"I know. I meant writing."

"What? I can't believe you are agreeing with my parents on this. You of all people!"

"Life is a crap shoot, Harper. Writing is just a way of copping out so you don't have to have a real job."

Harper was dumbfounded. "Do you honestly believe that, Finn?"

Finn took a long drink. "Oh, don't be so naive, Harper! What do you expect? Nothing comes easy so you might as well get something worthwhile in the end. That whole romantic notion of the destitute writers not caring about money because they're doing what they love is pure bullshit. Everyone cares about making enough money to keep a roof over their head and food on the table."

"Are you saying that your books haven't been worthwhile? They were valuable to me. I told you how your book inspired me to be a writer."

"Maybe that wasn't such a good thing."

Harper bit her lip and gulped down the lump in her throat. "I don't want to spend my days doing something I hate."

"I don't want to burst your Pollyanna bubble about writers and writing but we are a loathsome bunch," an unsympathetic Finn sighed.

Harper's voice cracked, "I thought you understood." Her eyes filled with tears. "I thought we had a real connection—a bond."

"I'm sorry, Harper. I don't know if I'm capable of having a bond with anyone."

Finn downed his coffee and they sat in silence for a few minutes. Finally he whispered, "By the way, Harper. Do you know where I can uh, score some, uh you know, uppers?"

Harper was dumbfounded. "For you?"

"Yes," Finn nodded.

She fidgeted a bit in her chair. "Well . . . I could probably get you some Adderall. Is that what you mean?"

"Sure. That'll work."

"I'll try. I'll bring them tomorrow."

"Thanks." Harper watched Finn stand up somberly, pick up his paper bag and stumble out of the coffee shop.

21

FINN STOOD AT THE KITCHEN SINK THAT EVENING, washing the dinner dishes with unnecessary thoroughness. His mind was a million miles away. Kate entered, dressed to go out, and smiled with curious amusement. "You are certainly putting an awful lot of effort into scrubbing them clean."

"Yeah," he grunted.

"Oh, and don't forget to put the trash out."

"Okay, okay. I've lived here long enough to know when garbage day is."

She bit her tongue and tried not to be confrontational. "Is Jed coming tonight to write?"

"I don't know. Maybe he's working at the restaurant."

"It's not like you really need him to write. You could get plenty done without his input."

186

"Stop nagging, Kate. Mind your own business and I'll take care of mine."

She stopped struggling to stay calm. "I'm not nagging, Dad! For God's sake, the publisher isn't going to wait forever for the rest of your book! I'll be home late," she snapped as she walked out in a huff.

After she left, Finn finished the dishes and pulled out the garbage pail from under the sink. He went out the back door and dumped it into the trash bin. As he dragged the container to the curb, he heard a cat meow. He looked up and down the street but saw nothing. He walked back to the house and as he opened the back door, Mother darted inside. "Mother!" Finn exclaimed.

He followed her into the kitchen and she rubbed her head on his leg, meowing incessantly. "What's wrong? Are you hungry? Where's Jed?" He opened the cabinet and looked around, sliding cans and boxes around. "I don't see any tuna fish." He opened the refrigerator and peered in. "Hmm. How about an omelet?" He took a carton of eggs and a package of cheese out of the refrigerator and set them on the counter. He knelt down and opened a cabinet next to the stove. "Where does she keep this stuff? Bear with me, Mother." He found a frying pan and set it on the stove. He broke a couple of eggs into a bowl and stirred in a little water. He found some oil in a cabinet and poured it into the pan and then put the eggs in, turning the pan from side to side to coat the bottom. Mother watched him curiously and patiently.

He found a shredder and grated the cheese into the eggs and used a spatula to fold the omelet. "I haven't cooked for anyone in a long time, Mother. If truth be told, I haven't done much cooking for myself in several months either." He slid the omelet onto a plate and set it on the floor. "Here you go." Mother ate ravenously. "It looks like you haven't eaten for awhile." He watched her fondly for a couple of minutes, but even a ravenous cat is a slow eater so he soon tired of waiting for her to finish.

He entered his office and sat down in front of the computer. He knew full well that he probably wasn't going to get any writing done tonight, but he didn't know what else to do. As he waited for it to boot up, he refilled his glass and took a couple of swigs. He clicked a few icons on the screen and a solitaire game came up. As he played, Mother entered and climbed onto his lap. Finn stopped clicking the mouse and sat back in his chair. "Oh well, I didn't really want to play anyway." He closed his eyes and petted her as she purred.

22

KATE ENTERED FINN'S OFFICE, dressed for her run, and found him in what had become his usual early morning position, still wearing the clothes he had on the day before. She saw the empty whiskey bottle and scowled, nudging his shoulder trying to wake him up. He woke with a start and Mother, who had been asleep on his lap, scampered away. "What?" he growled.

"Is Jed here?"

"No."

"Then why is Mother here?"

"She knows where to get a good meal."

"So Jed came over last night?"

"No," Finn scowled. "Jeez, I'm half asleep. Stop all this questioning!"

"Mother came over by herself?"

"Apparently."

"Is this becoming a ritual? Staying up all night and sleeping on top of your computer?"

"For Christ's sake, I'll sleep when and where I want." She tried to look at the computer screen, but he covered it with his arm. "Are you checking up on me?"

"Yes," she snapped.

"It's really not your business whether I'm writing."

"I think it is my business. When you moved in you were supposed to help out with the mortgage and food. I haven't seen a penny."

"I'll give you money when I get it from the publisher."

"I thought you already got some."

"I had bills to pay and I gave some to Jed."

"Gave some to Jed?" she cried. "You're supporting him and his cat?"

"Stop it, Kate," he mumbled.

"Why don't you stop drinking and write the damn book! You're ruining both of our lives!" She stomped out.

Finn angrily shoved a pile of papers off the table and they scattered over the floor. "Damn bossy woman!" He made no move to pick them up. Mother scampered to the other side of the room. She sat rigidly, cautiously watching and waiting. He went to the front porch and picked up a newspaper, not even bothering to see which one it was. He brought it in and dropped it on the floor of his office. After a trip to the bathroom he grabbed the newspaper off the pile of papers and left without a word to Kate.

He left the house, still wearing yesterday's clothes, and looked for Harper at the cafe. He spotted her at a table and sat in the chair across from her. "Did you get them?" he blurted.

"Good morning to you, too, Finn."

"Yeah, good morning."

She reached in her bag. "Yes. I got some."

"How much?"

"Well, I couldn't get a whole prescription bottle—"

Finn interrupted. "No, no, I mean how much do I owe you?"

"Just take them." She handed him a plastic bag with about half a dozen pills.

He took one out of the bag and put the rest in his pocket. "I'm sorry I've disappointed you, Harper." He swallowed the pill. "I've been doing a lot of that lately."

She decided to change the subject. "Did you finish the puzzle?"

"Why? Do you want to cheat from it?"

She smiled feebly. "Well, if you were just going to throw it away . . ."

He handed her the whole newspaper. "Here, you can have it."

She opened it and took out the section with the crossword puzzle. She found the right page and then looked at him inquisitively. "You didn't even start it?"

"I'm a bit preoccupied. You can save your dollar. Keep my paper."

"Wait. This is the *Los Angeles Times*. Have you switched your allegiance?"

"No. I guess I didn't even notice."

Harper put the crossword puzzle in her bag and opened the local news section. "You might want to see this, Finn." She read the headline aloud. "'New York Woman Attacked in Venice Motel Room.' It says she was a hospice nurse from New York City named Antoinette Delon. Isn't Antoinette the name of the nurse who took care of your wife? The one you had that letter from?"

He looked at her stunned and took the paper from her. "Jesus!"

"Is it the same person?"

"Yes. It is."

"Is she dead?"

"It doesn't say."

"I'm sorry, Finn."

"There's no need to be sorry. No need at all," he replied with a hint of a smile.

"You can keep that section. I'll just take the crossword puzzle," Harper said as she watched him walk away. She didn't know how to react; she wasn't even sure how she felt about him now. She was concerned about his depressed state, sad that he had let her down, a little afraid for herself, but mostly she felt disappointed by someone she had considered a mentor and even a bit of a hero.

Finn stopped at a liquor store and came out with his customary brown sack. He crossed the street against the light, causing a bit of ire in the drivers who had the green. He entered a small grocery store where the choices were limited and the prices outrageous. He paid the clerk and walked out with a bag of cat food under his arm.

When he got back to Kate's and entered the kitchen, Mother came scurrying up to him just as the phone rang. He set the cat food bag on the counter and answered it. "Hello? Judith! What did they say?"

He picked up Mother and set her on the counter. His eyes and his mouth narrowed. "But I can't wait. I need the money now! Did you tell them that taking care of Maggie wiped me out?"

He took a bowl out of the cupboard. "Okay, okay. Tell them I'll have more in a week." He slammed the phone down and brooded as Mother meowed at him.

He tried to open the top of the bag by pulling it apart but it wouldn't open. "Damn fucking bag!" He got a knife out of the drawer and angrily slashed the cat food bag. The kibbles poured out unto the floor. "Here, eat!" He threw the bowl into the sink, shattering it into pieces. He grabbed the brown sack from the liquor store and stomped out of the kitchen, leaving Mother to eat the food off the floor.

When he got to his office, he fell into his chair and took out the bag of pills. He swallowed two more pills and chased them down with a mouthful of whiskey. He stared at the blank computer screen for several minutes, cursing at it and himself. The doorbell rang. "Oh, good. Maybe that's Jed."

He hurried to the front door and opened it. A man in a suit flashed a badge at him. "Finnegan McGee?"

"Yes?"

"I'm Lieutenant Bukowski. I'd like to ask you a few questions."

"About what?" Finn asked cautiously.

"May I come in?" Finn hesitated at first, but then realized he had better cooperate and opened the door wider. Lieutenant Bukowski followed him into the living room and sat down. He kept his eyes focused on Finn, observing his demeanor carefully. Finn squirmed and averted his eyes. "I believe Antoinette Delon was your late wife's hospice nurse?" the lieutenant asked.

"Yes." Finn figured a brief answer was the best way to reply.

"Did you know she was here in Venice?"

Finn didn't know how to answer this. He didn't want to say yes and then have to talk about the blackmail, but he didn't know if she had said anything to the police about having seen him. He thought he'd try to stall. "You mean she's living here now?"

"No. She was apparently visiting for a few days."

"Oh," Finn replied.

After a few minutes the exasperated lieutenant asked again. "So did you see her in the last couple of days?"

Finn took a deep breath and took a chance, finally answering, "No."

"Had you heard from her since your wife died?"

Now what should he say? If he admitted to that, then he would incriminate himself. He decided to tell a half-truth, although he was not at all sure it was the right thing to do. "I think I got a letter from her but I figured it was a request for a job reference and didn't open it." That way if the lieutenant knew anything, Finn could just claim ignorance.

"She didn't call you?"

"Uh, I don't think so." Finn hoped his quivering voice wasn't noticeable.

"Hmmm. That's interesting. Her cell phone record shows that she called your daughter's number more than once."

"Really? Well, I guess I wasn't home."

"Did you know she was attacked in her motel room?"

"Oh, was that her? I think I read something about that in the paper." Was he being a total fool and making things worse? He hoped the lieutenant didn't see through his charade.

195

"When did you see her last?"

"The day my wife died."

The lieutenant smiled. "She didn't come to the funeral? Or contact you at all after your wife died?"

"There was no funeral."

"And the answer to my second question?"

"You mean when I was still in New York? No."

The lieutenant wrote on his pad. "How long did Ms. Delon work for your wife?"

"About six months."

"Did she live with you?"

"No. She came in the morning and left at night." Finn shifted uncomfortably. He started to realize that it was more serious than he thought. "Why are you asking me these questions?"

"We found the address and phone number of your daughter, Kate, among her things. As well as a copy of a letter written to you." Finn stiffened but remained silent.

Finn stood up. "I don't think I have to answer these questions."

"You don't have to, but it would be wise if you did."

Finn walked to the door of the living room and turned toward the lieutenant. "I think we're done here."

When they got to the front door, Finn opened it and waved the lieutenant out. "Thanks for your time, Mr. McGee. By the way, it might not be a bad idea to call a lawyer. Miss Delon died this morning." The lieutenant smiled and sauntered out. Finn watched him drive away and then went back to his office to obliterate his panic.

That evening Kate came home through the back door into the kitchen and saw the cat food all over the floor and the broken bowl in the sink. "What th—Dad?" She walked around the house calling for him and when she got to his office, she noticed the papers scattered around and the empty whiskey bottle by the computer. She picked up the papers and put them in a neat pile and threw the bottle in the wastebasket.

She got a broom and dustpan out of the kitchen closet to sweep up the cat food. She smiled for a moment when Mother darted in and started eating the food off the floor as Kate swept. When she heard the front door slam, however, the smile turned sour and she glared at Finn as he staggered into the kitchen, holding a bag.

He looked at the floor and then up at Kate. "I was going to clean it up." Kate said nothing and swept with such fervor that Mother ran away. He stumbled to the cabinet and got a clean glass.

"You don't even try to hide it anymore?"

He looked at her forlornly. "I'm sorry, Kate," he said as he stumbled out. "For everything."

23

THE NEXT DAY A DISHEVELED AND UNSHAVEN FINN watched Davion and Ty entertain a crowd on the boardwalk. After they finished their performance they noticed him and danced over. "You sick, mon?" asked Davion.

"Just tired. I didn't sleep well last night."

"Smell like you had a good time last night," Ty chuckled. He winked at Davion. "He must have a pretty lady friend."

Finn's face remained somber. "Hey, I really need to find Jed. Do you have any idea where he might hang out?"

"We told you. Jed a very private person. Especially when he get in his mood."

"Have you ever known him to be without Mother?"

"What you mean?" Ty asked.

"Mother is at my house."

"Not like Jed to leave Mother. You try the restaurant?"

"I'll check." Finn's body wobbled back and forth, almost falling into Davion and Ty.

"You okay, Finn?" Ty asked while holding his arm.

"I'm fine. If you see him, let him know I have Mother." Finn staggered down the boardwalk.

"He don't look fine to me," Davion said to Ty.

Bella was sifting through a trashcan and she looked up when he stumbled by. "If it isn't Finnegan's Wake. So how are things in Glocca Mora?"

"Not so good, actually." Finn found a bench to sit on.

"Maybe you need to find a pot of gold."

"That would help. Maybe I should start rummaging through these trashcans with you." Bella gave him a sharp look.

"I'm sorry, Bella. Don't pay any attention to me."

"I won't."

He took a pint out of his pocket. Bella stared at him with disdain as he drank. Her displeasure turned to compassion and then pity as he lay down on the bench and closed his eyes. She watched him for a minute, waiting for some kind of explanation, but none came. She turned around and walked away. Finn opened one eye but let her continue walking. When she was far enough away not to turn back, he sat up, took another swig, and lay back down.

The boardwalk was emptying as the merchants and performers closed up for the night. Finn awoke and took a few minutes to get his bearings. He got up slowly, hanging on to the bench to steady himself, and then started walking. It was dark by the time he got to Kate's front porch and opened the door. An anxious Kate appeared in the doorway to the living room. "There's a detective here to see you."

The lieutenant watched Finn stumble into the living room. "Your daughter was kind enough to let me in. Can we go somewhere to talk?"

"I told you I was done talking to you."

"Would you rather I get a warrant to search your house and force you to come to the station for questioning?"

"What do you mean, force me to go to the station? Are you arresting me?"

"If I determine that you are obstructing justice by interfering with an investigation, I can bring you down to the station and keep you for forty-eight hours if necessary."

Finn was silent as he motioned him to follow. Kate watched nervously as they walked into Finn's office. "Dad?" she asked timidly. He ignored her plea.

"I have a few more questions for you," the lieutenant announced as he scanned the piles of papers and books all over the floor.

Finn shut the door. "What questions?"

"Your wife was a diabetic, correct?"

"Yes."

"And you were giving her insulin after she couldn't do it herself?"

"Yes." Finn sighed and flopped into his chair.

"You know that the nurse kept track of how much insulin she got?"

"That was her job," Finn sighed. His head was pounding and he had a hard time concentrating.

"According to the Coroner's report, your wife had too much insulin in her body the morning she died."

Finn paused. "My wife died of cancer."

"Where were you when Antoinette was murdered?"

Finn's face reddened as his exasperation turned into anger. He stood up abruptly. "That's it. Get a goddamn warrant. I won't answer any more questions without a lawyer."

The lieutenant observed Finn's demeanor coolly. "Suit yourself. I was just trying to keep everything friendly. These are just routine questions."

Finn fell back into his chair. "Jesus Christ! Are you kidding me? You think I killed her?"

"Killed who, Finn? Antoinette? Your wife? Or both?"

Finn shook his head in disbelief and shouted at him. "Get the hell out of here!"

"Can you give me the names of some people besides your daughter who may be able to give you an alibi?"

"Kate's a goddamn schoolteacher—how much more of an upstanding citizen do you need?"

"Well, she's your daughter."

"She wouldn't lie!"

"Just give me some other names. That will help your case. And one more thing, do you know a man named Jedidiah Gibbons?"

Finn took his hands away and glanced up at the lieutenant warily. "Why?"

"He's also a suspect and according to your daughter, you two are writing a book together."

"I've interviewed him a few times."

"I understand you're taking care of his cat."

"His cat just wound up here. And leave my daughter out of this. Maggie was not her mother."

"I know."

"You certainly do know a lot, don't you! Is there anything else?"

"I think you should know that Jed's fingerprints were found in the motel room." Finn's mouth dropped. "Did you hire Jed to kill Antoinette?"

"No!" Finn exploded.

The lieutenant stood to leave. "Call my office to give me those names. I can see myself out."

He was barely out the door when Kate rushed in. "What's going on, Dad? Why is he asking you all these questions?"

"I'll tell you later. Please just let me be right now."

"You're frightening me."

"It's okay, Kate. I'll take care of it."

"Please, Dad. Tell me what's going on." Her voice was trembling. "I've never seen you like this. What's happened to you?"

He put his arms around her and held her. They stood like that for a minute, neither speaking, until Kate pulled away and wiped her tears. "You really reek of alcohol."

Finn smiled feebly. "Hey, I never promised you a rose garden."

"I'll make some coffee." After she left, he took the bag of pills out of his pocket and swallowed two before heading to the shower.

A cleaner, more respectable looking Finn approached the front door of Luis' restaurant and tried the door but it was locked. He knocked loudly and Luis opened it. "Senor Finn! What are you doing out so late?" Finn followed Luis inside where a busboy was clearing tables and Mercedes was counting money. "Can I get you a beer?"

"Do you have any whiskey?"

"No, just beer and wine."

"Okay, I'll have a beer."

Luis brought two bottles of beer and sat down at the table. Finn reached for his wallet but Luis stopped him. "No, no. It's on me."

"Thanks." Finn put his wallet away.

"So, Senor Finn. Have you heard anything from Jed? We miss him around here. I can't find anyone who works harder and faster than him."

Finn downed half the bottle of beer. "I haven't heard anything. I was hoping you had. Please take my phone number in case you see him or hear from him. It's urgent that I talk to him." He handed Luis a piece of paper.

"Do you think something's happened to him?" Luis asked anxiously.

"I don't know." Finn finished his beer. "Do you have a dishwasher tonight?"

"No. They only work til payday. Then I don't see them again. Poor Jose, here, has to do two jobs."

"Where are the aprons?"

"Senor Finn! You don't have to—"

"I want to," Finn interrupted. He looked down at the floor and took a deep breath. "More than that, I need to."

Luis looked at him, bewildered. "You need a job?"

Finn smiled. "Well, yes, but no, that's not what I meant. Washing dishes relaxes me. I just want to do it."

"I couldn't let you," Luis objected.

"Please, Luis. Just show me where the aprons are." Luis shrugged his shoulders and took Finn into the kitchen.

24

FINN WAS UP EARLY THE NEXT MORNING.
He was already showered and dressed and making
coffee when Kate, in her jogging clothes, entered the
kitchen. "You're up? You got home so late last night I
figured you'd still be sleeping."

"I have some things to do today." He took his
coffee and went to his office where he made a beeline
for the cabinet to spike his coffee before sitting down
at his computer. He was about to take a sip when he
reached into his pocket and took out a pill and
shrugged, "What the hell." He swallowed the pill and
followed it with a swig of the coffee.

He heard the phone ring and Kate's muffled
voice. She called from the kitchen, "Judith is on the
phone. She's very anxious to speak to you."

"Tell her I'll call her back later," Finn shouted
back.

Kate entered his office. "You'd better speak to her."

"I told you—"

Kate interrupted. "The publishers want more chapters. Do you have any?" He stared at her and then exhaled deeply, more with resignation than irritation. "Dad?"

"Just tell her I can't talk to her now," he said quietly.

Kate shook her head. "You can't go on like this." She went to the phone and Finn heard her muffled voice and then the back door slamming as she went out for her morning jog.

He played a couple of games of solitaire while he guzzled some more reinforcement. When he finished that he stood up abruptly and bolted out the door.

He got to the boardwalk and stopped to talk to Charlie. "A detective might be asking you some questions about me."

"Why?"

"Nothing important, I just wanted to give you a heads up that I'm giving him your name."

"What's he going to ask me?"

"Just whether you've seen me around the boardwalk on a certain day."

"How am I supposed to remember what days I've seen you?"

"Just say yes. What the hell difference does it make to you?" Finn replied.

"Are you okay, Finn?" Charlie patted him on the arm.

"Yeah. Just dandy."

He walked further down and watched Davion and Ty perform. When they finished he started to walk toward them, but they were surrounded by admirers. He turned around and walked the other way. He wasn't too worried about them. He knew they'd figure out the right thing to say to keep him and Jed out of trouble.

He saw Bella at a trashcan and approached her. "I am going to give a police lieutenant your name as someone who could vouch for me. He may come looking for you."

"Vouch for you how?"

"That you were with me on a certain day and time."

"You want me to lie for you?"

"No. I'm sure you did see me that day."

"Do I see you every day?"

"Just about."

"Okay, Mr. Abie's Irish Rose."

"You sure know all the Irish songs."

"I told you my husband was in show business."

"What's this about, anyway? Why is there a cop asking about you?"

"I'd rather not say, Bella. All I'm asking you to do is tell him the truth."

She shook her head and frowned, "This is meshugana and you are meshugana!"

"I appreciate it, Bella." He hurried off.

His next stop was the cafe. He looked around the patio, but didn't see Harper anywhere so he exited out the back door. "Damn, I hope he doesn't get to her before I do. She might get all flustered and say the wrong thing."

By the time he got to Luis', the restaurant was bustling. Mercedes ran around waiting on tables while Luis bussed and manned the cash register. Finn found Jose, the busboy, in the kitchen where he was frantically washing dishes. Finn put on an apron. "Go ahead, Jose. You go bus tables. I'll wash."

Luis hurried in with a tub of dirty dishes and saw Finn at the sink. He smiled gratefully, but said nothing as he lowered the tub into the sink and rushed back out. A couple of hours later, Luis and Finn sat at a table drinking beer. Mercedes counted her tips while Jose vacuumed the room. "Gracias, Finn. An angel must have been looking out for me today."

"I'm glad to help. Now I need to ask something from you."

Before Finn could say anymore, the door opened. Lieutenant Bukowski entered the restaurant. "Well, well, well. Fancy meeting you here, Finn."

Finn started to leave but then took out a piece of paper and handed it to the lieutenant. "This is a list of people who can vouch for me. I don't know their addresses or phone numbers. You'll have to use your brilliant detective skills to track them down. You can start here with Luis."

He exited the restaurant and walked down to the boardwalk, stopping at the liquor store on his way. He figured Bukowski was at Luis' to ask about Jed and was probably shocked to see Finn there. He didn't know for sure how Luis would react to Bukowski's questions. He might be used to being evasive, though, having to respond to the immigration authorities about his undocumented dishwashers. He hoped Luis would say just enough to look like he was answering honestly without letting on too much. After all, he didn't want to lose his two best dishwashers.

25

IT WAS LATE AND THE HOMELESS AND THE STREET URCHINS HAD TAKEN OVER THE BOARDWALK. The drone of a drum circle alternated with the rhythmic crashing of the waves on the beach. Finn sat by himself on a bench with his eyes closed, periodically taking sips out of a bottle in a brown paper bag. A dark figure sat down next to him, but Finn was in his own world and didn't notice. "Your daughter's worried about you."

Finn's eyes opened wide. "Jed!"

"Thanks for taking care of Mother." Jed had Mother in his arms.

"Where have you been?"

"I needed a vacation."

Finn took a gulp of whiskey and offered the bag to Jed who declined. "You know Antoinette was murdered a couple of weeks ago."

"I heard."

"A police detective came to my house asking me all kinds of questions."

"What kind of questions?"

"He knows all about Antoinette and how she's blackmailing me."

"He thinks you killed her?" Jed asked.

"Actually he thinks we did it together. He said your fingerprints were found in her motel room. He also has a copy of the letter she sent me." He turned and faced Jed. "What the hell's going on? Why were your fingerprints in her motel room?"

Jed stared at his lap for a few minutes and finally spoke. "I knew Antoinette at Jonestown."

"What! Antoinette was at Jonestown?"

"She was a leader in the organization, one of Jim Jones' loyal lieutenants."

"My God!" Finn took a deep breath.

"She was one of the nurses who administered the poison."

"What do you mean by administered?"

"Antoinette gave it to my mother and sister."

Finn couldn't speak. He could barely breathe. The enormity of the situation had sunk in and he didn't know what to say or do. They sat quietly for several minutes while Finn tried to regain his composure.

"So you knew as soon as I told you about her that she was the same person?"

"Yes."

"How did you know she gave your sister and mother the poison?"

"I was there. I saw her do it. And then I ran."

"Jesus . . . fucking . . . Christ! I don't know what to say. You watched your own mother . . . and sister . . . " Finn's voice trailed off. He took a deep breath. "I have to ask, Jed. Did you kill Antoinette?"

"No!" Jed stood up abruptly, causing Mother to scamper off his lap. He paced around the bench, trying to calm himself and finally sat back down. He picked up Mother, placed her on his lap and petted her until they both relaxed.

"So what happened in her motel room? Why did you go see her?"

Jed took a deep breath and shook his head. "I just wanted to understand why. Why she murdered my family and countless others. Why she didn't commit suicide herself."

"Did you get an answer?" Finn asked quietly.

"Not a satisfactory one."

"Did you really expect to?"

"I didn't know what I expected. It was impulsive, a knee-jerk reaction to finding her after all these years."

"Nothing she could have said would have helped. I don't think anyone, then or now, can answer why."

"I also wanted to get her to leave you alone, Finn."

"How were you going to do that?"

213

"I thought I could bribe her right back with all I had seen at Jonestown."

"What were you going to do? Go to the FBI?"

"I told you," Jed replied angrily. "It was impetuous. It's not like I had some premeditated plan worked out. You showed me the card from the motel and I just went there."

"And how did she respond to your threat?"

"She was only interested in collecting money from you."

"Is that how you got her to let you in? You told her you had the money from me?"

"She assumed it." Finn took another swig while Jed petted Mother and breathed in time to her purring. "Ironic, isn't it?"

"What do you mean?" Finn asked.

"That Antoinette injected my mother and sister and then tried to blackmail you for injecting Maggie."

"I suppose there's some irony in this whole ugly situation," Finn replied.

They sat quietly, each lost in their own thoughts. Finn finally spoke. "So what do you think happened to Antoinette that they think we killed her?"

"She was wearing my mother's necklace." Jed stopped talking. He decided not to say anymore to Finn. Not because he didn't trust him, but he didn't want Finn to know too much. He didn't want Finn to have to lie to the police and perjure himself.

"And?" Finn asked.

214

"I took it and left her room. I don't know what happened after that." Jed stood and held Mother firmly to his chest. "I need to ask you for a favor."

"What's that?"

Jed reached in his pocket and took out the necklace and handed it to Finn. "Would you hold this for me?"

Finn looked at Jed warily and then pocketed it. "Of course. This is the necklace in the picture, isn't it?"

"Yes." He kissed Mother lightly on the head and handed her to Finn. "And could you keep Mother a little while longer?" He walked toward the mountains without waiting for an answer.

26

BELLA WALKED DOWN THE BOARDWALK, pushing her shopping cart and sorting through trashcans. The sun had barely risen and it was still too early for the tourists. The shopkeepers had opened their doors and were hosing down the front of their establishments. Artists, craftsmen and political activists were setting up their tables. Bicyclists, rollerbladers and skateboarders whizzed past and the homeless were rolling up their sleeping bags. Finn was asleep on a bench with Mother curled up at his feet. Bella shook him awake. "What are you doing here, Finn? You look like dreck."

"I feel like dreck."

"Would you like to come for a walk?" Finn shrugged his shoulders and got up. Mother brushed up against his legs as if to remind him that she was there and Finn picked her up. "Is that your cat?"

"Sometimes." Bella stopped to take things out of trashcans as they walked. "What do you do with all the stuff?" Finn asked.

"It comes in handy," she answered irritably.

"I'm sure it does."

"Since when do you know everything?" Bella snapped.

"Sorry. You don't have to get all bent out of shape." They walked in silence for a while.

"So what do you do, mister haimisher mensch? And why are you sleeping on the boardwalk?"

"I'm a writer."

Bella laughed. "Well then that makes sense. So you're sleeping on a bench because you haven't published anything?"

"Actually I have."

"Have I heard of any of them?" she asked.

"I had a best seller."

"What was it called?"

"*Ode to Forgiveness*".

"I know the book. That was published a long time ago. If it was a bestseller, why are you sleeping on a bench?"

"It does make sense. In some metaphysical, existential, metaphorical kind of way."

Bella laughed. "If that statement is an example of what you're writing these days, then I guess it does. I doubt that kind of Bullsgeshichte would be bestseller material."

Finn smiled. "How right you are. I've become a total embarrassment to the world of literature. Leave it to the Germans to come up with the perfect technical term for bad writing."

"Don't be so hard on yourself. Are you working on a book now?"

"I'm making a half-hearted attempt at it."

"What is it?"

"A book about Jonestown."

"Jonestown. Oy vey, that was quite a story."

"You remember it, then."

"Of course I do. When was it . . . the late seventies?"

"1978."

"Killing that congressman and all those people committing suicide. Such a waste."

"They didn't all commit suicide," Finn replied.

"Not the children, I suppose."

"Not adults either. Many were forced."

"Forced to drink the Kool Aid?" Bella asked.

"Yes, in a manner of speaking."

"If I remember correctly, it had become a nightmare living there for these poor souls. But suicide is not an answer. You have to fight against tyrants like Jim Jones and Adolph Hitler!"

Finn watched Bella's face turn red with anger and pensive at the same time. He calculated her age and wondered about her own past. Before he could ask whether his conjecture was correct, Mother meowed loudly. "You must be hungry, Mother. I'm sorry."

"What does she eat?"

"Anything and everything, apparently."

"Well then, let's find her some food."

"Good idea."

They continued walking in silence for a few minutes until Bella asked, "Why are you writing about Jonestown?"

"I have a friend who was there and escaped."

"I didn't realize people had escaped."

"There were about thirty survivors."

When they got to the bathroom pavilion, Finn put Mother on top of the pile of junk in the shopping cart. "I'll be right back." He joined the throng of homeless washing up in the public restrooms. Bella petted the purring cat. When he came back he lifted Mother off the pile.

"Leave the cat," Bella said. "I think she would like riding in the cart."

Finn took a Styrofoam container out of a trashcan and opened it. "Perfect. The remnants of a breaded fish sandwich." He put it next to Mother on the cart and she ate voraciously as they continued their journey.

Bella stopped at various trashcans, but when they reached a bench she said, "Let's take a rest." They sat down and Finn took Mother onto his lap. He petted her and kept his gaze on the cat while Bella tried to catch her breath. She finally spoke. "So what is your Jonestown book about exactly?"

"It's basically my friend's story. He lost his mother and sister there."

Bella shook her head and let her mind wander. She finally spoke. "I lost both my parents . . . at Auschwitz."

Finn had been correct. "I'm sorry."

"My brother and I escaped."

He stopped petting Mother and turned to face her. "How did you escape?"

"Did you ever see the movie, *Schindler's List*?"

"Oskar Schindler helped you escape?"

"No, not him. But there were others who helped. Especially the children."

They didn't speak for several minutes. "Do you still have nightmares about the camp?" Finn asked quietly.

"Sure. You never forget. But survivors live to tell the world so it will never happen again."

"Never again, the famous Holocaust quote, and yet—"

Bella interrupted, getting visibly angry. "And yet it keeps happening again. A million people died in Rwanda in 1994! But not six million people! Two-thirds of the total European Jewish population, and two-fifths of the Jews in the entire world!"

"So that's what you meant before? About suicide not being the answer?"

"Yes," Bella said. "People need to know the truth."

"Those who forget the past are condemned to repeat it."

"Exactly." She sighed deeply, more with bitterness than with sorrow.

Finn returned to petting Mother and looked away. He wiped his eyes with his sleeve. "Thank you, Bella." He stood. "I have something important I must do." He walked away with Mother in his arms.

Kate sat at the kitchen table reading the paper and drinking coffee when Finn entered through the back door. "Dad! I thought you were upstairs asleep. Where have you been? Are you okay? You look terrible."

"I need to talk to you, Kate."

She took Mother from him. "Why do you still have Mother? Didn't Jed find you?" She filled a bowl with cat food and put it and Mother on the floor, but Mother rubbed against her leg and didn't eat. Apparently the fish sandwich had been enough to satisfy her.

"He did find me, but then he left again."

"What's going on? Does all this stuff with the police have to do with Jed? Why does he keep leaving Mother here?"

"That's what I want to talk to you about."

"I don't mind that Mother's here. I was just wondering why. I have to leave soon for work. Can it wait 'til later?"

"I'd like to talk to you now. It's important and I . . . " He stopped speaking.

"And you what?"

"I don't want to chicken out."

She looked at the clock and then sat back down. "I have a little time, I guess."

Finn took her hand and kissed it. "Maggie was so sick. She was in so much pain."

Kate looked at him warily. She was unsure where he was going. "Yes, Dad, I know she was."

"She was a good woman. I loved her." He smiled. "She put up with my craziness and my moodiness . . . never let it get to her . . . she trusted me."

Kate looked at the clock and nodded. This was very unlike Finn. He wasn't one to open up about his feelings and his relationships. "I liked her too, and I knew she was good for you."

He took a deep breath and put his head in his hands. Kate reached over and put her hand on his shoulder. He obviously had something important to say to her but what was it? And should she call the school and tell them she would be late? He finally spoke but his head was still in his hands, his eyes on the table and his voice barely above a whisper. "We had talked about it. I didn't just make this decision on my own."

"What decision?"

He raised his head and looked deeply into her eyes. "I gave her an extra shot of insulin."

"I don't understand."

He continued looking into her eyes for a minute and then with a choked sob he answered her. "I killed Maggie."

Kate gasped and sat back in her chair. "What?"

"She wanted it that way. Please believe me. She was in a coma but we had both decided we didn't want to live like that. We had talked about it." He cried openly and Kate wasn't sure if she wanted to comfort him. She waffled between feeling sorry and angry. He stopped crying and took a deep breath. "Antoinette saw me do it."

"Oh, God. What did she say?"

"Nothing at the time. But then she wrote me and called here asking for money."

"She's blackmailing you? I thought you said she was a good nurse! You liked her!"

"A good nurse but apparently not such a good person. She knew how sick Maggie was." Kate got up and went to the phone. "Who are you calling?" Finn asked with alarm.

"Just school to tell them I'll be late."

"Good. Because there's more."

Kate's eyes widened in disbelief and then she spoke into the phone. "I'll be late today. Please get my first two periods covered. Thanks." She hung up and sat back down exhaling loudly. "What else?"

"Antoinette came here in person."

"Here? To my house?"

"Yes. She said she was going to the police if I didn't give her money."

"Good lord! What did you tell her?"

"I said I didn't have the money."

"So what's going to happen? Is she going to let it go?"

Finn stood and paced the floor before answering. "She's dead."

"Dead?"

"The cops say she was murdered but I don't think so."

"What do you mean you don't think so? How do you know? Were you there? In her room?"

"No. But Jed was."

"Jed?"

Finn's head went back in his hands. "This is so unbelievable."

"You're not kidding!" Kate said angrily.

"Antoinette was a nurse in Jonestown when Jed was there. He saw her inject poison into his mother and sister."

"Oh, God! Now I get it! The police think you did this together? Dad!" She started to cry herself and Finn tried to put his arms around her but she pushed him away.

"Kate, I did not go to her motel. And Jed says he didn't kill her and I believe him. He just went there to talk to her and get this." He took the necklace out of his pocket. "This was his mother's necklace and she was wearing it."

Kate composed herself. She stopped crying and took a deep breath. "How did she die?"

"The newspaper said from a head injury."

"So what makes you think Jed didn't hurt her?"

"I know him. He's not a murderer."

"I told you to be careful with him! I can't believe this is happening!" She rushed out of the room.

Finn sat at the table staring into space. He hadn't thought about how Kate would react to all this. He just wanted to be honest with her. He didn't realize she would be so angry. Now that she knew everything, he didn't want to put her in the position of having to lie or defend him. He stood up and went to his office. He opened the cabinet but it was empty. He tore his boxes apart, throwing paper and books all over the room. "Fuck!" he yelled as he threw the last book across the room. He searched his pockets and opened his wallet, but there was nothing: neither drugs nor money. He returned to the kitchen and saw Kate's purse on the counter. He opened it, hesitated for a minute, but took out her wallet and emptied it of cash. He picked up Mother and bolted out the door. He knew he wouldn't be coming back anytime soon.

27

THE SUN HAD BARELY COME UP so it was still too dark for the joggers, bicyclists and rollerbladers to start their morning routine. Charlie was the only person setting up a table. He was handing out donuts and coffee to a line of homeless men and women, as well as cards and pamphlets for various social service agencies. Finn emerged from an alley between two stores, a sleeping bag in one hand and Mother in the other. He walked up to Charlie's table and placed the sleeping bag under it. "Thanks again for the use of the bag."

Charlie handed him a cup and a donut with a sympathetic smile. "It will be here tonight for you. I should be packing up about six. But you know, the shelter is only a few blocks away."

"It's okay. I'd rather not."

"Does Mother need some milk this morning?"

Finn nodded silently as he took the cup of milk and continued to walk down the boardwalk. When he got to Muscle Beach, he sat down to watch the few bodybuilders who got there early. He set the cup of milk down for Mother and gazed at her affectionately as she lapped it up.

Finn had been on the boardwalk for a couple of weeks, guilt-ridden and embarrassed to return to Kate's after stealing her money. He had established a daily routine and was amazed at how quickly time passed. He poured some whiskey from his flask into the cup of coffee and watched Bella scrounging through a trashcan. She took out a couple of newspapers and looked through them until she found what she wanted and put that one in her shopping cart. She hobbled over to Finn's bench and sat down with difficulty.

Finn nodded to her as she silently handed him the newspaper from her cart. "Do you want to come over for a shower?" she asked.

"Yes." He stood and helped Bella up and then placed Mother on top of the piles in the cart. They hobbled off together, looking like a couple that had been married for many years. Finn's agile gait had morphed into a shuffle.

He left Bella's house a couple of hours later with a clean body, a full stomach, and a book to read. Mother trotted at his side. He walked through the canals for a while, admiring the architecture of the multimillion-dollar houses and then headed down

Venice Boulevard. He stopped in a liquor store to fortify his stash with a few dollars Bella had given him. He picked up Mother to protect her from the heavy traffic on the boulevard and subsequently the throngs that had invaded the boardwalk. He set her down to watch Davion and Ty perform for a while, knowing the crowd surrounding them would be mesmerized with their performance and wouldn't bother her. They danced over when they were finished.

"I ney Finn. Remember that man's card you gave us?" Davion asked.

"What man?"

"The samfi who gonna be our agent?" Ty added.

"Oh, yeah. You said he was a shyster."

"Turn out he not a samfi. He really work for American Talent Search."

"No shit. You going on the show?"

"We go for audition, then we see."

"That's great. I'm sure you'll get on the show."

"What's the prize?"

"A lot of cheddar."

"Cheese?"

Davion and Ty laughed hard. "Money, mon." Finn smiled. "Enough to get out of hellhole garage we living in."

"Is that where you live? I wondered. I never see you on the boardwalk after the drum circle breaks up."

"Yeah. Ooman lets us rent it."

228

"Ooman?"

"A lady. She bashy. Good woman."

"When's the audition?"

"Couple days."

"Well, good luck." Finn picked up Mother and sauntered down to visit with Derek. He helped him hand out brochures about global warming and recycling, but most of the tourists were less than interested. "I'm not sure if these tourists are the right audience for your message," Finn said.

"I don't like to preach to the choir. I got you hooked, didn't I?" Derek winked at Finn.

Several other activists, performers and craftspeople chatted with him, as he sauntered down the boardwalk. When he got to his customary bench near Muscle Beach, he sat down and took out the newspaper Bella had given him. He opened it and ignored the news section, going directly to the crossword puzzle. He zipped through it, as usual, and carefully dumped it in the recycling bin, before walking over to watch and marvel at the strength and flexibility of the bodybuilders. It was a motley crew of muscular men, toned women, and one powerfully fit athlete of indeterminate gender. He opened the book Bella had loaned him and immersed himself in *The World According to Garp*.

After a while, he closed the book, scooped up Mother and went up the street to Luis'. Although the cat had lived on the streets probably all her life, Finn was always worried she'd get hit by a car or stolen like that first day on the boardwalk. "Are you hungry, Mother?" Mother purred loudly. When they got to Luis' restaurant, Finn put Mother down before entering. "Wait here." Mercedes greeted him and led him to a table. "What's on the menu today?"

"Let me go ask my father." She went to the kitchen and came back with a plate of food. "Enchiladas."

"Beef or chicken?"

"Beef," she answered.

"I like chicken better," he teased.

"Beggars can't be choosy," she teased back and left him to eat. Luis came to the table with a beer and set it down. "Thanks for the meal, Luis. Mother's outside but she doesn't like beef."

"I've got some shrimp for her." Luis returned to the kitchen and came back with a Styrofoam container and put it on the table.

"You know, Luis, you really should look into using cardboard rather than Styrofoam. It's much better ecologically-speaking."

Luis laughed. "Maybe so, Senor Finn, but more expensive."

When he finished eating, he brought his plate into the kitchen and put it in the sink on top of the piles of dishes and pots. He put on an apron and started washing.

Luis came in the kitchen just as Finn was hanging up his apron. "I hope Mother enjoys her dinner." He handed Finn a twenty-dollar bill.

"She loves your cooking." He bid Luis and Mercedes goodbye and took the shrimp outside for Mother. When she had finished eating, he lifted her up and trekked back to the boardwalk, stopping at another liquor store on the way.

Most of the tourists, street performers and merchants were gone. Charlie was packing up when Finn approached his table. "Here you go," Charlie said as he handed the sleeping bag to Finn. "See you in the morning."

A drum circle had formed and Finn sat on a bench watching. A man handed him a small bongo and invited him to join the circle. He took it hesitantly and started to tap quietly on the drumhead. It didn't take him long to get a rhythm going and his taps became louder as he got more confident. At about 11 p.m. the police cruised by and broke up the circle. Finn sat on the bench to wait for the police presence to be gone before he went to his hiding place in the alley between the sunglass store and the Kush clinic. He took out the sleeping bag and curled up with Mother for the night.

28

FINN AWOKE AND SAW THAT THE BOARDWALK WAS ALREADY BUSTLING with people setting up tables. He sat up abruptly, surprised he had slept so long. Mother was nowhere in sight. He scanned the area, but to no avail. He rolled up his sleeping bag and continued the search, not 100% sure she would return to him as she always did to Jed.

When he arrived at Charlie's table, the coffee and donuts were gone. "Sorry, Finn. All out. You're too late."

"That's okay, Charlie. I'm not hungry. But do you at least have some coffee left?"

"Busy morning." He reached into his pocket for a couple of dollars and offered them to Finn.

"Thanks anyway, but no. I'm fine." He handed Charlie the sleeping bag. "Hey, did Mother stop by without me this morning?"

"Haven't seen her, Finn."

He walked away and saw a crowd gathering around Davion and Ty rehearsing. "Hey, have you seen Mother?" he called out to them.

"No, mon," Davion shouted back.

"Well, keep your eyes open, will you? She seems to have wandered off."

"Irie, Finn." He and Ty continued to practice their dance moves as Finn continued his search, calling her name and asking random people he passed if they had seen a black and white spotted cat. Most people didn't answer him at all, wondering if this unkempt man in rumpled clothing was possibly mentally ill.

After walking up and down the boardwalk looking for Mother, he decided to try the cafe. When he got there he glanced around the room and saw Harper sitting at a table typing on her laptop. He approached the table and Harper jumped up and gave him a big hug. "Finn! I haven't seen you in ages. I've missed you."

He followed her to her table and sat down. "Why? Need help with the crossword puzzle?"

"Well, yes, that too. But I could have used some of your input on my writing."

"I don't know how much help I'd be." Finn took a pint of Old Crow out of his pocket and chugged it. He had found it necessary to downgrade his brand of whiskey.

Harper looked worried. "You're just drinking it straight now? You don't even need to add it to coffee?"

233

"You sound like my daughter."

"I guess all children sound the same." She shrugged and looked down at her laptop screen. "I would really like it if you could critique my latest story."

"Another time, Harper. Not today. Have you seen Mother, by any chance?"

"No, sorry. Has she been missing long?"

"Just this morning. She'll probably turn up."

"Have you been writing? Is that why you haven't been to the cafe?"

"I, uh, haven't had access to a computer."

She looked at him warily. "Is your computer broken?"

He looked away. "I haven't been living at my daughter's for awhile."

"Why not?"

"It's complicated."

"I'll bet she misses you terribly."

"Who are you to talk? You didn't even tell your parents when you won the contest."

"Actually I've been showing them my writing lately." She winked at Finn. "Sometimes I listen to wise old men."

Finn smiled and patted her hand. "I'm glad to hear that."

Harper smiled back, confused yet empathetic. "Is everything okay? I've really missed you."

"I'm fine. I need to apologize, Harper. I said some terrible things to you."

234

"That's okay. Don't worry about it."

"I shouldn't have said what I did. You have your whole life ahead of you. Maybe you will make a huge difference by writing the books you have inside you."

"I hope so. You have."

"You're a good writer, Harper. Don't pay attention to the ramblings of an old man. You just write the truth. That's the most important thing."

Harper blinked back tears. "Do you want to borrow my computer so you can write?"

"That's very kind, but no. I don't feel much like writing right now."

He looked over her shoulder at her laptop and read aloud the quote she had up on her screen: "*Whatever we think of the past, we must not be prisoners to it. Barack Obama, June 4, 2009.* Smart advice."

"I was researching how most wars are started by religious fanaticism and this speech he gave in Cairo came up."

"Many religious leaders become tainted by power, just like politicians."

"I don't think Obama has."

"He's unusual." He stood up and patted Harper's shoulder. "Keep writing. You have a lot of good things to say." He squeezed her shoulder and left.

He walked by Luis' but the restaurant hadn't opened yet. He searched for Mother in the back alley, under and inside the dumpsters, thinking she was

235

hungry. Then he decided to check out Kate's house. He knew she would be at work by now, so he figured it was safe to take a look for Mother on the porch. When he arrived, he explored the front and back but no Mother. He peered in the window. He hadn't been back for quite awhile and seeing the house gave him a sinking feeling he didn't want to have. Anyway, the best place for him to be was back at the boardwalk. That's where Mother would look for him.

He stopped by a pizza parlor, another one of his haunts. It was a good place to look for leftovers. Many people couldn't finish a whole pizza so there were often intact pieces that no one had taken a bite from. Since most of them were tourists staying in motels, they didn't take the rest home for another dinner. The manager knew Finn often stopped by for food for Mother and saved it for him. Sometimes Finn would earn a whole pie for himself by washing the dishes.

"Hi, Maria," Finn said as he walked in.

"Ah, Finn. No dishes yet today but here's a couple of pieces. I'll heat them up for you."

"Thanks, Maria. You're a doll."

She put them in the microwave. "Where's Mother?"

"I don't know. Keep your eye out for her, will you?"

"Sure thing." She took the pieces out of the microwave and put them in a container. "You want a cup of water?"

"That would be nice." He took the water and pizza and left to go sit on his bench in front of Muscle Beach.

He watched the bodybuilders go through their routines as he ate. A stocky, muscular Pacific Islander especially intrigued him. It was the one he couldn't identify as either male or female. When Finn's gawking became obvious, the performance turned into a particularly outrageous flaunting of muscles and sexuality. After putting on a show became tiresome, the bodybuilder approached Finn and sat down next to him. "Wha'cha looking at, old man?"

"I'm admiring your athleticism," Finn replied. He avoided the bodybuilder's eyes and looked up and down the boardwalk."

"Do I make you nervous?"

"Not at all. I'm looking for my cat."

"A hip cat or a feline cat?"

Finn smiled. "A feline cat."

"What does he look like?"

"It's a she and she's white with black spots. Or black with white spots." He laughed. "I guess it doesn't matter. You get the picture."

"Yeah. She's black and white. Haven't seen her."

"Would you like some pizza?"

"Nope. Don't touch the stuff. White flour, canned tomatoes, fatty cheese."

"You too? I've never seen so many people obsessed with healthy eating."

"I take care of myself."

"You might say I do the opposite. I seem to make a point of not taking care of myself."

"You're a funny man."

"Funny? Hardly."

"What do you call yourself, funny man?"

"Finn."

"What kind of a stupid name is that? Sounds like a fish."

"It's short for Finnegan. My mother had a thing for Irish surnames."

"You Irish?"

"Born there but moved to New York when I was eighteen."

"So why did you leave New York?"

"My wife died."

"So? That doesn't answer my question."

"You ask a lot of questions. What's your story?"

"Name's Savali. Born in Samoa."

"Have you lived here long?"

"Long enough to call this place home. You lived here long?"

Finn sighed and glanced around. "I guess the same. Long enough to call this place home."

Savali stood up and stretched. "Got to get back to work."

"What work do you do?" Finn asked.

Savali looked at the bodybuilding machines and then back at Finn. "I play rugby."

"Tough sport."

"Yep. It's big in my culture."

"Do you play for a team here in Los Angeles?"

"You ever hear of fa'afafine?" Savali asked, ignoring his question.

"Is that the name of your team?"

"Look it up. See you later, Flipper."

Finn watched Savali for several minutes, trying to understand his new friend. The build was definitely masculine, but he thought he detected small breasts under the sleeveless muscle shirt. The voice was low, but the sarcastic tone had a female edge to it. At least it kept his mind off Mother's disappearance. Savali glanced over at him several times and winked, enjoying the audience. He winked back, enjoying the show.

He stayed there most of the afternoon, expecting either Mother or Bella to show up. Neither of them did, though, so he decided to walk over to the skate park and the public art wall. That wasn't their usual hangout, but maybe the pickings were slim at Muscle Beach. Mother was probably looking for food and Bella was probably looking for more crap to clutter up her house.

New murals had been painted on the walls since Finn had been there last. They were professional and colorful and he thought it was somebody's good idea to create a place for the graffiti artists to hone their craft rather than all over the storefronts. Derek walked over while Finn was admiring the artwork.

"That one was done by a friend of mine," Derek said, pointing to a large dragonhead.

"It's very good. Can anyone come here and paint?"

"You need a permit. And I think they just started charging the artists."

"Why would they charge them to paint?"

"Upkeep, I guess. I don't think they charge much."

"Say, Derek, have you seen Mother?"

"Can't say I have. Not since the other day when I saw her with you. You lose her?"

"She wasn't with me this morning when I woke up."

"I don't know, man. I hope she's not looking for Jed. He hasn't been around in a long time."

Finn wished Derek hadn't brought that up. He had always been afraid that Mother would go searching for Jed in the mountains and would get lost, or worse, eaten by a coyote. At least on the boardwalk she only had to watch out for wealthy, meth addicted punks. "Well, let me know if you see her," Finn finally said. He thought he saw Bella over by the skate park so he said his goodbyes to Derek and sauntered over there. It wasn't Bella, though, rummaging through a trashcan. It was just a tourist who had apparently lost something or thrown it away by accident.

He turned his attention to the skateboarders. The skill and artistry in every milieu on the Venice Beach boardwalk still amazed him. The performers,

240

the artists, the bodybuilders and the skateboarders could all hold their own in professional competitions. He managed to fritter away the rest of the afternoon watching the skateboarders, taking a few minutes every now and then to search the beach and the boardwalk for Mother.

When it started to get dark, he strolled back over to the restaurant. He walked in as Luis, Mercedes and Jose were hustling about and went straight to the kitchen where he donned his apron and did his job. As the night wound down and the piles of dishes did too, Luis came in. "Jose will finish them. Come on in and sit down."

Finn took off his apron and followed Luis into the dining room to a table where a plate of food was waiting for him. He sat down to eat while Luis helped Mercedes and Jose finish up the closing duties. After Finn finished his meal, Luis sat down with a couple of beers.

"Thank you, Luis. Delicious as always. Mother hasn't been by, has she?"

"I haven't seen her. Maybe Jed is back. I've known him a few years and I've never seen him without Mother. I'm quite surprised that he would leave her for so long." Luis patted Finn's arm. "Not that you haven't been wonderful to her."

"That's okay, Luis. I didn't take it as a criticism." Mercedes sat down next to her father.

"Hola mi anegelito." He put his arm around her.

She put her head on his shoulder. "I'm tired Papa." Finn smiled and watched them fondly.

"Pobre bebe," Luis cooed tenderly.

Finn turned pensive and melancholy. He watched the comfortable interaction between Luis and Mercedes. He thought about the way Harper had come around to showing her parents her work. He remembered when Kate was young and the easy affection between them back then. He downed the rest of his beer and stood. "Are you leaving?" Mercedes asked.

"Yes. If Mother comes by, will you give her some food? She's probably starving."

"We'll feed her and keep her until tomorrow." Luis patted Finn's shoulder.

"Thanks." Finn left the restaurant and looked through his pockets for some change, but found none. For one fleeting moment he thought about asking for spare change from anyone who passed by, but quickly dismissed the thought. He realized that Charlie had probably already left the boardwalk and taken the sleeping bag with him. It was getting a little too chilly at night to be on a bench with nothing to cover him. He wondered about Bella and thought he could pretend that he was worried about her and could go to her house. Maybe she had a tiny corner he could curl up in that wasn't completely stuffed with garbage and crap. He doubted there was any room.

As he neared the boardwalk, he thought about Luis and Mercedes. He took a deep breath and walked away more purposefully than he had in weeks.

When he got to Kate's front porch, he walked up the stairs and rang the doorbell. Kate opened the door. She was in her bathrobe and had Mother in her arms. Her eyes filled with tears as she opened the door wider for him to enter.

29

FINN SLEPT FOR 15 HOURS STRAIGHT. When he finally woke up and went downstairs, it was already starting to get dark. He made a cup of coffee and went to his office. It was just as he'd left it, which surprised him. He thought surely Kate would have gone in and cleaned it up. He sat sipping his coffee and went online to check his email, but was totally discouraged from doing so when he saw how full his inbox was, mostly filled with junk mail and spam. He was still sitting and sipping when Kate got home from work. She put her head in the door and smiled at him but didn't say anything. He heard her knocking around the kitchen. Mother had been in his office with him but scurried out when she heard the sound of cat food filling her bowl. "Have you eaten dinner?" Kate called from the kitchen.

"No," Finn called back.

"Do you want to?"

"Whatever you're having is fine." He waited for a cynical remark from her, but it never came.

He went to the cabinet and noticed a couple of empty whiskey bottles. He threw the bottles away and looked through his records until he found the specific one he wanted. He put it on the turntable and went back to his chair. Kate entered just as Richie Havens' voice filled the room singing "Follow."

Kate sat down across from him and took his hands in hers. They sat like that for a few minutes until the song finished, tears coming down both their cheeks.

"Have you listened to it lately?" Kate asked.

"Not for many years. You remember it, then."

"Of course, Dad. You played it over and over all through my childhood."

"Your mother loved Richie Havens. And this song had so much meaning then."

"It still does." Kate got up and put the needle back on the beginning of the song and went back to the table, this time pulling up a chair next to Finn. He put his arm around her as they listened to the rest of the verses.

They sat in silence for a few more minutes. "Let's eat." Finn said. They got up and went to the kitchen.

After dinner Finn was in his customary spot at the sink rinsing the last of the dishes. Mother was stretched out on the counter, feeling quite at home and basking in the warmth of being inside. Kate sat at the kitchen table, her students' essays spread out in front of her.

"You didn't used to work at the kitchen table. I thought you liked to correct at your desk."

"I do. I guess I just want to be near you, now that you're back home."

Finn smiled at her and swallowed the lump forming in his throat. "Do you want any help? It's been a while but I think I can remember how to edit high school English papers."

"That's okay. I'm almost done."

He finished the dishes and wiped his hands on the towel. "Then I guess I'll go see if I can remember how to write."

When he got to his office he turned on the computer and waited for it to boot up. He stared at the screen, got up and paced, walked to the cabinet and glanced at his boxes. He thought about taking a walk, but was a little afraid where he might end up. He had started to repair his relationship with Kate and he was determined not to harm that in any way. He knew he had to stop drinking if he was ever going to finish the book. He sat back down and started to reread what he had written. Mother entered and climbed on his lap. That cemented it. He was more than determined, for everyone's sake.

He worked nonstop for a couple of hours until Kate entered. "I'm turning in," she announced.

"I'm not tired yet. I had quite the marathon sleep last night, as I'm sure you know."

She stood next to his chair and put her hand on his shoulder. "Is the writing coming easily?"

"Yes. Maybe I just needed a break."

"I don't need to go to bed yet. I mean, if you want to talk . . ."

Finn turned his face to look at her. "If you want to."

She pulled up a chair and sat next to him. Mother jumped from Finn's lap to hers. "I don't need to know where you've been these last weeks. In fact, I probably don't want to know."

He took a deep breath and exhaled loudly. "I agree."

"I do need to tell you, though, that the police are looking for you. Actually, I'm surprised they didn't find you. They were sure crawling around here all the time."

Finn laughed. "They probably never thought to look where I've been."

Kate looked at him curiously, but still didn't ask. "Well, it was good that I didn't know where you were. They didn't believe me and I didn't need to be arrested for lying to them."

"It is convenient that I don't know where Jed is, either, so I don't have to perjure myself."

"Well now you're back. What are you going to do?"

"Did that Lieutenant Bukowski tell you anything more?"

"About what?"

"If they found out any more?"

"About Antoinette?" she asked.

"Yes. Like what exactly she died from."

"No. Head trauma is all I know." Kate squirmed in her seat and Mother jumped back onto Finn's lap. "Dad . . . do you know anything that you're not telling me?"

"You think I killed Antoinette?" He didn't know whether to be angry or shocked.

"Of course not. But Jed?"

"I told you. I asked him and he said no and I believe him. And that's what I will tell Bukowski when he asks."

"It doesn't look good for him. He had a motive, two actually if you count yours. The police told me his fingerprints were found there. I don't think they're after you except to get to him."

"I hope you're right. I gave him the names of people who saw me on the day she died but it's not really an alibi."

"Are you going to call the police or wait for them to come back here?"

Finn took Kate's hand and looked into her eyes. "I honestly don't know. I'm a bit scared."

"So am I." They sat for a minute in silence and then Kate pulled her hand away and placed Mother back on Finn's lap. "I guess I'll go to bed now." She went to the door and turned around. "I want you to know, Dad, that I think you did the right thing for Maggie."

248

"Thank you, Kate. That means a lot to me."

She nodded and left. Finn petted Mother, trying to keep from rummaging through the kitchen for anything Kate might have in a cupboard. He had done it before cold turkey and he knew he could do it. He had never felt that it was an addiction. He could always stop when he truly wanted to. He was not an alcoholic, or so he told himself. He was Irish and he was a drinker. He was not his father. He turned back to the computer and was pleasantly surprised at how quickly the words came.

30

IT WAS ALMOST DAWN WHEN FINN DECIDED TO TAKE A BREAK. He had been writing all night. He wasn't sure what the strongest motivator had been: relief at being back with Kate, the comfort of being warm and fed, his sobriety, or his determination to prove something to Judith and the publishers. He glanced over at Mother sleeping peacefully on Kate's chair. Perhaps it was that he wanted to give Jed a chance to tell his story. Or maybe it was simply because he needed the money. Whatever it was, it worked.

He stood and stretched, and went out the front door to look for the elusive newspapers. They were both there, neatly stacked on the porch. "Well, look at that! They finally learned how to deliver a newspaper." He picked them up and took them into the kitchen. He pushed the button on the coffee maker and took a mug out of the cupboard. He yawned and realized that he was a lot more tired than he thought. He should probably sleep first. He put the mug back and went to bed.

Kate came into the kitchen shortly after he left and saw the newspapers on the counter and the full coffee pot. She peeked into Finn's office and saw it was empty other than the still sleeping cat. For a brief moment she was afraid that he had gone out to buy some whiskey, but glanced at his computer screen and saw that the page number was in the high two hundreds. He had obviously written quite a bit so she decided not to let her mind go there. She heard the flush of the toilet and breathed a sigh of relief. When she heard the door to his bedroom close, she realized he had written all night. "He may be on an odd schedule but at least it works," she said to herself. She gave Mother a pet and a kiss and sprinted out the front door onto the sidewalk.

The ringing of the doorbell woke Finn out of a deep sleep. He glanced at the clock and was surprised to see that it was already two in the afternoon. He had expected to take a short nap and then get back to work. He knew he had missed several deadlines and he wasn't so sure the publishers even cared anymore. He made a mental note to call Judith and see what was what. "Hold your horses!" he yelled as he climbed out of bed. The ringing was incessant. "Shut the hell up— I'll be right there!" Apparently whoever it was heard him because the ringing stopped. He got to the front

251

door and opened it. "I figured you'd be here soon," he said, rolling his eyes.

"Well, well, well. You've decided to come home and face the music."

"You're an idiot, Bukowski."

"Thanks for the compliment. I have that search warrant. Did you get yourself a lawyer?"

"No."

The lieutenant took a piece of paper out of his pocket and showed it to Finn. "What shall we do first? Search the house or bring you down to the station for questioning?"

Finn thought about the chance that there might still be some drugs left and decided it would be better to go down to the station. After all, he had nothing to hide. He hadn't done anything to Antoinette and he had no idea where Jed was. He wouldn't have to lie. And it would only make him look guilty if he refused to go without a lawyer present. He certainly didn't want to pay a lawyer if he didn't have to. "All right. I'll go. Can I take a shower and change my clothes first?"

"Where you're going, no one is going to mind if you smell or look like a derelict."

"Full of flattery as always." Finn followed him out the door and into the car.

When they entered the police station, the lieutenant left him in an interrogation room. Finn knew the trick. He'd read enough crime novels and watched enough TV to know the routine. He didn't care how long he had to wait to be questioned. He just wished he had a laptop so he could write while he was waiting. He was on a roll and he hated to break the momentum. Surprisingly, he didn't have to wait that long. Bukowski entered with a black woman in her thirties and a couple of paper cups. Finn gladly took the coffee but almost spit it out after the first sip. "This is disgusting."

"Welcome to our world," Bukowski smiled disdainfully. "We don't get to frequent the fancy cafes like you."

Finn thought it best not to answer with another sarcastic wisecrack. "So who's your friend?"

"This is Detective Washington."

"She doesn't merit a cup of coffee?"

"I know better, but thanks for your concern," she answered.

Bukowski turned the chair around so he was straddling the seat and leaning on the back of the chair. Finn couldn't resist. "Is that your Matthew McConaughey imitation?"

"Woody Harrelson, actually."

"Can we get started here?" Detective Washington sighed.

"You're making it very difficult for me to decide who's the good cop and who's the bad cop in this scenario," Finn quipped.

"So, Finn, do you want to tell us what happened in that motel room?" Bukowski got serious.

"How do I know? I wasn't there."

"Okay. How about telling us what happened in your wife's bedroom the day she died."

"That was in New York. You can't ask me that. You have no jurisdiction."

"I can ask you anything I want if I think it's relevant."

Finn weighed again whether he should call a lawyer but decided to see where this questioning was going. "She was in a coma and she died. What else is there?"

"Did you give her too much insulin?"

Finn thought he had nothing to lose since Antoinette was dead. He could say whatever would help his case. "I gave her the usual morning shot. I don't know what Antoinette did when she got there. I was in the kitchen." Why hadn't he thought of this before? He's definitely in the clear now that she can't refute it.

"Then why would she blackmail you? She claimed in her letter to you that she saw you give her an extra dose."

"How do I know? Anyway, she didn't know it was an extra dose. She was just jumping to the conclusion that I had given her one earlier." He was beginning to like this; he was feeling quite smug.

"Are you aware that she had talked to the New York City Police before she spoke to you. She had covered her tracks quite well. She had also made her concerns known to her bosses and the hospital personnel."

Finn's arrogant confidence took a hit. He started to have some misgivings about whether he would get away with this. But he was damned if he was going to let Bukowski know it. "So what if the hospital knows she had extra insulin. They don't know who gave it to her. That goes for the police too so move on."

"*We* will decide when we move on!" Detective Washington retorted.

Finn now knew who was in which cop role. "Whatever you say, Ms. Washington." There was an uncomfortable silence and he didn't know whether it was on purpose or whether they were regrouping. He knew he was right and they probably didn't want to let on that they knew he was.

"When did you get the letter from her?"

"I don't know. Quite a while ago. I didn't pay much attention to it."

"You didn't? Why not?" The detective actually seemed curious.

Finn shrugged. "I thought she was a nut case."

"Really? I heard from your daughter that you liked her very much and that she was a good nurse to your wife," Bukowski chimed in.

Dammit Kate. You talk too much. "She was. But wouldn't you think it a bit crazy if you got a letter like that?" Finn thought he had made a good comeback.

"Doesn't matter what I think, Finn."

"Well, I just figured she was crazy. It wasn't until she showed up at my door that I worried about it." Right away he knew he had said the wrong thing. He could see it in both their eyes. Maybe he'd better get that lawyer after all.

"So she paid you a visit? That's not what you said earlier," Bukowski sneered.

"I guess I forgot."

"What made you worry about it then?" Ms. Washington gleefully jumped into the conversation.

"Who likes to be around really crazy people? You don't know what they might do." He hoped this twist in the discussion would work.

"You could also say that about scared people, grieving people, and angry people." Bukowski knew how to turn the conversation too.

Finn decided to keep quiet and wait for the next question. It didn't take long for Detective Washington to ask it. "Did you set up Jed to take the fall for you?"

"No." He answered it calmly and softly. It was time to go back to short answers.

"Where is Jed? It would help your case if we could talk to him."

"I don't know."

"Isn't he your friend? And isn't he your co-writer?"

"He's a friend but not my co-writer. I interviewed him for my book. Do you always know where all your friends are at any given time, Ms. Washington?"

She glanced at Bukowski as if to say, "I believe him. He doesn't know Jed's whereabouts." Even Finn could see that much.

"We're not going to keep you here, even though we could. I don't think you're a flight risk. I don't trust you 100% but I do trust your daughter to do the right thing."

"Thanks for the endorsement." Sometimes he wished he didn't have such a sardonic streak. It didn't always serve him well.

"We'll be in touch."

Finn stood up. "Great. I'll look forward to it." There it goes again.

Detective Washington walked him out. "Do you need a ride home?"

Finn was truly astonished. He thought she was right there with Bukowski in her disdain for him and yet her demeanor was actually kind of warm. "Uh, that's okay. I can walk."

"Are you sure?"

Now he wondered what she was up to. Was she really concerned about his well-being or continuing to play a role? Maybe she thought she could find out something if she took a different tactic. But he was tired and Kate's house was a few miles away and he hadn't brought any money with him. He'd accept the ride. He just wouldn't talk much. "Okay."

They walked to an unmarked car in the parking lot behind the police station. He started to get in the back when she laughed. "You are not under arrest, Finn. You can ride in front."

He caught himself before he could make a cynical wisecrack. "Thanks." He wasn't quite sure what to make of her.

She started the car and pulled out of the parking lot before she spoke. "I read your memoir. It hit home for me."

Now he was really perplexed. What was she getting at? "Oh, yeah?" Now that was a bland response. Perfect.

"I'll look forward to this new one. When will it be out?"

Seemed like a fair and innocuous question. "Soon." And that was an innocuous response. So far this conversation was going quite well.

"What's it about?"

Aha! Now she was getting to the crux of it. This was how she was going to get information on Jed. But he was onto her and he would be careful.

"Jonestown."

"That's it? Just Jonestown? Aren't there already a lot of books on Jonestown?"

"A lot of books on Jim Jones. This one's more about the survivors."

"I see."

Finn couldn't resist asking how this thirty-something woman knew about Jonestown. "Most people your age don't know much about it."

"I'm a cop." He didn't know what to make of that answer, but he decided not to ask anything more. He didn't have to. "I wanted to be one all my life and I read as much as I could about all kinds of criminal minds."

"Is that how you view Jim Jones?"

She turned in her seat to look at him. "Don't you?"

"I guess so. But I hadn't thought of it that way. I had just thought of him as a wildly crazy drug addict."

"Isn't that a criminal?"

Now he was starting to squirm. Did she know about his drug and alcohol problems? Did she think Jed was part of Jim Jones' army of loyal followers? Now he was sure she had an ulterior motive for driving him home. He decided to change the subject. "Do you know where I live?"

"Yes. I've been to your house a number of times." She wasn't finished though. "So Jed's a survivor? That's why you're interviewing him?"

Aha again. Now she was showing her true colors. He had the perfect response. "You know, I don't like to talk about a book too much before it's published. We'll have to table this discussion until after it comes out."

The rest of the ride was silent. It was as he predicted. It had all been a ruse to get him to talk about Jed.

31

THE NEXT COUPLE OF MONTHS WERE SMOOTH SAILING with only occasional phone calls from Bukowski. Finn and Kate had settled into a routine. A playful and accepting atmosphere had replaced the tension and strained communication of the past. Every morning, Kate entered Finn's office and placed a cup of coffee on the table next to him as he wrote. She kissed him on the top of his head; he winked at her; and Mother purred as Kate set a saucer of milk on the floor. Finn ate all the dinners Kate fixed and was, of course, the chief bottle-washer afterwards.

He took time out from writing every day to visit with his boardwalk friends. Davion and Ty had auditioned for American Talent Search and had gotten to the semifinals. Finn was sure they would make it to the finals and be on their way to Las Vegas and the big time. Derek had moved on to Portland, Oregon where he felt his message would be more accepted. He finally agreed with Finn that the tourists on the Venice Beach Boardwalk were not interested in saving the planet. They were on vacation and didn't want to be disturbed by dire predictions of the end of the world. The indomitable Charlie was at his post with a smile as always. One day he had spilled the beans that he had been a down and out addict himself at one time and this was his chance for redemption. Finn had figured it had to have been something like that.

Harper had started her own novel and Finn critiqued it as she went along. Her parents had relented and became supportive, sending her a few bucks now and then so she could waitress a few less hours and devote more time to her writing. Bella kept up her usual activity and their friendship grew deeper and closer. She was the one Finn could trust and confide in since Jed was gone. He liked being able to have someone in his circle who was older than he was and could mentor him for a change. And then there was Savali. Finn would go by Muscle Beach every day but it was only once a week or so that he found Savali working out. He never did find out whether Savali was male or female, nor whether transgender or transsexual would be the correct description. He tried to get into a conversation but Savali would merely smile and tell him to research Samoan culture.

Finally one afternoon, he typed the last word of his latest draft, stuck it in an envelope and mailed it off. As he was walking home from the post office, he decided to take a detour. He hadn't been to Luis' for ages. He greeted Mercedes at the cash register and found Luis in the kitchen where he was showing a new dishwasher how to scrub a pan. "Hey, I don't come for several weeks and I lose my job?"

"Finn! Good to see you! No worries, you can always have a job here."

"I don't suppose you've heard anything from Jed?"

"Nada. That detective's been around a few times looking for him, too."

"Yeah. He's also been bothering me."

"Can I get you a plate? I have some nice chicken fajitas."

"No, thanks. I just wanted to say hello."

"How about a beer?"

"I'm good, Luis. Take care," Finn called over his shoulder as he left.

He climbed the stairs of the front porch and put his key in the lock, excited to share with Kate that he had finished and mailed his manuscript. But Kate opened the door before he had a chance to turn the key. "Dad. That lieutenant is here!" She looked frightened and worried.

He held her arm a little too tightly. "Did he ask you any questions? Did you say anything?"

"He just said he had some information for you, but wouldn't tell me what it was. He's in the living room." Finn dropped her arm and Kate started to follow him into the living room.

"Let me talk to him alone, Kate. I don't want you mixed up in this."

"I'm already mixed up in this, but okay."

Bukowski stood when Finn entered. "Hello, Finn. It's been a while."

"Yes, it's been quite pleasant. So what's this information?"

"Do you want to talk in here?"

Finn looked around the room and saw that Kate had closed the door and stayed outside. "Yes."

"The New York case against you is closed."

"There was a case?"

The lieutenant smiled. "Of course there was a case. But lucky for you, New York has much more to deal with than the death of a woman who was already dying. They've decided not to investigate the circumstances of your wife's insulin overdose."

"Oh, I'm so relieved."

"I'll just ignore your misplaced sarcasm."

"Aren't you the scholarly detective."

"However, your case here in Los Angeles is still open."

"And what case is that?"

"As an accessory."

"And how do you reckon I'm an accessory?" Finn could feel his rage rising.

"The definition of an accessory is 'one who aids, abets, commands, or counsels another in the commission of a crime.' Do you understand what I'm telling you, Finn?"

Finn was furious but managed to keep his wits about him. "Let me get this straight. You think I had Antoinette killed? And you think Jed killed her?" Finn asked, his anger rising rapidly. "This is ridiculous! Jed wouldn't do that. You're all wrong about him."

"We'd like to find him so he can prove that to us."

"I told you. I don't know where he is and—" Finn stopped himself.

"And if you did you wouldn't tell me? Is that what you were going to say?" Finn just glared at him and then looked away.

"There are things you can do to get your case as an accessory closed."

"I thought I've been vouched for by several people."

"I don't think you went to her motel room, Finn, and pushed her down. Your fingerprints were not the ones we found."

"What are you saying?"

"I think you know what I'm saying."

"Yeah, that you think I sent Jed there?"

The lieutenant raised his eyebrows. "You did have a reason."

"That's bullshit! Jed didn't kill her! And I had nothing to do with any of it."

"You're still in a heap of trouble, Finn. But you can do yourself a big favor and give us Jed. We just want to talk to him."

"Get out!" Finn was furious.

"We're willing to cut you a deal."

"I have nothing more to say to you." Finn stood up and opened the door, his eyes ablaze and his body trembling.

Lieutenant Bukowski walked out and called over his shoulder, "You'd better get yourself that lawyer and he'd better be a good one."

Finn paced for a few minutes. He checked his wallet and found a few dollars inside. He grabbed his coat and stuck his head in the kitchen. "I'll be back later." He rushed out before Kate had a chance to ask where he was going. Not that he would have told her. He ducked into the liquor store and grabbed a bottle, paying no attention to the friendly owner who inquired on how he hadn't seen him in such a long time.

Finn spent most of his days at the boardwalk, hobnobbing with Charlie, and with Ty and Davion and Savali whenever he could. Sometimes he visited Bella at her house when he didn't see her on the boardwalk. He was the only person she allowed inside her house. Many mornings he would have a cup of coffee with Harper at the cafe, mentoring her with her writing as well as the crossword puzzles.

In the evening he would sit at his computer, researching ideas for another book. He thought about the homelessness idea again but threw that one out. This particular evening he had looked up euthanasia and toyed with the idea of going up to Oregon to interview some of the family members of those who had chosen to end their lives under that state's "Death With Dignity" law. But then he thought it was a little too close to home and he wasn't keen on the possibility of reopening any kind of investigation by the New York police department. Just as he scrapped that idea, the doorbell rang and who should Kate escort into his office but Lieutenant Bukowski.

"Long time no see, Finn."

Finn quickly shut down his computer. "Always a pleasure."

"Just thought I'd check in and see if you'd heard from Jed."

"Like you'd be the first to know if I had!"

The lieutenant sat down at the table and picked up the necklace Jed had asked Finn to hold for him. "Nice necklace. Is it your daughter's?"

Should he say yes? Bukowski might ask Kate and he didn't want her to have to lie. "It was my wife's. And I'd appreciate it if you'd leave it alone."

The lieutenant dropped it back on the table and put his hands up in fake surrender. "Sorry."

Finn composed himself and said assertively, "Is there anything else? Now you know that I haven't seen Jed, I'd like to get back to work."

Bukowski stood up. "No problem. Just keep me in mind if you see him." He walked to the door and added, "Don't bother getting up. I can see myself out." He walked out but Finn figured he had better make sure that he actually left through the front door instead of looking for Kate to grill her about any of this. She had apparently made herself scarce because even he couldn't find her. Good. He didn't want to talk to her just then anyway. He went back to his computer and his buddy, the whiskey bottle.

After leaving Finn's, Lieutenant Bukowski went back to the station to sift through the evidence they did have on Antoinette's murder case. Other than Jed's fingerprints in the room and the letters she had sent to Finn, there wasn't much to go on. He didn't really care that much about pinning anything on Finn, although he certainly had a motive. Rather, he was convinced that Jed had pushed Antoinette and caused her death. But he wondered if there had been some connection between Jed and Antoinette other than Finn. He knew her death was no accident and he did not want the case closed.

When he got to the station he found the evidence box and brought it to his desk to sift through again. He was thumbing through Antoinette's wallet when he noticed a picture hidden in one of the compartments. He took out the picture and examined

267

it closely. It was a photograph of Antoinette and another woman at a party. He took a magnifying glass out of his drawer to get a better look at the necklace around Antoinette's neck. It was exactly the same as the one Finn had claimed was his wife's. Could Antoinette have stolen it from Maggie? Then how did Finn get it back? Would Finn have wanted it back that badly? Certainly he must have plenty of his wife's jewelry. What was so significant about this necklace? And why was it sitting out on Finn's table? He put the picture in his pocket. He would pay Finn another visit and ask him about it.

32

THE NEXT DAY LIEUTENANT BUKOWSKI tried several times to contact Finn. He wasn't sure what he was going to say, but he couldn't keep his mind on his other cases. He stopped at Kate's house four or five times throughout the day but no one was ever there. He figured he'd have to wait until evening. Even if Finn wasn't there, Kate would most likely be home from work and he thought he could easily cajole her into telling him where Finn was.

Kate cleared the table after dinner while Finn started the dishes. The phone rang and Kate answered it. "Hello?" She looked at Finn. "Really? That's great. I'll tell him. He's washing the dishes right now and hates to be disturbed doing his favorite activity." She hung up and grinned at her father.

"I'm glad I can provide you with a target for your wit and merriment."

She put her arms around his waist. "That was Judith. The publishers love what you sent them."

Finn hugged her back. "I knew they would." He didn't really, but he wanted to sound confident.

"By the way, I won't be home for dinner tomorrow. It's Awards Night at my school and I have a student who's getting special recognition. He's only been in my class a few months and his mother just died. I want to make sure someone's there for him when he accepts the award. He's a great kid."

"What's it for?"

"It's the Steiner award—named after a teacher who had been at the school for something like forty years. It's for students who've worked hard and improved a lot, good attendance. That kind of thing."

"You sure are one extraordinary teacher." Finn kissed her on the cheek.

"I learned from the best." She kissed him back and left.

He finished the dishes and returned to his office to continue his Googling. He hadn't found anything that piqued his interest as much as Jonestown had; something he was willing to devote the time to learning about. Maybe it was time to write fiction for a change of pace. The doorbell rang and he waited for Kate to get it but when he didn't hear any movement from her, he went to the door himself.

"Oh terrific! My favorite visitor!" he grumbled when he opened the door.

"Great to see you too, Finn. May I come in?" Lieutenant Bukowski asked.

"What now?" Finn didn't budge.

"Do you really want to talk about this out here?"

Finn turned his back and walked into his office without a word, but left the front door open as a signal that the lieutenant should follow.

Finn closed the office door after the lieutenant entered and sat down. "Okay. What piece of damning evidence have you found that will put me in jail for thirty years?"

"I wouldn't be so flippant if I were you." Bukowski took out the picture and shoved it in front of Finn.

"I see that you have a picture of Antoinette. And that proves what exactly?"

"Look at the necklace she's wearing."

Finn looked at the picture again and stiffened. Should he play dumb or make up a story. He decided to do the latter. He shrugged his shoulders and handed the picture back to Bukowski. "She borrowed it from Maggie to wear, I guess." Then he thought he could add something to make Antoinette look bad. "She probably took it from Maggie's jewelry box without telling her or me. At least she had the decency to put it back."

"Look again, Finn. Antoinette was at least twenty years younger in this picture." The lieutenant handed him back the picture and Finn glanced at it

271

briefly. "Then I don't know what to tell you. Maybe she had one like it."

"Come on, Finn. Don't be ridiculous. Let's get to the truth here. Whose necklace is it and why do you have it now?"

Finn was silent. He really didn't know how to answer without incriminating Jed in some way.

"Remember I do have a search warrant," Bukowski continued. "Why don't you give me the necklace and save us both the trouble of having to go through all the crap in your office. We do not offer a cleanup service when we're done and I doubt Kate would be keen on us messing up her immaculate abode."

"Shut up, Bukowski! I'll give you the goddamn necklace!" Finn knew he had no choice. He was sure there were traces of cocaine powder in his things and who knows what else he may have misplaced during his drinking binges. If the police found the pill container that Harper had given him, she could get in trouble. Not to mention Davion and Ty, if the cops were to find any evidence with their fingerprints on it. Anyway, he had a lot of faith in Jed's abilities to escape detection. After all, he'd been honing his craft for many years. He took the necklace out of his pocket. "Can I get it back?"

"Sure thing, as soon as the case is concluded. The sooner the better for both of us, eh Finn? Any help from you would certainly get it done faster." Bukowski took the necklace and put it in a plastic evidence bag. "We can dust for prints and I will take into consideration that you are touching it now. We just want to see if Jed's prints are on it." He gave Finn a knowing look, hoping he'd take the bait, but Finn knew what he was doing and didn't bite.

"Are we done here now?" Finn sighed irritably.

Bukowski stood. "For now. Have you found a lawyer yet?"

"None of your fucking business." Finn led the way to the front door and opened it wide. "Good riddance." The lieutenant left with a wink and a fake smile.

Finn went back to brood in his office. Kate stuck her head in the door. "Is he gone?"

"Yes."

Kate was dying to know what Bukowski said but she knew it would not be a good idea to ask Finn. He would tell her if and when he was ready. She started to leave when Mother scampered in and jumped onto Finn's lap. Kate smiled and quietly shut the door.

"You have food in your dish, what do you want?" Mother snuggled into his lap and purred. "Oh, just some affection. Okay."

After a few minutes he got up and put Mother down on the chair. He went to the cupboard and leafed through his pile of records. He found what he was looking for and put it on the turntable. He poured himself a glass, put Mother back on his lap and settled into his chair. He closed his eyes, and let Bob Dylan's raspy rendition of "I Shall Be Released" soothe his soul.

Jed arrived at Miss Ruthie's after dinnertime that same evening. He put his ear to the door, listening for the sound of crying infants, but it was quiet. He knocked and Malcolm answered and threw his arms around him. "Jed!"

They hugged tightly. "The babies are quiet."

"There's only one here right now and Miss Ruthie just got her to sleep." Malcolm looked outside to the left and right of the door. "Where's Mother?"

"She's okay. She's being well taken care of." They walked inside together. "How are you doing?"

Malcolm's happiness at seeing Jed vanished and he sniffled, wiping his nose on his sleeve. "My mom died."

Jed put his arms around him. "I'm sorry, Malcolm."

They embraced silently without a trace of awkwardness. Malcolm pulled away first. "Miss Ruthie said she's gonna try to adopt me."

"That's wonderful!"

"And guess what? I'm getting an award at school tomorrow!"

"That's also wonderful."

"There's a ceremony and everything. Can you come?"

"I don't know . . . maybe . . . what time?"

"7:30."

"What school?"

"Venice High. Do you know where that is?"

"I'll find it."

"It's on Venice Boulevard."

"I'll try to be there."

Malcolm grinned. "Want some dinner? I think there are some leftovers."

"No, I can't stay. I just wanted to see you."

"Hey, Jed, how come you go away for so long?"

"I have business to attend to sometimes. Say hello to Miss Ruthie for me." He gave Malcolm one more hug. "I'll try real hard to get there tomorrow night." Malcolm watched him walk out the door.

33

THE NEXT EVENING AT THE HIGH SCHOOL, Kate stood to the side of the stage as the auditorium filled with excited students and proud parents. She scanned the crowd and found Malcolm, dressed in a polo shirt and khaki pants, sitting next to his foster mother. She smiled at how much pride he took in his clean, well-pressed outfit. Miss Ruthie had a baby on her lap. Kate was relieved that Malcolm had a "family member" to celebrate his award with him.

When the principal walked up to the podium, the crowd quieted down. Jed slipped in the door silently just as the principal started speaking. After the typical welcome address to the students and parents and praise for the recipients, the principal started calling out names and awards. When Malcolm was recognized as the winner of the Steiner award, the most meaningful prize of the night, the teachers stood and gave him a standing ovation. They all knew

Malcolm's background, and that his mother had just died. Although the parents there didn't know that, they also stood to applaud the young man who had probably never been acknowledged for anything in his entire life. It was a special moment and Kate had tears in her eyes as she snapped his picture when he accepted the trophy. Jed couldn't have felt prouder if Malcolm was his own son.

After the ceremony, Jed waited at the door to congratulate Malcolm and noticed Kate hugging him and talking to Miss Ruthie. How's that for a coincidence. He knew Kate was a teacher but he had no idea what school and that she was Malcolm's. Maybe he should leave. He didn't really want Kate to see him and tell Finn. But he wanted Malcolm to know he had come. Before he had made a decision on whether or not to exit as quietly as he had arrived, Malcolm saw him and squirmed out of Kate's hug to run to him. Kate's eyes followed him and her mouth dropped when she noticed that it was Jed whom Malcolm had gone to. Jed's eyes met hers but he turned to Malcolm with a high five and a bear hug.

Miss Ruthie watched Malcolm run as well and grinned when she saw who was there. "Oh, look. Jed's here. Come meet Malcolm's good friend." Ruthie took Kate's arm and brought her over.

"Hey, Miss McGee. This here's my friend Jed," Malcolm said excitedly.

Jed and Kate smiled and shook hands. "Nice to meet you," Kate said.

"Likewise," Jed answered.

The baby had been quiet up until then, but chose that moment to start wailing. "Come Malcolm. I'm afraid we have to go now." Miss Ruthie placed her hand gently on Malcolm's arm.

"But what about the cookies and punch?"

"I'll drive him home," Kate offered.

"Oh, that's very nice of you. Are you sure that's okay?"

"I'd be happy to."

"Goodbye, Jed. Will you be over soon?" Miss Ruthie asked.

"I'll try."

Kate gave Jed a puzzled look, but kept her questions to herself. Miss Ruthie left with the baby. "Malcolm, why don't you get yourself some cookies and punch? And I know some of the other teachers and students would like to congratulate you," Kate said.

"Okay." Malcolm headed to the refreshment table.

After Malcolm and Miss Ruthie walked off, Kate turned to Jed. "I'm not sure why we pretended not to know each other."

"I don't know either."

"I guess it just seemed easier that way."

"I guess so."

"My father misses you."

Jed smiled. "How's Mother?"

"She's fine. She misses you too."

"I know she's happy to be with you." He looked away for a minute and then turned back to Kate. "And I, too, am happy she's with you."

"Dad told me everything. I assume you're laying low."

"I think it's best. Maybe you shouldn't tell Finn you saw me."

"That will be hard."

"I just don't want him to have to lie to the police."

"I think he already has."

"Oh, no. About what?"

"I don't know exactly. That lieutenant won't leave him alone and I think there was something about the necklace—"

"What about the necklace?" Jed could feel himself getting agitated but worked hard at keeping it contained.

"Honestly. He wouldn't tell me. It's just what I overheard."

"Well, what did you overhear?"

"The lieutenant took the necklace like it was some evidence."

Jed wrung his hands and breathed heavily. "I really think it's best if you don't tell Finn you saw me."

"If that's what you want." Kate decided to change the subject. It was too distressing for both of them. "So, how do you know Malcolm?"

"He used to hang out on the boardwalk before he started living at Miss Ruthie's."

"Was he homeless?"

Jed stopped for a minute. He didn't want to get Malcolm into trouble. But now he was at Miss Ruthie's and all was well. It shouldn't matter. "When his mother was in the hospital, they were kicked out of their apartment. He didn't know where to go."

"It only makes him even more of a success story." She smiled at Jed. "Something tells me you had something to do with getting him and Miss Ruthie together."

Jed shrugged. "I just introduced him to the right person. Malcolm's the one who should get all the acclaim."

"And he has. He's one of my favorite students."

"He's a great kid."

"He seems to think you're pretty great too, Jed."

"I feel sorry for him. Losing his mother and having no one else to turn to."

"A familiar story to you," she said.

Jed looked at her warily.

"I read the manuscript."

"I need to go, Kate. It was nice seeing you. Would you tell Malcolm that I'll come see him soon?"

"I will. Take care of yourself, Jed. And I know Dad would really like to see you soon, too. So would Mother."

Jed nodded, smiled, and disappeared into the crowd.

34

LIEUTENANT BUKOWSKI WAS RELENTLESS in his harassment of Finn. But the more he pestered him, the more determined Finn was in proving that there was no case. It was an obsession for both of them. Finn reveled in being able to show Bukowski up, and that just pushed the lieutenant to look harder. Meanwhile, Jed stayed away and it soon became impossible for Bukowski to stay focused on this one case.

First of all, the evidence was circumstantial and weak. Secondly, there was no certainty that Antoinette's death had been a homicide as opposed to an accident. There was no weapon and no clear motivation on Jed's part. After all, the lieutenant knew nothing about the Jonestown connection between Antoinette and Jed. Nor did he know that Finn had paid for Mother's veterinary bill so he couldn't prove that Jed "owed" Finn anything. All that Bukowski knew was that he had started this investigation and he had put a lot of time and energy into it, and it had gotten nowhere. He did not want to drop it. But there were other murders, and other investigations, and plenty of other police business to attend to. And most importantly, his captain decided that it was a cold case and he needed to move on. But Bukowski was a stubborn man. If the captain wanted him off the case, he would continue with it on his own time. He made sure the necklace and the picture were in an easy-to-reach place in the evidence room, not in storage with the rest of the cold cases. He was not done with it, no matter what the captain said.

Meanwhile, Finn tried to get excited about his book's release. Judith wanted to set up some interviews, but he had told her that he wasn't interested. The publishers were not pleased, but as Judith put it, they were used to his cantankerousness. She didn't argue about it too much either because she knew that his drinking had interfered in the past with his speaking engagements. She had noticed the telltale slurring and irritability in their phone conversations.

Finn busied himself searching for book topics and visiting his boardwalk friends. He thought a lot about Jed; partly just missing him, but also concerned that he had to stay in hiding. He didn't know what to believe about the circumstances surrounding

Antoinette's death. If she did die while Jed was in the room, he was sure it was an accident. But he doubted the police would see it that way. Many evenings he noticed a car drive by the house slowly. He knew it was Bukowski either trying to annoy him, scare him, or just remind Finn that he was keeping an eye on him. He doubted the lieutenant presumed he would find Jed stopping in for a visit.

One morning Finn entered the kitchen and found Kate drinking coffee and reading the newspaper. He poured himself a cup and sat down at the kitchen table. "And good morning to you, too." She was so engrossed in the article she was reading, that not only didn't she answer him, she didn't seem to know he was there. "Kate? Hello? Earth to Kate."

"Sorry. Uh, good morning, Dad." She looked up at him, her face panic-stricken.

"What's wrong? You look like you just saw a ghost."

She handed him the *LA Times*. "You'd better read this."

He took the paper and looked down at the headline: "Probable Drowning Off Venice Beach." He read further. "Authorities are asking the public for help in identifying a man whose body was recovered from the Pacific Ocean early Thursday morning. The body was found floating face down in shallow water near the Venice Beach Pier. The African - American male appears to be between forty-five and fifty. He was dressed in black jeans and a black long sleeved shirt. There was no identification on the body and nothing was found on the beach or the pier at Washington Boulevard. He appears to have been in the water for several hours before being spotted by a jogger about 5:30 a.m. Anyone with information is asked to contact the Pacific Community Police Station of the Los Angeles Police Department." He put the paper down and looked up at Kate. She hadn't moved, watching him intently to see his reaction. He took a deep breath and exhaled loudly as he sat back in his chair. They didn't speak for a couple of minutes. "Aren't you going to be late for work?" he finally said.

"What do you think?" she answered, ignoring his effort at skirting the issue.

"What do I think about what?"

"Dad! Stop it. You know what I'm talking about!"

"I don't know what I think."

"Should you go see if you can identify the body?"

"Go to the police?"

"Yes, Dad," she sighed.

"No."

"But—"

Finn interrupted her. "I'll go talk to some people first."

"You mean on the boardwalk?"

"Yes. You better get to work."

284

Kate shook her head in annoyance and got up. "Sometimes I don't get you at all. Do you really think things will just go away if you don't deal with them?"

He shrugged. "I can hope."

"Apparently you still have a lot to learn." She left the kitchen.

Finn sat quietly for a few minutes. He heard the front door slam and Kate's car start up. Mother moseyed in and rubbed against his leg, looking for food. He ignored her, lost in his own thoughts. She meowed loudly and finally he snapped out of his daydreaming. "Oh, I guess you're hungry." He got up and took a bowl from the cupboard and set it on the floor. He looked for the cat food bag but found nothing. "Well, I guess we're going for a walk whether I'd like to or not." He checked his wallet for money but it was empty. "I guess it's time to visit some of our old haunts." He scooped up Mother and walked out.

The first stop was Charlie's table, not just because he was always the earliest one to set up, but also because Finn thought he would know more than anyone about what happened. He would also probably have some milk for Mother. That could keep her going until the pizza store or Luis opened up for some real food. "Finn! I haven't seen you in ages! How have you been?" Charlie exclaimed as he poured Mother a cup of milk without even asking. Mother was extremely grateful and lapped it up.

"I'm okay, Charlie. Hangin' in. And yourself?"

"Superb!"

Charlie was the most optimistic, contented person Finn had ever known. But it was never too syrupy sweet. He was just one of those all-around good guys you had to like and admire. "Have you heard about the body that washed ashore?"

Charlie's face took on a serious bent, which was very unusual. "Yes. The police stopped at the shelter right away to see if I knew him."

"And did you?"

"I didn't look at the body. I just told them that no one was missing of the regulars that stay with us."

"Oh, that's too bad."

Charlie looked at him curiously. "Huh? Are you saying that it's too bad that he wasn't one of our guests?"

"No, no. That's not what I meant. I—" Finn stopped himself. He didn't know what to say without coming right out and asking about Jed. "I just meant the whole thing was too bad. You know, the guy drowning and all."

"Oh, yeah. Very sad."

Finn thought it best to leave on that note. "Mother and I thank you for the milk."

"Great to see you. Don't be a stranger," Charlie said.

"I won't. See you soon."

Finn continued down the boardwalk. Davion and Ty might know something. They seemed to have inside info on everything. But they were nowhere in sight. Now that was really weird. Finn's mind started jumping to all sorts of conclusions. Maybe they went to the police because they knew who it was. Even if it wasn't Jed, they seemed to know everybody on the boardwalk. Actually they seemed to know everyone in all of Venice Beach. He bet the police had come to them and taken them to the morgue to see if they could identify the body. Finn would ask Harry, the Kama Kosmic Krusader. He was one of the boardwalk regulars who played electric guitar while rollerblading. "Hey Harry!" he called out to him.

Harry made a wide turn on his skates and rolled over to Finn. "How'd you do, my friend. What can I do for you?"

"Do you know where Davion and Ty are this morning?"

"You haven't heard?"

Finn's face took on that grim, panicked look of dread. Could it have been Davion or Ty? But didn't the article say a middle-aged man? "Heard what?" he asked tentatively.

"They won the finals on American Talent Search. They're going to Las Vegas, man!"

Finn's face broke into a grin. "You're kidding! That's wonderful! Is that where they are now? Vegas?"

"No, just probably meeting with some bigwigs or rehearsing somewhere. They're around still. Just not their regular hours like all day every day."

Finn debated about asking Harry if he saw anything, but thought it best to talk solely to the

287

people he knew best. He'd wait to speak with Davion and Ty. "Do you know when they'll be around?"

Harry shrugged. "I don't keep tabs on my competition, man." He rollerbladed away, doing figure eights and strumming a Jimi Hendrix tune.

Finn got to Muscle Beach to sit for a spell while waiting for the pizza place to open. He took a quick look for some Styrofoam containers in the trashcans, but the garbage had all been emptied. Bella wouldn't find much to fill her cart. She probably knew when the best times to search were, so he suspected he wouldn't see her around. Savali wasn't there, either. Neither of them would know anything, anyway. They weren't boardwalk denizens. They came for a purpose and left when they had accomplished their tasks.

He placed Mother on the bench beside him when he sat down but she would have none of it. She crawled onto his lap and snuggled into his stomach as if it would open up for her. "You are becoming quite spoiled," he smiled as he stroked her. "I don't know who's done this to you, if it was Kate or me." He peered down the boardwalk toward the pier. It was several blocks away so he couldn't see much. Maybe he would take a walk down there. He got up and took Mother in his arms. He never could quite figure out how to get her comfortably on his shoulders as Jed had always done. Maybe they weren't the right shape for carrying a cat. Or maybe they were too bony or something. But neither he nor Mother lasted long in that position.

As he neared the pier he saw a couple of people standing next to the yellow police tape identifying that this was a crime scene. The closer he came the more he worried that Bukowski would be one of those two people so he slowed his pace. It looked like a black woman dressed in street clothes standing next to a police officer in uniform so he breathed a sigh of relief. He could handle Detective Washington, if that was indeed who the black woman was.

She noticed him before he could identify her for sure. "Hello, Finn," she called out to him sounding downright friendly.

"Just wondering what all the commotion was." What a stupid thing to say. He was trying to be nonchalant, as if he didn't know what had happened at the pier, and it only made him sound like he was guilty of some unknown crime. Maybe he couldn't handle her. Now they would think he had something to do with this man drowning, even if it wasn't Jed. Thankfully, she approached him so he could stop his obsessive mind going to ridiculous places.

"Haven't you heard?" she asked.

Does everyone think he's a moron who never listens to the news or reads a newspaper? Okay. He will not dig himself any deeper. "Sure I have. I was just taking a walk." Now he was attempting to explain himself? Like he couldn't take a walk anywhere he pleased? What an idiot he had become in this whole debacle.

"We haven't identified the body yet. Do you have any thoughts? I know you spend a fair amount of time on the boardwalk."

Now she was baiting him! Damn her. He wouldn't fall for it. "Nope. Do you?" Ha! He'd turn the tables.

"Some. We know the body had been in the water for several hours and there were no signs of any trauma. We're pretty sure it was a simple drowning."

Was she giving him some information to taunt him further? Did she think if she gave some, then he'd open up? Actually, everything she told him was probably what he could read in a newspaper article about it. "Where's your partner in crime?" He laughed after he said it. He meant it merely as a clichéd expression, but it was pretty funny as a description for a police duo.

She smiled. "He's not on this case."

That gave Finn a sense of relief. If they had thought it was Jed, wouldn't Bukowski have been assigned to it? "Lucky you."

Detective Washington laughed. "You and he have quite the warm, fuzzy relationship."

"Yeah. A real love fest."

"Do you want to come down to the morgue and see if you can identify the body?"

She's good! She got him after all! He took a deep breath, trying to waste some time before he answered, not being sure how he should. "I doubt I could help you." There. That sounded innocuous enough.

"I think you could and I think you should."

Finn started to feel angry now. He felt trapped. She was trying to work on his guilt. What if he could identify him? But he didn't want to. "No thanks."

She stared into his eyes as if she were piercing through them with needlelike laser beams. "Don't you want to know if it's Jed?"

Damn her! Damn her for saying it. Damn her for insinuating it. Damn her for knowing how to get to him! He pulled Mother to his chest so tightly that she squirmed and meowed. Detective Washington gently placed her hand on his arm to help loosen his hold. Finn's reflexes kicked in and he let her adjust his grip on Mother. He looked back into the detective's eyes and they were soft with compassion. "He would never . . ." Finn couldn't finish.

"I don't know Jed, but he seems to fit the description. You need to do this, Finn. Not for the police, but for you. And for your friend. Maybe it wasn't a suicide. Maybe it was foul play."

"The article said the police did not suspect foul play."

"That's just what we always say. If it was a crime, it's easier to capture the perpetrators if they don't think we're looking for them." He closed his eyes and shook his head, not to say no he wouldn't, but to say no he didn't want to but he knew he should. She seemed to know that and pulled gently on his arm. He instinctively followed her. "Let me drive you there now," she added. "Joe!" she called to the officer. "I'll be back in a couple of hours." The policeman waved.

They walked to her car and got in. As they drove away Finn turned to her, "What do you honestly think?"

"That it's not Jed." She sounded definitive.

Finn sat quietly for the entire half hour drive, looking out the window and petting Mother. He got out slowly and followed her inside the building. It took several minutes to get to an office where there was a computer set up because so many people had to stop and admire Mother. She ate it up, purring and burrowing even more into Finn's chest. "You can sit here, Finn," the detective pointed to a chair in front of the computer.

He looked at her questioningly. "Don't I go to that room like on TV where they pull the bodies out of those drawers?"

She smiled. "It's a database now. You see pictures of the bodies to identify them. Are you ready?"

"I suppose." He put Mother on the floor next to him. Strangely enough, he didn't want her to see the pictures of the body. It was instinctual and maybe a bit farfetched, but that's what he did.

She typed some information into the computer and up came an "Unidentified Persons List Search" page. She typed the case number, sex, and race, and then turned to Finn to answer the last question. "Date last seen?"

Finn panicked. What should he say? He doubted she'd believe him even though it had been so long since he had seen him. And anyway, he wasn't sure he even remembered. But what did it matter? He was alive until he wasn't, whether he had seen him or not. He answered truthfully, "I don't remember. Way before the day before yesterday and that was apparently the last time this man was alive."

"I'll just type in a week ago."

"Oh no," Finn protested. "It was way before that."

"It doesn't really matter, does it, Finn? This has nothing to do with your case with Bukowski."

"Doesn't it?" he retorted.

"No. It doesn't."

Finn relaxed somewhat and let her finish typing. He stared at the computer screen, waiting for the picture to come up. He got up from the chair and paced around it, wishing he had never walked down to the pier in the first place. What was he thinking? Finally the picture came on the screen and she beckoned him over. He inhaled deeply and looked at the monitor. Then he exhaled with relief. It wasn't Jed. "No." That's all he said.

She logged out of the computer. "I'll drive you home."

He scooped up Mother and followed her out, walking with a much lighter step.

35

THE SUMMER CAME AND WENT WITH NO SIGN OF JED. Finn had gone back to researching homelessness but lost interest quickly. He decided the issue had already lost its luster as too many other writers had taken it on. Anyway, he didn't really want to revisit that time in his life. He had always written nonfiction, memoirs or historical-based ideas. Maybe it was time to switch to fiction. He started a couple of novels, but nothing came easily so he gave up on that.

His drinking had gone back to "more than he should but not over the top" and he had given up the drugs altogether. He had a love/hate relationship with alcohol but in his mind there was no such thing as an Irish alcoholic; drinking was innate to the species.

There was still no exact date for publication and it was exasperating but there wasn't a thing he could do to speed up the process. He was comfortable in the rut of drinking too much and writing too little.

He still met with Harper at the cafe most mornings to discuss her novel. He usually brought nothing to the meetings other than ideas that had not materialized into any typed pages. Most afternoons he and Mother could be found on his favorite bench by Muscle Beach. He had his trusty brown paper bag when finances permitted.

Davion and Ty, however, spent less and less time on the boardwalk. They had parlayed the American Talent Search success into several gigs: Las Vegas, state fairs, music and dance festivals. It had been enough to get them a decent apartment so they didn't need to be on the boardwalk all day every day. Finn saw them about as often as he saw Savali: every week or two. It wasn't the same for Finn without Jed or Davion and Ty on the boardwalk. But at least Bella usually came by for her trashcan search.

Sometimes late in the evening he would sneak out to see Luis and Mercedes. He had to be clandestine about it because Kate had become a real "Jewish Mother," not wanting him to go out by himself after 9 p.m. She always offered to drive him there, but it made him feel ridiculous and he always refused.

One afternoon he and Mother walked up and down the boardwalk and found only Charlie in his usual spot. Davion and Ty had gone to Miami. They were invited to be part of a reggae cruise for seven days. Finn wondered if they would go to Jamaica to see their families since Miami was so close. He smiled remembering those first conversations about dawtas and pickneys. He looked forward to their return. He wanted to hear how they managed to do their acrobatic performances on a ship that may not always be smooth sailing. Savali hadn't been around for more than a week and Derek, of course, was up in Portland as far as Finn knew. There were the other boardwalk denizens, but Finn had never nurtured any close relationships with them. They were like neighbors: good for a smile and a nod and occasional chats about mundane things.

Finn sat on the bench feeding Mother a piece of pizza. People were always leaving parts of their slices at the pizza parlor, so he didn't feel bad about asking for the leftovers. Mother didn't care if they were half eaten and they would only be thrown away. He had received his entire advance so no more checks would be coming until the book was actually published. Kate would occasionally give him money, but he hated to ask for it. The only thing he bought with Kate's money was his beloved whiskey and she'd be furious if she knew. He planned to give her a nice bonus check after the book was published, assuming it sold well, of course.

As the sun started to set, he realized it had been quite a while since he'd seen Bella. It was definitely more than a week. That was extremely unusual. As far as he knew, she never went anywhere else. She had long ago lost touch with her friends and had basically become a hermit, only venturing out to gather new items to add to her collection.

Lately when he walked her home, she refused to let him in. He knew better than to pester her about it so he stopped asking after the first couple of times. He was able to catch a glimpse when he held the door open for her, and he saw that it had gotten much worse. The newspapers were stacked past the windows. There were piles and piles of bags, books, paper goods, boxes and cans of food long since expired. The path that went from the front door to the kitchen, living room and bathroom was just wide enough for her and the shopping cart. The dust was no longer just sprinkled on everything; it was more than an inch high. What amazed him the most was that she wasn't sick with some kind of lung disease, breathing in all the dust and mold and who knows what else. She was, after all, in her eighties.

Maybe she was ill. He wondered if she had anyone who would get her medicine or take her to the doctor if she needed to go. Money didn't seem to be an issue for her. Morty had probably left her a tidy trust fund. She certainly didn't spend much money and the house was probably long since paid off. Maybe she had a neighbor or old friend who looked in on her. But she never spoke of anyone. She could always call 911 if she needed help, he supposed. If she could find her phone, that is. He knew so little about her. She had talked of her life with Morty when he was a big time agent, and about her life as a little girl in the concentration camp. But she had never shared anything about her friends or the rest of her family.

She must have some relationships with her neighbors, having lived there for over thirty years. But what if she didn't. And what if she couldn't find her phone. And what if she didn't even have a phone. Or worse, what if she couldn't get to her phone.

He stood abruptly and picked up Mother who was sprawled on the bench in typical lazy-fat-cat fashion. "Let's go, Mother. We need to check on Bella." He started out toward the canals and quickened his step the nearer he got. He had worked himself into a frenzy of worry. He remembered reading several news stories about hoarders who had died in their houses, either from piles toppling over onto them or the floor falling through and them tumbling along with it. By the time he reached Bella's house, he had become somewhat frantic.

"Bella! Bella!" he shouted as he pounded on her front door. Mother even hid under a bush, not sure what to make of Finn. He ran around the house, trying to peer into windows but he couldn't see anything with all the piles of crap in the way. He tried opening windows and the back door while yelling her name, but it was futile. After several minutes of pounding and yelling, several neighbors came out of their houses to find out what all the commotion was.

"Have any of you seen Bella lately?" he called out to them.

They glanced amongst each other and shook their heads. "We don't see much of her anyway. She keeps to herself." One of the women came forward. "Are you a friend of hers?"

"Yes. I'm concerned. I usually see her every week or so and it's been awhile."

"She used to be friendlier. She became something of a recluse after her husband died. He was such an outgoing fellow."

"Do you know if she has any friends or family in the area?"

"I don't think so." The neighbor shook her head. "When Morty was alive, the house was in good repair. None of this was here." She spread her arm to encompass the junk-filled yard.

Finn wanted to call the police to break down the door. But he didn't want to bring any more attention to himself. Not with all that had gone on. He certainly didn't want Bukowski on his tail again, if he had ever left it. He could call Detective Washington, but he didn't know if that would be possible: calling and asking for a specific person to come out on a case. But he didn't want to ask these neighbors to call either. Did these people have any idea of her hoarding? He started to feel very protective of her. He didn't want them to know. But then, how could they not? Before he could think of an alternative one of the other neighbors spoke. "Maybe we should call the police?"

"No!" Finn surprised himself, as well as the others, at his emphatic response. "I mean, maybe she's just a little under the weather. I'll call her later."

They seemed to welcome Finn's plan and returned to their homes. He, however, could not accept it at all since he didn't even have her phone number. He wasn't sure what he would do, but he couldn't just leave. He found Mother's hiding place and joined her on the ground. She climbed into his lap and he leaned against the side of the house, petting and pondering.

It was quite dark when an idea came to him. This was a time he wished he had a cell phone. Kate had been after him to get one, but he hadn't felt the need. He got up slowly, knocked one more time and called Bella's name, this time softly. He put his ear to the door to listen for any movement or breathing. He heard nothing so he and Mother set off for Kate's house. He didn't want to ask to borrow a neighbor's phone and he couldn't use a pay phone. First of all, he had no money and secondly, they were hard to find these days. He would call the fire department and rush back here to meet them. Maybe, just this once, he'd even ask Kate for a ride.

36

HE DIDN'T KNOW HE STILL HAD IT IN HIM. Even Mother was impressed that he could run, although she may not have been that enamored with the jiggling her body had to endure. He made it to Kate's house in less than fifteen minutes. Of course, he didn't really have to run. It wasn't like it was a real fire. But there was something about calling the fire department, though, which made speed a necessity.

"Kate, are you home?" he yelled breathlessly as he rushed to the kitchen.

She was standing at the stove stirring a pot. "What's wrong?" she asked, alarmed.

"How do you call the fire department? Do you use 911 even if it's not a fire?"

"What's going on?" She was getting quite nervous at this point.

"Just answer my question, dammit!"

"I guess so. I don't know. What do you need the fire department for if there's no fire?" She was relieved to see Mother; glad he wasn't calling for a cat trapped in a tree.

Finn ignored her, waiting for a 911 operator to answer. He just looked at Kate, panting heavily and holding his hand to his heart to stop the pounding. "Hello? Yes. I need to get inside someone's house. She doesn't answer and I think something's wrong."

Kate stared at him, trying to fathom what he was talking about. Meanwhile, Finn started to feel protective again, not wanting Kate or even the operator to know about Bella's problem. But he had no choice.

"She may be stuck under debris that may have fallen on top of her. No. There wasn't an explosion or fire." He paused as the operator spoke. "No! I don't want the police. I need the fire department to come out and check. Please don't call the police." He looked at Kate whose expression had changed from alarm to concern. "Why do you have to call the police?" Kate's concern was now wariness. "They have to do a welfare check first?" He sighed. "It's on the canals." And then he realized he had no idea what the address was. "I, uh, don't know. It's a brown house, rundown. You can't miss it. It's the only one dilapidated and badly needing a paint job." He hoped Kate wouldn't ask questions. "She's a hoarder and her house is full of stuff. I'm afraid she's buried under it." Kate was frowning by this point. "I'll go find out the address.

Do I have to give my name? Good. I'd rather not. I'll call you back in a few minutes." He hung up and turned to Kate. "Would you drive me there and can I use your cell phone to call in the address?"

"Okay, Dad, but who is this person?"

"Her name is Bella. She's a Holocaust survivor and a hoarder and a friend." He waited to see how Kate would react to his truthfulness.

"Thanks for being honest with me, for once."

He started to make a wisecrack about her snide response but decided to leave it alone. "You're welcome."

She gathered her purse and car keys and he followed her out the back door. When they got to the canals, they parked on Venice Boulevard and Finn ran out to the house. When he returned, Kate handed him her phone without a word and waited for him to relay the address to the dispatcher. After he hung up she asked him, "Are you going to wait for the police?"

He was silent for a minute, trying to decide what he should do. Would they break down her door? Would they call the fire department to do it? Would they call an ambulance to be waiting in case she was hurt inside? Would they need to ask him questions? "I want to stay, but—"

Kate interrupted, "I'm sure Lieutenant Bukowski doesn't do welfare checks, Dad. It will just be a random policeman who has nothing to do with the investigation into Antoinette's death."

"You're right. But you don't have to stay. It's late and you have work tomorrow. Just leave me here. I'll be fine."

"Are you sure?"

"Yes."

"I'll leave you my phone and you can call me for a ride."

He doubted he'd do that but he did feel better having her phone with him. Maybe he would get one of those contraptions, after all. "Good idea. Thanks." He didn't know who was more shocked by his newfound acquiescent attitude. He figured Kate didn't know that he was using it as a manipulative device. But actually, she was fully aware that he was doing that. But it didn't matter. They both went along because it diffused tension and made their interactions a whole lot more comfortable.

Kate left and Finn waited by Bella's house for the police to come. He was still uneasy about talking to them so he found himself hiding behind a bush rather than standing by the front door. He hadn't totally made up his mind about whether or not he would hang around or make himself scarce. The police showed up quickly, before he had time to decide. He came out of his hiding place as an instinctual response because deep down he really did want to be there when they went inside Bella's.

Two police officers showed up and they were startled when Finn came out from his hiding place. They composed themselves immediately, however, and asked "Are you the man who called in for the welfare check?"

Finn didn't answer that question directly. "She's a hoarder. I'm afraid she's buried under debris or fallen through the floor."

One of the officers peered inside through the window. "I can see that."

"How long has she been missing?" the other officer asked.

"I haven't seen her in more than a week."

"Have you called other family members or friends?"

"I don't know anyone to call."

"What's her name?"

"Bella."

They knocked loudly, calling her name and then turned to Finn when they got no response. "Are you sure she didn't go on vacation or isn't just visiting someone?"

"I don't know. Can't you just call the fire department or something to break down the door?"

"Look, we don't just go breaking into people's houses willy-nilly. Give it more time. She'll probably show up soon."

Finn's voice got louder. "You saw those piles! She could be buried underneath them. What does it take to get you to do a welfare check for Christ's sake?!"

"Now calm down, sir. Have you talked to the neighbors?"

"Why should I? They don't necessarily have anything to do with her."

"You'd be surprised how much neighbors know about each other. Go ahead and knock on some doors. Maybe she just doesn't want to see you for some reason."

"What the hell!" Finn shouted at them but then stopped himself. He could see the officers getting heated up too.

"Go home, old man, before you do something stupid you're going to regret."

Finn turned around abruptly and started to walk away. He certainly didn't need to get arrested and brought down to the station to face old Bukowski.

One of the officers came over and took Finn's arm. "You know, you might call the hospitals in the area."

He nodded and walked home. He went straight to the kitchen. Kate came rushing in. "Well?"

"They wouldn't go in." He opened drawers and cabinets, messing up Kate's coordinated orderliness.

"What are you doing besides causing chaos in the kitchen?"

"Looking for a phone book."

"No one uses them anymore. Why do you want one?"

"I need to call hospitals."

"Why don't you use your computer?"

"How?"

306

"Google hospitals in Los Angeles. If she's one of your down and out friends, she's probably at Harbor."

She's not down and out!" Finn answered sharply. "She lives on the canals for Christ's sake!"

"Okay. Sorry."

Finn left a meowing Mother in the kitchen and called over his shoulder as he entered his office, "Would you feed her please? She hasn't eaten much today." He sat down at his computer with paper and pencil and started writing down hospital phone numbers.

Los Angeles is a big city and by 11 p.m. he was exhausted. Kate entered the kitchen as he hung up the phone for what seemed like the hundredth time. "Any luck?"

"Nope."

"She's probably fine, staying at a friend's or something."

"I didn't think she had any."

"How do you know? Did you ever ask? You're just assuming it."

"Maybe you're right."

"Well, I'm going to bed." She kissed the top of his head. "You should too." She left and Finn retired to his office again. The whiskey was low but there were still a couple of swigs in the bottle. Maybe it would be enough to get him to sleep.

37

KATE'S ASSUMPTION HAD BEEN CORRECT. She got up at six and found Finn asleep in his chair, his head on the keyboard. She looked for the telltale signs and sure enough, there was the empty whiskey bottle on the table. She wanted to wake him up and send him to bed, but decided she didn't want to put up with his crankiness. She knew his reaction would be less than loving so she sighed and went out for her morning jog.

Mother, on the other hand, was less concerned about irritating Finn and rubbed against his leg, meowing loudly. He awoke with a start and reaffirmed Mother's perceptiveness by petting her and bringing her in the kitchen to eat. He then showered, dressed, poured his coffee, got the papers, and when Kate came back, he looked and acted like the picture of health and good-naturedness. "Good morning," he smiled at her.

"Uh, good morning." Kate was understandably a bit taken aback.

"Would you like some breakfast?"

Now she was totally confused. He was offering to make her breakfast? "Are you going to cook?"

"No," he laughed. "But I'll go out and get some scones or muffins or something."

She laughed. "I don't think so. But thanks for offering."

Damn. His ploy hadn't worked. He knew full well that she wouldn't eat bakery goods, but he was hoping she'd give him some money for them. He thought he would conveniently come back after she left for work with his own idea of a good breakfast. Today he would call Judith. Too much time had passed without a word from her. Okay. He would just be direct. "Could I borrow some money? I'm going to call Judith today and see what the holdup is."

Kate went to her purse and took out a twenty-dollar bill. She handed it to him silently, trying not to look disdainful or annoyed. It didn't matter how hard she tried though. Finn took it that way.

"I'm sorry to bother you," he added sarcastically.

She didn't respond right away, but finally she decided to say what had been on her mind for a while. "Maybe you could do some tutoring. I could see if my school has something available. There's a state-sponsored tutoring program starting up. I mean, just for some spending money until the book takes off."

Finn stared at her as if she had asked him to jump off a cliff. That's how farfetched it sounded to him. He wasn't angry, just flabbergasted that she would ask him that. He had enough of his wits about him, though, to respond appropriately. "Sure. Why don't you find out?" That might appease her enough to buy him a few more bottles.

He had to buy an off-brand bourbon since twenty dollars wasn't quite enough for a whole bottle of Jameson. At this point he had to stop being loyal to his favorite brand. He wanted to get to Bella's in the daytime and see if he couldn't figure out a way to get inside. Even if she wasn't there, he wanted to see if he could find something that would give him some clues to Bella's life and people he might call. Maybe she had an address book. Or a scrapbook. She must have friends if not any family. Then he thought about Jed. Not necessarily. Not everyone has friends and family. But Bella had lived a more normal life. Wouldn't Morty have had family? Unless he, too, had been a Holocaust survivor and had left them all behind. How little we know about people.

He had been a bit of a hooligan himself growing up in Ireland. He was known to tag along with some of his friends when they broke into houses. Maybe he could remember some of the tricks of the trade. When he got to Bella's he went straight to the back door. That was usually the one that people were less careful about keeping in good working order. Sure enough, as old and dilapidated as the front door was, the back door was worse. It wasn't difficult at all to break the lock. He was a little afraid of letting Mother scurry around the house, worried she might get lost or hurt in the piles of junk, so he held her as he walked the narrow pathways.

There was no way he could find anything in this mess. It made his office look like the embodiment of neatness and organization. He picked up a newspaper from the top of a pile and read the date. It was ten years old. He opened a plastic garbage bag and gasped when he saw it was filled with ketchup, mustard and sugar packets. He called Bella's name a few times as he looked for legs and feet sticking out like the bad witch in *The Wizard of Oz* when Dorothy's house landed on her. At any rate, the piles were still standing, the floor hadn't caved in, and he was pretty convinced that she wasn't at home. He was also sure that he wasn't going to stumble upon any address books or scrapbooks so he left.

He thought about calling someone to fix the door, but soon recognized how unnecessary that would be. No one else would be able to find anything of value in there either. He took a quick swing by the boardwalk, checking out the vicinities of all the trashcans, and then went back home. He thought about stopping at the cafe. Harper was probably wondering where he was. But he just wasn't interested in helping an aspiring author today. He was full of too much insecurity and self-doubt. Besides that, he knew she had all the potential to be better than him. He just didn't want to have to deal with her success while his own was waning. So he went home to brood and drink.

And that's what he spent the rest of his morning doing. He wondered when the police would consider her truly a missing person. He sipped his whiskey and decided it was easiest to sit and do nothing. But then it wasn't. By early afternoon it weighed on him that something terrible could be wrong and he was doing nothing about it. Or even just the fact that he had broken her door and now anyone could go inside and rob the house. He decided the least he could do is try to get the door fixed or at least boarded up.

He would go and assess the damage. He left Mother home. She didn't need to tag along on what might be a busy afternoon. She was quite happy to sleep peacefully on one of her favorite places, the computer keyboard. Finn wondered if maybe he would come home someday and find out that she had typed the great American novel. Or at least the greatest one written by a cat. It felt good to smile.

He had no idea where a hardware store was since he didn't drive. Not that it mattered since he was not the least bit handy having lived in New York City all those years. Other than changing a light bulb, most residents in rented apartments just called the Super when something needed fixing. He obviously couldn't pay anyone to fix it either. Well, he did know where to find large pieces of wood: the alleys off the Venice boardwalk were a treasure trove of things that could be made into makeshift lean-tos. And he could probably figure out how to nail it across the doorway. This is where his mind wandered as he walked to Bella's house. He didn't want to worry about her so he worried about her damn door.

Well, he needn't have worried. Everything looked just as he had left it a few hours earlier. On almost every house on the canals except Bella's, he saw those little signs that say "protected by a security company" or "video cameras and burglar alarms on the premises." So even if Bella didn't have all that fancy surveillance, her neighbors did. He tiptoed inside, smiling when he realized that he was doing exactly what he wanted to prevent: entering Bella's house when she wasn't there. He tried to assess the door lock damage, but he started sneezing and coughing from all the dust and newspapers so he went back outside and sat on her front step to contemplate what action he should take. Maybe he should just sit there and guard it.

He closed his eyes and leaned back against the wall. The canals were always very quiet. Apparently the people living there did not have screaming children or barking dogs. They certainly didn't use loud lawnmowers or leaf blowers. This was not a place with normal city or suburban noise.

He was almost asleep when he was startled awake by the sound of his name being called. "Finn? What the hell are you doing here?" He opened his eyes to the sight of Bella, walking slowly toward him followed by a Pakistani man pulling a suitcase. As if that wasn't weird enough, she was dressed in a black skirt and a white blouse and even wore a pair of black shoes instead of her normal attire of housedress and slippers.

"Bella?" he asked. He was dumbfounded. Not so much that she was there; more for the way she was dressed.

"What's going on?"

"Where have you been?" Finn asked when he finally found his voice.

"I didn't know I had to keep you informed of my whereabouts at all times."

"You react to my worry with sarcasm?"

Bella realized he was genuine in his concern. She had never seen this side of him. "I'm sorry." They stood silently for a moment until the Pakistani man cleared his throat. "Oh yes." Bella reached in her purse and took out a twenty and a ten. She handed it to the Pakistani. "Does this cover the fare?"

"Yes. Thank you." The cab driver put the suitcase in front of the door and walked away.

"I broke the lock on your back door. I'll get it fixed."

"You what?"

"I hadn't seen you in more than a week and I thought—" He stopped himself.

"You thought I had been swallowed up by the contents of my house?"

Finn smiled. "Something like that."

"Well, how and when are you going to fix my door?" She was visibly angry. He wasn't sure about which. Probably both: that he caused her door to be broken and that he was being judgmental about her hoarding. She did not return his smile and didn't seem interested in telling him where she'd been.

Finn thought he'd try a different tactic. "You look nice all dressed up."

She didn't bite. "Don't bother fixing my door. I'll get it done myself."

"You can install a door lock?"

"Of course not. I'll call someone. Goodbye, Finn."

Finn was astonished by her reaction. He watched her pull her suitcase inside, unsure whether he should help her or walk away. This was a whole different Bella than he had ever seen, in every respect. There was her businesslike attire and the fact that she had been away from her familiar surroundings for over a week and willingly, no less. But more than that, her attitude and demeanor seemed angry and combative as opposed to playful and resigned. And he was dying to know where she'd been. He turned around and walked away, hoping that by tomorrow she would forgive him and maybe even be just a little bit appreciative.

When he got home he found a hungry cat and poured the nuggets into a bowl. He realized he hadn't eaten anything either. He opened the refrigerator and a few cabinets and closed them all without taking anything out. Food didn't interest him. He went to his office and found something more satisfying.

As he sipped from his flask, he contemplated how much things had changed since he first got to Venice. Jed was gone and he had no idea when or even if he'd be back. Davion and Ty were hardly ever on the boardwalk anymore. And now Bella seemed so different and so distant. And he was starting to question if his book was ever going to come out. Maybe he had misjudged Judith's comments. Maybe the publishers had changed their mind. His paranoia surprised him. It must be this whole police matter making him feel that way. He had never been in a situation before where he was investigated for a crime. And now he was suspected of committing or aiding and abetting two of them.

He drained the flask and looked through the cabinet for any forgotten bottles, knowing full well that he had long ago emptied them all. He thought he'd pay Luis a visit. The lunch shift should be winding down. Maybe Luis would offer him a beer or two in addition to a few dollars in wages.

He got to Luis' just in time to help with the dishes. When he finished he not only got a couple of beers and a twenty dollar bill, but also a beef burrito and some chips and salsa.

"Any word from Jed?" Luis asked as he sat down to count the take from the day's lunch. Finn was just finishing his first beer and had started nibbling on the chips. The burrito was untouched.

"Nope. It's been so long, I kind of doubt I will."

"You never know, Senor Finn. He's left and come back before. He may show up."

"I hope so." Finn smiled. "I miss him."

"Si. Yo tambien." Luis finished separating the money into piles and then stood up. "It's good to see you. It's been a while. But I need to get the dinner meal started."

"Do you need help later? I mean, is there a dishwasher coming after dinner?"

Luis wondered if Finn had hit the skids again and was sleeping on the boardwalk. He certainly didn't look like it. He was clean and neat. "Si."

"Okay." Finn looked disheartened by Luis' answer.

"Do you need the work?"

Finn wasn't sure how to answer. He didn't need the work. He needed the whiskey. He had enough empathy left in him to feel badly about taking a job away from someone who may actually have to pay rent with the earnings. "No, just if you were short-handed." He certainly didn't want Luis to be put in an uncomfortable position.

"Well, stay as long as you want and come back soon." Luis left Finn to finish his food.

Kate was making dinner in the kitchen when he got home. He said a cursory hello and went into his office to finish the day with his favorite companion.

38

FINN WOKE UP EARLY THE NEXT MORNING. He wanted to get to the boardwalk and wait for Bella. He was dressed and out of the house with the newspaper in one arm and Mother in the other. He stopped at the cafe for a cup of coffee and scanned the tables, looking for Harper, but she wasn't there. He felt badly that he hadn't been showing up for their writing critique sessions and hoped she hadn't given up on him. She should have, though. He had given up on himself.

He took his coffee to go and found a spot on a bench with a good view of most of Bella's usual haunts. He glanced around at the performers setting up, but no Davion and Ty. Then he eyed the machines at Muscle Beach but no Savali either. Only good old reliable Charlie was there, trying to cajole the diehard boardwalk sleepers to come to the shelter for a bed and some food and the resources that would get them off the street. Most of them didn't bite. They liked the freedom and power of being beholden only to themselves. Charlie waved at Finn and beckoned him. Finn waved back but didn't move off the bench. He took out his pen and worked on the puzzle as he sipped his plain coffee. He had emptied his flask last night.

It wasn't long before he spotted Bella pushing her shopping cart. She was back in her usual uniform. He rose to greet her and she smiled at him. She seemed to be back to her old self, as well. He'd try a lighthearted approach. "There's my Bella for Adano."

"And there's my Huckleberry Finn."

Finn beamed as he took her arm to help her down onto the bench next to him. "I'm really sorry about your door. Did you get it fixed?"

"I had a new door by dinnertime."

"That was fast. Do you have a handyman that does work for you?"

"Same one anyone has. Home Depot." She gave him a cynical smile.

He smiled back and decided to be frank. He really wanted to know where she'd been. "You certainly looked nice yesterday all dressed up. Was it a wedding or a funeral? Or maybe a job interview?"

"You are a nosy one," she answered hostilely. "But I guess I owe you an apology too."

"You do? For what?"

"It felt nice to have someone care that much." She shook her head and laughed. "But was it really necessary to call the police?"

Finn shrugged and smiled. "They weren't particularly helpful anyway."

She didn't seem to be forthcoming with any information on where she had been for a week and dressed up, to boot. He'd ask again. "So did you go on vacation for a week?"

"You never give up."

"I'm not known to."

"Have you ever been to the Museum of Tolerance?"

"Here in Los Angeles?"

"Yes. Over on Pico."

"No. I haven't."

"You should go."

"I will. I didn't know there was one here."

"I volunteer with them. I give talks about the Holocaust. They asked me to go to some schools in northern California and talk to the kids. There aren't too many of us left."

"That must be hard to do." Finn's voice was soft. He was impressed and even proud of her.

"It is hard." She sighed. "But people need to know before it's too late."

"You are one incredible lady."

"Just determined. For the dead and the living we must bear witness."

"Elie Wiesel?"

"Yes."

They sat silently for a few more minutes until Bella got up slowly. "I have work to do."

"Can I help you?"

"Nope." She padded off to rifle through the trashcans.

Finn watched her for a while, lost in thought, until Mother reminded him that she hadn't eaten. "Okay, okay. Let's go home and get you some food."

He spent the afternoon and evening in his office at the computer, Googling. He looked up the address of the Museum of Tolerance and decided to ask Kate if she had ever been. He thought it might be a good thing for them to do together. And anyway, that would mean they could drive and he wouldn't have to figure out how to get there on his own.

He also researched more about the Holocaust itself, as well as Elie Wiesel. He looked for similarities between Hitler and Jim Jones and then added other crazy-with-power leaders like Idi Amin and Josef Stalin. And then he added some pure lunatics like Charles Manson and Son of Sam to the mix. He spent a good six hours reading, but all he came away with was a heavy bout of depression and disgust.

Where the hell was Kate? He needed to borrow some more money. He remembered that he should call Judith and he was dialing the phone when Kate got home from work. Good. Now she could be impressed that he was talking to Judith. Maybe it would soften her up to give him some money without his having to ask.

"Hi, Dad."

Finn put his fingers to his lips to show that he was on the phone. He was glad that Judith wasn't there so he could just leave her a message. "Judith? It's Finn. What's happening? I thought everything was set to go yet I've heard nothing. Call me right away, will you?" He hung up and nodded at Kate as if to say, "Aren't you going to reward me for being such a good boy?"

"Have you eaten dinner?"

Damn. She didn't take the bait. "No." He'd try the father-daughter togetherness angle of going to the museum. Maybe that would work. "Have you ever been to the Museum of Tolerance?"

"Yes, I have. It's a fascinating place."

"Would you like to go again? With me?"

Kate's eyes widened in disbelief and she almost dropped her purse. Did she hear him right? Did he just ask her to do something with him? Not just for him? "You mean, together?"

"Yes. Together. You and me."

"Uh, okay." She looked at him warily, but deep down, she was also rather pleased.

"Would you like to go out to dinner at my friend Luis' restaurant tonight?" This was getting ridiculous. Now he was introducing her to his friends?

"Sure."

He put his arm around her and kissed her cheek. "Good. Let's go. Of course, you'll have to pay." He smiled sheepishly.

"I know."

They went out arm in arm and you could hear Mother purring with pleasure at this new turn of events.

Judith didn't return his call for several days but Finn wasn't fazed. Kate's and his relationship had reached such a good place that she willingly gave him the money he needed. He should have used this tactic long ago. They had enjoyed their dinner at Luis'. In fact, he and Mercedes had joined them at the end of the meal and Kate had fallen into teacher mode, or maybe it was pseudo-mother mode, giving much-appreciated mentoring to Mercedes.

He had returned to the cafe for his writing critique sessions with Harper and most days he found Bella for some intellectual conversation touching on philosophy, politics and history. Even Davion and Ty had resumed their act on the boardwalk with a hiatus from their new career in television, on cruise ships, and in other cities. Things were close to being back to normal, other than the absence of Jed.

39

JUDITH FINALLY CALLED FINN to say the book would be coming out shortly. There had been a delay due to some business issues the publisher was having with a certain distributor. She didn't offer any more information than that and Finn didn't ask. She couldn't give him an exact date, but she promised it would be very soon. That would give Kate enough of a measure of optimism to continue to subsidize him.

He sat at the kitchen table, sipping his coffee and watching Mother eat. He was contemplating whether or not he wanted to do some more topic research or head for the boardwalk to do the crossword puzzle. He should have been feeling happy that the book was finally going to come out, but instead the news just made him more melancholy about Jed. He ended up going back to his office and cracking open the bottle earlier than planned.

Jed had decided he couldn't leave things as they were with Finn and the police any longer. He needed to get that necklace. It wasn't just to get Finn off the hook. He wanted it back. He needed to formulate a plan and the best place for him to do that was at Miss Ruthie's. Rocking the babies gave him the chance to relax and let his mind go anywhere it needed to go.

She answered the door with a baby in her arms. "Good to see you, Jed. But you know Malcolm's at school at this hour."

"I know. I think it's probably best not to tell Malcolm I was here. I don't want him to be upset that I came over knowing he'd be at school."

"I won't tell him." She figured he had a good reason.

"Is there a baby that needs rocking?"

Miss Ruthie looked at the clock. "Sure. You have time?"

"A little." He followed her up the stairs.

After an hour or so, the babies were sleeping so they placed them gently back in their cribs and tiptoed out of the room.

"Will you have some lunch with me?" Miss Ruthie asked when they got back to the kitchen.

Jed glanced at the clock. "When does Malcolm get home?"

"In an hour."

"Okay then." Jed sat down and Miss Ruthie took out some bread, ham and cheese and set it on the table with a couple of plates and jars of pickles and mustard. They made their own sandwiches and started to eat, all without a word. Miss Ruthie knew better than to ask Jed too many questions. "How's the adoption process going?" he finally asked.

"It's a lot of paperwork but it's going. There shouldn't be any problems."

"Best thing that could happen to Malcolm."

She smiled. "He's a good kid. Just needs some guidance."

"I'm happy for both of you."

"You mean a lot to him, Jed."

"I know. I won't forget him. I'll be around. I promise you that. I just can't right now is all."

"That's okay. Just keep in touch when you can."

Jed finished his sandwich. He had come up with an idea and was ready to prepare for it. He stood to leave and took her hand. "Thank you. For more than you realize." Miss Ruthie nodded and he left.

He found Earl under the Santa Monica pier. "Hey Earl. How goes it?" Earl was admonishing some twenty-something tourists from Germany not to ride so fast on the bike path.

"Well, well, well. If it ain't Jedidiah. Where you been hiding? Haven't seen you in a blue moon."

"I've been around."

"Where's your cat?"

"Safe and happy."

Earl laughed. "You were always such a great conversationalist."

"I didn't come to see you to shoot the breeze."

"I figured as much. You ain't exactly a social butterfly."

"I have a problem and I think you can help me."

"Well, what do you know, Jed's asking for assistance. That's a first."

"I need to get something. It's in a police department property room. Do you have any ideas?"

"What precinct?"

"I don't know the specific one. Do you know a Lieutenant named Bukowski?"

"Yeah. I know him."

"Well, it would be his precinct I guess." Earl looked at Jed coolly for a few moments, but didn't speak. "Do you know anyone there?" Jed asked. Earl nodded a barely perceptible 'yes' but was still silent. "Yes I realize I'll need some big bills."

Earl smiled. "And where are you going to get them?"

"I think you can help me there too. I have an idea."

"What idea is that?"

"Do you know a couple of punks named Matt and Luke?"

"Those honky trust-fund-baby meth addicts who think their shit don't stink?"

Jed suppressed a laugh. "Yeah. Those."

"I know 'em. What about them?"

"You think they could loan me some cash to pay your friend?"

"Loan?"

"Well, maybe they won't get paid back. I think they kind of owe me."

Earl looked at Jed suspiciously. "How am I supposed to help you with those assholes?"

"Maybe we'll run across them buying some provisions. You can offer to help them out by taking the cash off their hands in exchange for keeping them safe from the man."

"And what's in it for me?"

"Some of the cash."

"And what are you going to be doing?"

"I'll be your strong-armed sidekick." Earl turned his gaze toward the ocean to ponder the possible consequences. "How much does your friend at the precinct need?" Jed added.

"A few C-notes."

"Whatever we get from those two creeps, the rest is yours. I don't want any of their dirty money."

"I guess that's doable," Earl finally consented.

"So what is it you want from the evidence room?"

"A necklace. The case is against me and a guy named Finn McGee."

"What's the case?"

"The murder of a woman named Antoinette Delon."

Earl stared at Jed with a hint of a smile. "Murder? You?"

"I didn't do it."

"I'm sure you didn't."

"I don't want to talk about it."

"Come by about ten tonight. I'll have the buy set up."

"What if Luke and Matt aren't here tonight?"

"There are plenty more just like them."

"But those two are the ones I want."

"You got a beef with those particular two?"

"They're the ones that beat me up, but I don't care about that."

"What is it then?"

"They hurt Mother. She ended up needing stitches."

"Okay then. See you later."

Jed returned to the pier at 9:30 that night but Earl was not in his usual spot. He walked up to the pier and watched the tourists and teenagers playing arcade games and riding the carousel. He kept his eye out on and under the pier, as well as on the beach. After awhile he went inside the Bubba Gump Shrimp Company to ask the time. When he found out that it was after 10:00, he hurried off the pier but still there was no sign of Earl or the two punks. He waited for what felt like an hour before he saw Earl moseying up the beach from the south, the Venice direction. He was alone.

"Sorry I'm late," Earl said as he approached Jed.

"You didn't find Luke and Matt?"

"Yeah, I found them. Everything's taken care of." He handed Jed the necklace.

"What th—" Jed started to ask.

Earl interrupted him. "I didn't need you. I handled it myself." Jed looked at the necklace and then back at Earl with pursed lips and narrowed eyes. "What? You're pissed?" Earl asked.

"I, uh, would have liked to have been there." Jed tried to keep his anger in check.

"What do you care? You got what you wanted."

"Not everything. I would have liked a few minutes with those creeps."

"You know, Jed, I figured I was doing you a favor because you're not the fighting type. Those two ain't worth getting your hands dirty. Just take the necklace and get out of here. I've got a couple of bills burning a hole in my pocket."

"Thanks, Earl."

"Anytime."

40

ONE MORNING, A COUPLE OF WEEKS LATER, Finn entered the kitchen and found Kate drinking coffee and reading the newspaper. He poured himself a cup and sat down at the kitchen table. "I doubt the *NY Times* is here yet so can I have a section of the *LA Times*?"

She handed him the whole paper, got up and kissed the top of his head. "I have to go to work. See you tonight."

Mother jumped up on Finn's lap and purred. "Okay, I know. It's breakfast time." He fed the cat and went out to the front porch, just as the carrier threw the *NY Times* on the lawn. "So not only are you two hours late, you can't even get it on the porch, you lazy bastard?" He returned to the kitchen and sat down at the kitchen table to read both papers and drink his cup of plain coffee. After he finished, he went to shower and get dressed. Just as he entered his office, the doorbell rang. He went to the front door and signed for the delivery. He lugged the box into his office and set it on the table to open. "It's been a long and winding road, but we made it." He took a stack of books out and set them on the table to make some room, and then put Mother inside the box. "Let's go for a walk."

His first stop was the cafe where he saw Harper sitting at a table, typing on her laptop. He took a book out of the box and placed it in front of her. "It's out!" She jumped up and hugged him.

"They came this morning."

"How exciting! When does the book tour start?"

"You'll be the first to know. By the way, do you have another chapter for me to read?"

"I do." She fumbled through her backpack and handed a pile of papers to Finn.

"I'll read it tonight." Harper opened his book to leaf through it as Finn walked on to his next stop.

He entered Luis' restaurant and saw Mercedes counting money at the cash register. "Is your father in the back?" She nodded so as not to lose her place. He found Luis cooking at the stove and offered him a book.

"Felicidades!" Luis wiped his hands before he took it. "Cuanto?"

"Nada. It's a gift."

"Oh, gracias. I look forward to reading it." He looked at the front and back and then opened it to the author's bio on the inside cover. "I only wish Jed was here."

"I know. I do, too," Finn replied wistfully.

"This is the longest he's ever stayed away." Luis' face showed his concern.

"He'll be back for Mother."

Luis brightened considerably. "That's true."

Finn walked down to the boardwalk and saw Bella rifling through a trashcan. "The books came today."

"Mazel tov. Can I have one?"

"Of course." He handed her a book and she placed it carefully in her cart. She looked at the cover.

"Very appropriate title."

"How so?"

"Considering all we've talked about these last months."

"You're right. But the title was the easy part."

"Well, yes, considering you didn't even have to create it." She winked at him.

He laughed. "Ah, there's Davion and Ty. See you later Bubba."

"Gay ga zinta hate, Zeyde."

As he turned around and started to walk toward Davion and Ty, he noticed Savali resting on the bench in front of Muscle Beach. He went over and sat down.

"Well, if it isn't Mr. Fish Face."

"How ya doin', Savali."

"Wha'cha' got in your box?"

"Copies of a book I wrote. Would you like one?"

"Sure." Savali took the book and looked at the title on the front cover. "I think I've heard that before."

"Yes, it's a quote from George Santayana."

"Never heard of him, just heard the saying."

"Other people have used this quote in various contexts."

"It's definitely true in my culture."

"In what way?"

"Did you ever look up that word I asked you to look up?"

"What word was that?"

"Fa'afafine."

"No, I didn't. What is it?" Finn asked.

"Look it up. Then you'll get it." Savali stood up. "Gotta get back to the grind."

"Catch you later, Savali."

He found Davion and Ty finishing up their performance and held the book up in the air. They came dancing over.

"My mon, Finn, your book is here!" Ty took the book. "Too bad Jed not here." He winked at Davion.

"He be back. He always come back." Davion smiled. Jed had appeared behind Finn and gestured to them not to let on he was there.

"So I always thought, but it's been a long time," Finn sighed.

"Sometimes it takes a long time before you can stop running and find peace," Jed said.

Finn grinned and turned around. He reached into the box of books and took Mother out and handed her to Jed. "I knew he'd find you, Mother." Mother leaped into Jed's arms.

"That's not necessarily true, you know."

"What's not true?" Finn looked puzzled. "Mother always finds you."

"The title of your book. *Those Who Forget the Past are Condemned to Repeat It.*"

"You don't believe that anymore?" Finn asked, puzzled at Jed's statement.

"I'm not sure. Sometimes I think it's okay to forget. Sometimes the past holds you hostage."

"But understanding the past helps to define the present."

"That may be true, but you also have to learn to let it go."

"I guess so. But that's a very personal decision."

"You don't have to worry about being involved in this Antoinette case anymore."

"What do you mean? Why not?" Finn asked.

Jed took the necklace out of his pocket. "There's no evidence to connect you to it."

"How'd you get that? You spoke to Bukowski?"

"Let's just say you're off the hook."

"And you?"

335

"Not your concern."

"Sure it is." Finn said.

"I have it under control."

Finn handed a copy of the book to Jed who put it in his backpack. "So does this mean you're back for good?"

Jed didn't answer. He just gave Mother a final pat on the head and handed her back to Finn. "Do you mind keeping her?"

Finn was stunned that Jed was going to leave Mother. "Of course not. But . . ." Finn stammered.

Jed smiled, turned toward the Santa Monica Mountains, and headed north.

"Thanks for everything, Jed," Finn called to him.

Jed raised his hand over his head and waved, but didn't turn around.

Finn and Mother watched Jed walk away until he was too far away to discern. Ty and Davion stood quietly by, also a little shocked that Jed was leaving Mother. Davion patted Finn on the shoulder and took Ty's arm. Ty nodded and they left Finn alone to his thoughts.

He put Mother back in the box and noticed Charlie at his table. He walked over and gave him a copy and then headed home, his step definitely having lost most of its bounce.

When he got home, he filled a glass and sat down with a heavy heart. He wrapped his fingers tightly around the glass and set it down on the table.

Then he turned on his computer and waited for it to boot up, his eyes on the glass of whiskey. Mother jumped on his lap, as if she knew he needed a distraction, and he started to pet her. She purred as if to say, "We'll be fine."

He Googled fa'afafine and read from Wikipedia, "*Fa'afafine* *are the gender-liminal, or third-gendered people of Samoa. A recognized and integral part of traditional Samoan culture, fa'afafine, born biologically male, embody both male and female gender traits. Their gendered behavior typically ranges from extravagantly feminine to mundanely masculine.*"

He smiled, sat back in his chair and pushed the glass away. "I do believe, Mother, that I have my next book!"

Acknowledgements

I would like to thank the following people and places:

Dave Elliot - my first writing critic and screenwriting friend who got me started on this journey

Nora Profit - founder of The Writing Loft where I honed my craft

David Zietz - producer and partner extraordinaire

Daniel Nauman - for his immeasurable critique and advice

The *Derelict Voice* writing group - Andy Hanson, Michael Long, Alex Patrone, Ben Mielke, and Scott Clark for their guidance and support

My book club members - Liz Stewart, Carol Meurer and Kris Kidd for validating me as a writer

Tin Roof Bakery and Cafe - where I spent many hours writing over endless cups of Earl Grey

Friends who have given me valuable input - Ellen Winder, Laura Joplin, Jim and Jane Stripe, Charlotte DeWitt, Trudy Duisenberg, Idie Adams, Jeffrey Miles, Ann Cowles

Dan O'Brien - for advising me on the publishing process

My daughter, Eva Saur, who inspires me more than she knows

And so much appreciation to my husband, David Gallo, and to my son, Chris Saur, for reading innumerable copies of *Venice Beach* in various forms and for endless conversations about it - there are no words . . .

Emily's next novel, *The Columbarium*, is a sequel to *Venice Beach* and takes Jed's story to San Francisco. It will be published soon. An excerpt follows.

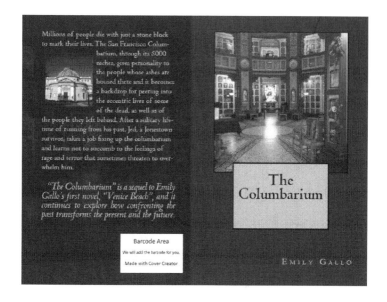

Millions of people die with just a stone block to mark their lives. The San Francisco Columbarium, through its 5000 niches, gives personality to the people whose ashes are housed there and it becomes a backdrop for peering into the eccentric lives of some of the dead, as well as of the people they left behind. After a solitary lifetime of running from his past, Jed, a Jonestown survivor, takes a job fixing up the columbarium and learns not to succumb to the feelings of rage and terror that sometimes threaten to overwhelm him.

"The Columbarium" is a sequel to Emily Gallo's first novel, "Venice Beach", and it continues to explore how confronting the past transforms the present and the future.

Barcode Area
We will add the barcode for you.
Made with Cover Creator

The Columbarium

EMILY GALLO

CHAPTER 1

IT HAD BEEN DUSK WHEN JED LEFT LOS ANGELES. By the time he got to Ventura where the 101 hugged the coast, all he could see of the Pacific were the sudden bursts of white foam as the waves tumbled toward the shore. It didn't matter, though. He had spent the last few years living on the boardwalk in Venice Beach and he needed sleep more than he needed scenery. He crumpled his jacket into a ball and put it against the window of the bus. He leaned his head into it and shut his eyes. It did its job: a warm soft barrier between him and the cold glass. He closed his eyes and started practicing his breathing techniques. Sleep didn't come easily to him. He had spent too many nighttime hours having to be vigilant and had learned to function on very little sleep. But it also meant that sleep evaded him on those few occasions when he felt safe and secure in his bedtime circumstances.

He had learned the breathing techniques when one of the boardwalk denizens had brought him to the Venice Buddhist Temple. They taught these techniques called Pranayama as a vehicle for meditation, but Jed wasn't interested in that. He didn't care much for the spiritual benefits of the Buddhist religion, or any religion for that matter. He used the exercises purely to release tension. He didn't care much for the yoga part either. He just liked to walk.

The bus pulled into San Francisco just as the sun rose. It felt good to stand up and stretch his legs. He wasn't used to sitting for long periods of time. Most of his days had been spent walking on the beach or in the Santa Monica Mountains. He made his way through the throng of passengers standing by the bus, waiting for their suitcases. All he had was his well-worn yellow backpack. Clean clothing was easy enough to come by in thrift shops or the free stores at the homeless resource centers.

Jed was a tall, thin, muscular African-American. He was pushing fifty but easily looked fifteen years younger. His hair, cut short, was barely graying at the temples and his skin was smooth. He was one of those people who turned heads, but not only because of his physical attractiveness. It was his air of mystery and aloofness that drew them in.

He had the stamina of a long-distance runner, but his gait and his demeanor were slow and deliberate. He had anger issues, but he was never physically aggressive unless someone threw the first punch. When he lost his temper he would walk for miles and it helped some. He worked hard at trying to stay calm; he didn't like to lose control but he did a little too easily.

It had been quite a few years since he'd been back to the San Franicsco. He thought it would be a good place to hide and get the proverbial fresh start. He had already had some fresh starts, but this one was different. This one was imperative. This time he was running from the law.

341